SILENCE

NATASHA PRESTON

Books By Natasha Preston

SILENCE SERIES

Silence

Broken Silence

Players, Bumps and Cocktail Sausages

CHANCE SERIES

Second Chance

Our Chance

THE ONE SERIES

Waking Up in Vegas

Just Like the Movies

Read My Mind

STAND-ALONES

Save Me

With the Band

Reliving Fate

Lie to Me

After the End

YOUNG ADULT THRILLERS

The Cellar

Awake

The Cabin

You Will Be Mine

The Lost

The Twin

The Lake

The Fear

The Island

Visit my website at www.natashapreston.com

Cover Designer: LJ Designs, www.ljdesignsia.com

Editor: Victoria L James, www.victorialjames.com

This book is a work of fiction. Names, characters, places, and incidents either are products of the author's imagination or are used fictitiously. Any resemblance to actual persons, living or dead, events, or locales is entirely coincidental.

❀ Created with Vellum

DEDICATION

There is one person who I can thank for making this book possible. Kirsty, there's no way I would have published without your encouragement. Thank you for making me be brave and talking me through a lot on this journey.

CONTENT WARNING

THIS BOOK CONTAINS REFERENCE TO CHILD ABUSE.

Chapter 1

Oakley

While staring at my reflection in the mirror, I brushed my hair repeatedly, trying to keep it simple and flowing straight down my back with no thrills or anything attached to it that would get me noticed.

Most girls at school used their hair to express themselves—though the principal was dull as hell and wouldn't allow us to colour it—with fancy plaits and updos that could take them from school straight to their wedding day.

I never did anything to mine. I left it down as a cape that disguised what I didn't want anyone to see...

That I was damaged.

"Are you ready to leave, honey? Cole's waiting outside," Mum said in a soft tone she used only for me, as if I was still a toddler.

It'd taken a few years for her to accept this new me—the one who didn't talk and barely communicated—but now she accepted who I was without question. And by that, I meant she held it in, occasionally tracking down a new doctor or form of therapy that she hoped would cure me.

It'd been almost eleven years now.

When would she finally give up? It would be easier for us all if she did.

She leant against my doorframe and smiled, but I could see how tired she looked. Dark shadows were now a permanent feature beneath her dulling blue eyes.

Her smile was as fake as my own, and it was all my fault.

Every single day, I would wake up wanting to tell her what had happened. To have her hold me in her arms and promise that everything would be fine, but reality stopped me from confessing every time. The fantasy I had in my head of how things would turn out was just that—a fantasy.

I'd lose *everything*. He'd told me so enough times. I knew he wasn't bluffing, so it wasn't something I could ever risk.

Placing my hairbrush on the dresser, I turned to Mum and nodded once. Then, with a deep breath, I followed her downstairs.

It wasn't until we reached the front door that she looked at me again. "Have a good day, okay?" Almost everything she said to me sounded like a question. As the words left her mouth, her eyes widened with the desperate hope that I would reply, and every time I responded with yet another brief nod, her shoulders would sag.

She'd still try again, though. Always.

I grabbed my schoolbag from by the door and swung it over my shoulder as I walked outside.

The blazing sun shone directly into my eyes, and I squinted at the brightness.

It was July, and almost time for high school to close for the summer holidays.

I couldn't wait.

Two more days.

Cole beeped his car horn even though he was parked right outside my house.

Thanks, Cole. Might have missed you without that alert.

He grinned through the window as I made my way to his car. His blue eyes glistened in the early morning light, making them look as pale as ice.

Cole Benson and I had been friends since we were babies. Mum had pictures of Cole holding my hand while I learned to walk. He was two years older than me, but he certainly didn't act like it. My mum Sarah and his mum Jenna met in high school, and they had been friends ever since.

"Good morning, sunshine," he said with a wide grin, reaching over to twirl a blonde lock of my hair around his finger. His car smelt like him, a mixture of outdoor and perfection.

Unlike Mum's, the smiles I received from Cole never changed. Grinning back at him was as natural as breathing. His happiness was infectious. Our friendship was always fun, affectionate, loving, and carefree.

He accepted me for who I was now.

I breathed him in and felt my body begin to heat. So many times, I'd wanted to get just a little bit closer, linger at his house a little bit longer, and have him play fight with me a little bit harder.

It hadn't always been a bed of roses, though. There were times in the past when Cole would beg and plead with me to tell him what was wrong—why I didn't speak anymore. I found it harder than when Mum asked.

He was the one person I still felt normal with.

I *hated* hurting him.

He released my hair and put the car in drive. It hadn't been long since he'd passed his driving test, but he was a good driver, and I trusted him with my life.

Still, I gripped the seat as he sped off.

Why was he so eager? I hated school with a passion, and the

way he was driving, we'd be there in just a few minutes. I wanted to prolong it as much as possible.

Cole talked almost continuously on the drive, chatting away about his car, telling me about parts he wanted to get, and then what we'd do later. Occasionally, I would nod or smile in response to something he said, but apart from that, I sat and listened to him speak.

His voice was smooth and calming. I desperately wanted to return his quick banter with something smart of my own, but I stayed tongue-tied.

I *had* to.

Not talking to him was hard.

As we pulled into the half-full car park, anxiety unfurled in my stomach. People whispered to each other whenever I was around, even though most of them had never known me to speak. Some spoke aloud, either thinking I also couldn't hear, or they just didn't care.

I was used to it, but I still hated being the centre of their jokes and bitchy comments.

"Oakley?"

I jumped and my head snapped up toward Cole.

"You going to be okay today?"

I nodded, grimacing slightly. I hated when we had to go our separate ways, and I wished I was in the same year as him. Most days, I could ignore the attention I got. Today, I felt off. So, that should be interesting.

"Message me if you need anything." He kissed me on the cheek, and I think my heart skipped about two full beats.

Feeling his lips against mine was another thing I wanted to do a little more.

He knew I wouldn't message him, but he still said the same thing every morning. It was our routine, and I kind of loved it, as much as it broke my heart.

We got out of the car, and the gloomy school building, all grey and depressing, loomed over us, blocking the sunlight out until midday, as if it wanted us to be miserable.

"See you later," he called as he walked towards the sixth form building next to the high school.

Once he was out of view, I let the smile slip from my face. There was no one around to pretend for now. It was almost a relief not to have to act like I was fine. I couldn't even figure out what was so wrong today, I just felt strange.

Walking towards the entrance of the school, I pulled my sleeves down over my hands and wrapped my arms around myself.

Keep your head down. Not long until the school year is over.

The shrill ring from the bell echoed off every wall, signalling the start of the day. My form room was at the end of a corridor that seemed to stretch on for miles with its harsh strip lighting. I walked quickly to avoid being caught up with the people still loitering around. Some days, when it was crowded and people stared, it was like doing the worst catwalk known to man.

I pushed the door open to the faded green room and took my usual seat next to Hannah Ross. Resting my arms on the desk, I inhaled a deep breath. Mornings were rubbish, and the first two periods always dragged on like this building had its own time zone.

Hannah smiled, and I returned the gesture. We weren't necessarily friends, but she was the closest thing I had to one here. She didn't judge or treat me any differently. I thought she just didn't know how to act around me most of the time.

"School sucks," she grumbled, tucking her black hair behind her ears.

Completely agreeing with you there.

"Oakley, what did you do last night?" one of the boys shouted from the back of the classroom.

I recognised his voice as Luke Davis's, one of the *biggest* idiots in my year, second to Julian. Seriously, he was even failing physical education. He was horrible to most people, but for some unknown reason, half of the girls in my class fancied him.

He wasn't even nice to look at.

"Sorry, I didn't quite *hear* you," he said, earning sniggers from a few people around the room.

I couldn't actually believe that he still thought those jokes were funny after five years. He didn't even try to come up with any new ones.

"Ignore them," Hannah whispered, sympathetically squeezing my arm.

Oh, I did.

I smiled at her as Mrs Yates walked into the room. With a quick greeting, she flipped the register open and pulled the lid off her pen. Like everyone else, she called my name, but unlike everyone else, she looked up at the same time. I never had any pressure from the teachers to talk; they kept everything as normal as possible for me, whenever it could be.

I was never going to do great on verbal assignments...

Mum had a lot of meetings when I moved from primary school to high school, ensuring that every member of staff was aware that I wouldn't speak to them. She didn't want me getting into trouble for being rude, and she wanted to make sure I was supported.

I might hate everything about my silence but at least I never got picked on for class reading. After the register and a pep talk from Mrs Yates, the bell rang again.

"Ready for maths?" Hannah groaned, standing up and grabbing her bag.

Nope. My expression mirrored hers. Maths wasn't my favourite subject, and today we had a double lesson. First thing... on a *Monday.*

"Do you think we'll ever use anything we've learnt in maths in the real world?" she mused.

Most definitely.

I had a lot of lessons with Hannah. We would sit together through them all, but she'd speak to her other two friends more since, unsurprisingly, they'd actually answer her. That was okay with me, though. I preferred to just do the work to pass the time faster.

One day I planned to be the CEO of my own company and turn people like Luke down when he applied for a job. Of course, I hadn't figured out how I was going to do that while mute... but I would. Maybe by that time, things would be much different.

"Good morning," Mr Spice greeted. "Pass these around and get started." He handed Georgie the stack of papers, and then he went to sit down. He's what was referred to as a paper teacher. Just shoved us some worksheets and let us get on with it, not even caring if everyone chatted throughout the lesson.

Obviously, that made him a favourite.

I tapped the end of my pencil against my lips and watched the clock for a bit. It didn't seem like it was moving.

The boredom was *actually* going to kill me.

I flipped the worksheet over, only to find another one. Sighing, I got to work on the new side.

Finally, the bell rang, and it was time for the first break of the day. Stuffing my pencil case into my bag, I mentally planned my route to the next class.

Helen, Laura, and Tina peered over their shoulders as they walked towards the door, snickering. My heart dropped, but I tried not to let them get to me. It wouldn't be long before we would leave school and I wouldn't have to see them again.

Unless they applied for a job, too.

I *really* hoped that would happen.

Heading straight to my third lesson, I kept my head down, hoping to go unnoticed. I took the longer route because there were usually fewer people were around.

The sun was even brighter than when I'd left home that morning, and as it shone on my face, I cradled my hand over my eyes to create a little shade.

England wasn't supposed to be this hot.

Suddenly, I slammed into someone who was walking around the corner. Gasping, I stumbled back.

"Sorry," a deep voice said.

I looked up and stepped back again, feeling sick as Julian grinned down at me. His smile wasn't a friendly one—more like that of a predator that had just caught its prey.

He was so much worse than Liam.

"Oakley," he said in what he probably thought was a playful tone.

No. Not now.

I gulped and straightened my back to try to appear more confident than I felt. My stomach burned with the hatred that I felt for this dickhead.

Look at him, I told myself, not wanting to give him the satisfaction of intimidating me.

"Miss me over the weekend?" Julian took one small step closer and towered over me.

I wanted to run, but I wouldn't let myself be that weak. Besides, running wouldn't help. Tilting my chin, I continued to stare into his cold eyes while my pulse thudded in my ears.

The corner of Julian's mouth curved into a sinister smirk. There was definitely something very wrong with him. The way he acted around me when we were alone was psychotic.

"Miss Farrell, Mr Howard, get to class.... Now!" Mr Simmons bellowed.

Startled, I jumped back. Break was over, thankfully.

Julian groaned, probably disappointed that he had to stop being a Class A bastard.

Pushing past him, I scurried off to biology, refusing to look back at a guy I wish would grow boils all over his face.

I'd be happy if I could just make it through *one* day without something happening.

Chapter 2

Oakley

At lunchtime, I walked to the exit to eat outside of the school grounds. It was easier. I was about to reach the front door when a manicured hand shot out, and I flinched to an abrupt halt.

"Oakley," Laura said with a fake smile, "I'm having a party on Saturday to celebrate the end of the year. You should come. What do you *say?*"

Laura and her friend Sally laughed under their breaths.

Oh, very witty...

I rolled my eyes, wondering how they never got bored of their own lame jokes. Same as Liam and Julian—especially Julian. It was their group that seemed to have it in for me. They must be so boring to have nothing better to do.

Sidestepping her, I broke out into a jog towards the door. The laughter stopped as soon as I was outside. I'd already had enough of today, and I needed to leave. Blinking the tears back, I walked quickly through the car park.

I swallowed the watermelon-sized lump in my throat and willed myself not to cry. I'd survived *much* worse, and I was stronger than this, so it frustrated me when their jibes cut deep.

"Oakley?" Cole's voice called out, bringing me instant relief.

I turned around to see him jogging towards me, his messy hair blowing across his forehead. I drew on the strength that his friendship gave me.

I took a shaky breath and smiled. I was *not* going to let them make me cry again, and I really didn't want Cole to see me upset, either.

He strode across the car park and stopped right in front of me. "Hey. Are you okay?" he asked, scanning my face with X-ray eyes. I was certain he saw more than I wanted.

Not *everything*, obviously.

I nodded my response.

He arched an eyebrow. "No, you're not. Hold on a minute. I'll come with you, and we can talk."

As he went to turn away, I grabbed his arm and shook my head. I didn't want him to come with me. He didn't need to be the boy who hung out with the freak girl who didn't talk. I nudged him in the direction of his waiting friends, telling him to go with them.

He looked to them for a second before returning to me. "It's fine. I'd rather come with you."

I both loved and hated that.

I shook my head more fiercely and clenched my jaw, hurt and frustrated. Of all the people in the world, I did not want *him* to feel sorry for me.

I should've just stayed in bed today.

Cole gave an exasperated sigh, his eyes tightening a little. "Either I'm coming with you or you're sitting with us. Doesn't bother me either way, so make your choice." He crossed his arms beneath his chest and raised a brow, challenging me to argue with him.

"Cole, you coming or not?" his friend Ben shouted.

I'd seen Ben plenty of times before but only in passing when

Cole was walking with him to his own car. He seemed cool, but I was younger than them, so we never hung out.

"Come on, babe. I'm hungry," some girl called.

Babe? *Babe!*

What the hell?

My eyes flew to Cole.

Who was she? It couldn't be his girlfriend because he definitely would've told me something like that. But then *why* was some skank calling him babe?

I really, really needed him to address that *right now*.

Instead, he mumbled something under his breath that I couldn't make out, and a vice around my heart squeezed.

Well, that was just perfect. I was jealous as hell. The burning in my stomach returned for a whole new reason. All I needed now was for a dog to come pee on my leg and make this the best day ever.

The thought of him being with someone made me feel sick. And, uncharacteristically, I wanted to gouge the girl's eyes out.

It was a new rage, and I wasn't sure what to do with it.

I couldn't actually mess up her face.

"I'm going with Oakley!" he shouted back.

I slapped his chest and pushed him again, which only made him laugh.

Why won't you just leave?

"All right, eating with us it is." He smirked, grabbing my hand, and pulling me along with him.

I tugged my arm, trying to get my wrist out of his iron grip, but he was too strong. His fingers were warm around me. Either that or it was the physical contact that was making me a little hot.

Whatever it was, it was time to start lifting. Gymnastics kept me fit and toned, but I couldn't match Cole's strength. He was able to manhandle me too easily.

"Oakley's sitting with us," he told his group of friends.

My cheeks heated. He made me feel like a three-year-old. Clenching my jaw, I averted my eyes and refused to look at the arsehole. He knew I didn't like being in a group of people, especially one full of strangers.

They accepted it with a nod, and we walked around the building to the field at the back, but I still felt out of place.

The girl with a face like thunder who'd called Cole *babe* didn't look happy that I was there. That made it a bit easier. Her hair was tied in a tight bun on top of her head—literally right on top like a cherry on a cake.

Same, mate. I'm not happy, either.

As we walked, she kept shooting discreet glares my way. I hadn't even wanted to bloody sit with them in the first place, and I certainly didn't want to sit with them if he was *with* her.

The school grounds stretched on for ages, thanks to the many sports fields and building blocks.

I strolled beside Cole until we come to the back of the field and sat under a huge oak tree. Ben dropped to the grass and grabbed a lunch box from his bag. Immediately, he started stuffing a sandwich into his mouth. The nameless girl—she looked a little like Meg from *Family Guy,* but with the silly hair instead of glasses—made a huge effort to shuffle as close to Cole as she could get.

She might as well have sat on his lap.

Frowning, I picked a blade of grass and wished the world would swallow me whole. Being angry at Cole was never going to last, and that kind of irritated me too. I wished I didn't *like* him.

The bun cling-on could give him so much more than I could.

"Oakley, you want?" Cole asked, holding his Pepsi out to me. A shake of my head answered his question, and he frowned, putting the can down on the ground. "You're annoyed with me."

What the hell was he thinking? His friends all fell silent, listening to Cole start a private conversation in a public place.

If I can get a do-over today, that'd be great.

He sighed, exasperated. "How long are you going to ignore me? Just so I know whether I should eat first."

The length of time would be directly linked to how long he kept airing our business in public. I shrugged my shoulders, still refusing to look at him, but glaring at the ground so he knew how annoyed I was. I felt ridiculous but this was new, and I didn't know how to react.

"What did you do to piss her off so much?" Ben asked, not even bothering to lower his voice so I wouldn't hear.

Cole snorted. "Nothing. She's just being impossible right now."

And you're being a dick!

How was I the one being impossible? I didn't choose to come over here. If he'd left me to go off on my own for a bit, I could've calmed down and sorted myself out. I'd come back to school, ready to ignore hateful shitheads, and get on with earning my one-way ticket to 'CEO who turns away old high school bullies'.

A shadow cast over my face, and I looked up to see Julian standing above me.

Oh, great.

"Oakley?" Julian sneered.

Get lost.

"Come out with me tomorrow night. *Say* yes."

He and his friends chuckled too hard over the lamest joke ever. Those friends were sheep. They did what he said, followed where he went, and laughed when they were supposed to. They spent their whole lives desperately trying to fit in with someone who didn't even like them. They had their own problems.

I painted a bored expression on my face and turned away.

Just as they went to leave, Cole jumped up and grabbed fistfuls of Julian's shirt, crumpling the perfectly ironed material.

I froze in shock. *What's he doing?*

"What did you just say to her?" Cole growled. His knuckles turned white around Julian's top.

Oh, crap.

"Whoa. Chill, man. I was only joking," Julian mumbled, stiffening his back, and pulling at his shirt to try and release it from Cole's grip. It didn't work, making Julian's dark eyes widen.

I couldn't watch, and I certainly couldn't let a teacher witness what looked like an argument turning into a fight. Cole would get in trouble, and I wouldn't let that happen over me.

Jumping to my feet, I pulled at Cole's arm, but he didn't budge an inch as if he was made of stone. It was as if he was too angry to even see me.

"Cole, let it go," Ben demanded. "He's not worth it."

Please, let it go, I begged with my eyes.

"A joke? I didn't find it very fucking funny. If you so much as look at her again, I'll kill you." Cole shoved Julian away from us and gently pried my hand from his arm.

As soon as I was no longer touching him, he launched forward and punched Julian on the cheek.

I flinched, and my jaw dropped open. Cole just *punched* someone. I'd never witnessed that from him before. He could hold his own—I knew that—but he didn't go looking for fights.

Julian stumbled backwards, almost falling over his own legs, but unfortunately, he somehow managed to correct himself. One of his friend's hands shot out and grabbed the top of his arms to steady him. For a second, Julian glared back at Cole. He looked like he was weighing up his options. Cole was bigger, older, and right now, a *lot* more pissed off. Julian didn't stand a chance.

I looked around at the crowd we were attracting.

My stomach rolled at the unwanted attention. All eyes were on us. My chest tightened as the feeling of claustrophobia wrapped around my neck. Grabbing my bag, I took off and sprinted towards the school gates.

"Oakley!" Cole shouted after me.

If I turned around, I would probably break, so I kept going, pushing myself to run at a pace my PE teacher would be proud of.

I sprinted out of the gates and towards the park. The muscles in my legs burned as I pushed myself faster and faster. I felt a stitch pinch at my side, but I didn't slow my pace.

All I wanted was to disappear.

Chapter 3

Oakley

"Hey, Oakley, stop!" Cole's hand circled my wrist, and he pulled me to an immediate halt. "Damn, when did you get so fast?"

Panting, I rested my hands on my thighs and tried to not hyperventilate. As I looked down, I felt a warm tear slide down my cheek and drop to the ground.

Ah, God, no.

"Hey, don't cry," he pleaded softly as he crouched down beside me.

His finger gently brushed my cheek, and without thinking or planning it, I rested my head against his hand and closed my eyes. The comfort I felt from him was out of this world; nothing compared to it. I *needed* it.

"He's not worth it. Just forget about him."

I was pulled into his strong, safe arms, and I breathed him in. His woody scent was all I needed to calm myself down. I regained control of my emotions after a minute and smiled against his chest.

Being wrapped up in his arms was my favourite place to be. I couldn't stay mad at him.

17

Cole didn't care that I no longer spoke. He just cared about me, and over the years, I started to feel much more for him than I should have. Perhaps it was always going to happen. We'd grown up together and been the best of friends for as long as I could remember.

That was bound to develop as we were getting older, right?

Eventually, Cole released me, and I met his eyes.

He grinned sheepishly. "You want to ditch the rest of the day? We could go eat our bodyweight in ice cream."

That was a tactical move. He knew I loved ice cream, and he was using it to get himself out of trouble. I already knew I was going to give in, though. Plus, I'd rather go to a dental appointment for root canal than go back to school this afternoon.

I rolled my eyes and failed miserably at stopping myself from smiling. He knew he had me now.

"Great. Come on, let's get out of here."

We crossed the road and walked along the footpath to town. A few minutes into the walk, Cole took my hand in his. My heart jumped as his fingers slotted perfectly between mine. The gesture was probably nothing to him, but it made my insides turn to mush.

Despite wanting to skip, I kept my head down, hiding slightly behind Cole. I was in my school uniform and didn't want to be seen by anyone my parents knew.

Dad wouldn't like my truancy at all.

We finally reached the place that served the best ice cream around—Julie's Café. Cole and I spent so much time there that it was like a home away from home. We would chill in one of the booths and eat our fill of ice cream. It looked like a typical diner-style café with light-blue walls, cream booths, and blue tables.

"Oh, there you two are!" Julie called across the café. She was in her mid-forties, and was one of the sweetest, friendliest, and most caring people I knew.

The first thing I noticed about her was her new haircut. It usually fell just below the small of her back but was mostly tied up. Now, it sat on her shoulders and flicking under. It made her look a lot younger.

"Take a seat. I'll bring over your usual." She ushered us towards a booth by the window.

It was the one we always chose whenever it was free. The few times it wasn't, Cole would glare at whoever had taken it like they'd just spat in his face. It was ours.

"Thanks," Cole said, laughing as Julie fussed around, swiping up a crumpled napkin from our table.

Everything had to be perfect for her customers; that was just how she was. We had barely sat down when one of the waitresses appeared with a chocolate milkshake and chocolate ice cream for Cole, and a strawberry milkshake and cookie dough ice cream for me.

I was just about to dig in when I heard a voice that made me want to throw something. It was the girl who liked Cole—the no-name, Meg-look-alike *babe* with the bun girl.

Cole winced when he noticed her.

"Why didn't you say where you were going?" no-name exclaimed, throwing her arms up in the air. Why couldn't I remember her?

Ben walked over to our table with her and smiled apologetically.

I wasn't sure if they'd followed us—though we didn't notice —or if Cole had told them about our hangout spot. Stupidly, that option stung. This was *our* place. I was as possessive about our traditions as he was over our booth.

"What are you guys doing here?" Cole asked, his carefree expression morphing into a frown. At least he seemed as put out as I was.

The girl sat down next to Cole. I wanted her name to go with the ridiculous hate I felt burning inside my heart. She was pretty, but the fact that she liked the guy I liked made her hideous to me. It was completely irrational, and I hated feeling that way, but that was how jealousy worked, wasn't it?

"Just wanted to grab a shake," she replied in her annoyingly whiny voice. "What would you suggest?"

That you leave.

"I don't know, Courtney," Cole replied.

Courtney. I didn't like it. To be fair, whatever her name was, I wouldn't have liked it.

"Can I get a vanilla shake, please?" Ben shouted across the room.

Julie frowned at him but nodded.

I stopped listening to what else Ben was saying when Courtney grabbed Cole's milkshake and took a long sip from the straw.

What the...?

"So, you've known Cole your whole life?"

I turned my attention back to Ben who had asked the question. He was smiling nervously and ran a hand down his tanned cheek. His lips pulled up into a half-smile. I dipped my head to answer.

"You'll have to tell me some embarrassing stories about Cole, so—" He stopped abruptly, and his eyes widened, horrified. "Shit! I mean...n–not tell but, er—oh, shit, I'm sorry, Oakley. I didn't think," he stuttered, grimacing.

I smiled and shook my head to tell him I wasn't offended. He hadn't said it as in insult. It wasn't a cheap shot at my expense. People just assumed that if someone was over the age of two, they could and would speak.

"Damn, I really know how to put my foot in my mouth, hey?" He chuckled, and his dark eyes lost the tension as soon as he knew I wasn't going to run off, upset, and Cole wasn't going to punch him.

"Anyway..." He shook his head and frowned, as if he was chastising himself internally. "You should come to my party this weekend. Cole's going to be there."

Is everyone having a party this weekend?

It wasn't often that I was invited to these things, but I wasn't even sure that I wanted to go, anyway. It wouldn't be much fun for Cole if I were there. He wouldn't be able to leave my side all night, but maybe it would be fun. If the other people going were half as cool as Ben, then I might even have a good time.

If Cole looked like he was bored, I could always go home early. All I would have to do was get my parents' approval, but I would be with Cole, and they trusted him, so that wouldn't be hard.

With a nod of my head before I could overthink things, I accepted his invitation.

"Great, I'll save a dance for ya," he said, winking at me.

Whoa. What?

I blushed and shifted in my seat, not liking that kind of attention... but not exactly hating it, either. Ben was playing around but it felt nice, normal.

"You ready to leave, Oakley?" Cole snapped.

Already? I hadn't even finished my milkshake or ice cream. I was about to shake my head until I noticed Cole's face was tense with irritation.

He got up, and I took that as my cue to leave. Cole quickly weaved around the tables and almost jogged away. I had to power walk to catch up with him.

What the...

As soon as he slowed down a fraction, and my breathing was normal again, we fell into a comfortable pace. I raised my eyebrows at him. He understood that I was asking him what the bloody hell was going on.

"It's nothing."

Nothing?

He didn't often lie to me. He shook his head, looking around to avoid me pressing the issue further, and I let it go. We walked on in an uncomfortable silence. I felt weird, hating anything being off between us.

"So... you coming to mine?" he asked when we reached his car in the car park at school.

I nodded eagerly. Spending some time alone with him was definitely what I wanted, what I needed, and I loved being at his place. Cole's parents and his sister Mia treated me like one of the family. I felt so at ease there, I preferred it to being at my own house—no question. Cole smiled, his eyes lingering on mine for a little longer than usual.

With the way my heart went wild, you'd think he'd just kissed me.

"Hello, sweetie," Jenna welcomed Cole as we walked through his front door. "Oh, hi, Oakley," she gushed, giving me a warm hug.

Cole mumbled something that sounded like, "Hi," and walked off to his room. He was probably annoyed about the 'sweetie' thing as well as whatever else had turned him moody.

"What's wrong with him?" she asked more to herself than me.

I shrugged anyway and smiled back at her. Jenna always smelt of coconut shampoo and peach moisturiser. She was sunshine.

"You should follow Mr Happy. I'll call you when dinner's ready."

She hadn't even asked me if I wanted to stay for dinner; she just knew I would. I'd never say no to spending more time at their house.

Cole's room hadn't changed much since we'd decorated it two years ago when he was fifteen. It was still the same shade of blue. He hated it now, though, saying it looked like a baby's room. I doubted he would change it anytime soon as he was too lazy. He'd just covered the walls with posters of motorbikes and cars that, unless he won the lottery, he'd probably never be able to afford.

He was lying on his bed with his hands behind his head, staring at the ceiling. His bottom lip was trapped between his teeth. Whatever was going on in his head was really bothering him.

He'd invited me over and left me. Not cool.

I lay down on my side, propping my head up on my hand, and waited. It didn't usually take too long for him to come around, but after just a few minutes, I became impatient. I gently nudged him in the ribs, prompting him to spill.

"What?" he whispered, still not looking at me.

I sighed and rested my head back, having absolutely no idea what was going on. Maybe the Julian thing was still weighing on his mind.

"Sorry," he eventually muttered with a sigh of his own.

Ah, he's back.

Sorry for what, exactly? I hated it when he was cryptic. It wasn't often that he could hide something from me, but when he did, it drove me *crazy*.

We laid beside each other in silence. As the seconds ticked by, my eyes started to feel heavy. His steady breathing, in and out, was like my own personal lullaby.

Without too much of a fight, I gave in and closed my eyes. A few seconds later, Cole grabbed my hand, interlacing our fingers, and then I fell asleep.

Chapter 4

Oakley

The mattress depressing woke me before Cole sat up on the bed and turned my way. Rubbing my tired eyes, I sat up.

"Sorry, did I wake you?" he asked softly, grimacing. "I tried to be quiet."

I shook my head even though he had. It probably wasn't a good idea to nap for too long anyway. I'd only end up wide awake until the early hours, and I liked sleep now the nightmares had stopped.

Smirking, he said, "Liar."

Oh, yeah, he knew when I wasn't being honest—most of the time.

"Anyway, your parents are coming over for dinner, too. We're having a barbecue... *again*."

Grinning, I stretched my arms up, unlocking my muscles. I loved sitting out in Cole's back garden eating barbecue food. Cole's dad David would always forget about the food, and he'd wander off, only to come back to it when it'd reached the point of no return. We'd end up having to smother the burnt bits in tomato sauce. It had become a tradition, though. I couldn't eat unburnt barbecue food anymore.

"So, that guy at school today—Julian..." Cole said, trailing off. His jaw tightened; eyes tensed. He was unsure if he should bring it up or not. *Not* would be the answer, so I shook my head.

School was over for the day, and I was with Cole. There wasn't anything in the world I wanted to think about other than a long summer of hanging out with him.

"Yeah, I know you don't want to talk about it, but tough. Does he do that a lot?" Cole's eyes pinned me with a steely gaze that was seeking nothing but the truth. A good lie wouldn't work this time. "We're doing this, Oakley, whether you like it or not. Does he always harass you?"

Closing my eyes, I reluctantly nodded my head once. There was no point in trying to fib and assure him that nothing was going on. He would see right through that.

Sometimes, I felt like he could read my mind... But then he had no clue about what happened to me, so obviously not.

"That bastard. I'm going to kill him," he growled angrily.

My eyes widened, and I raised my hands, desperately pleading with him not to do anything stupid. *Can't you see that it will just make things worse?* I didn't want any more fighting.

Julian, I could handle. When I left school, I wouldn't have to deal with him ever again. He was a tiny, insignificant, and temporary part of my life. He was nothing.

Cole's face softened, and he groaned. "I'm sorry, Oakley. I just fucking hate that people give you a hard time. I'll leave it, I promise... as long as he doesn't do anything like that again. You let me know if he does, okay?"

Sagging in relief, I rested my head on his shoulder. He wrapped an arm around me and pulled me closer to his side. My heart started drumming as he rubbed circles on my arm with his thumb. I loved his touch. Not once had I ever felt sick or scared with him. It was completely different to anyone else's touch, and I never wanted him to stop.

Cole was safe.

"Want to watch a film until dinner?" he asked as he picked up the remote and flicked through the movie channels.

I nodded against his shoulder, though he was already searching. I couldn't care less what we did, anyway. The movie didn't matter.

We chose a comedy and hid away in his room until Jenna called us down for dinner. I could have quite happily stayed in his room for the rest of the night, but I knew our parents would want us to be with them.

Cole leapt up, and I slowly climbed off the bed, preparing myself to go and act normal. Or as normal as it got for me. The pretending was exhausting.

"Finally. I'm starving," Cole exclaimed. "I'm having three burgers."

Smiling to myself, I followed Cole at my own pace.

Mum was standing at the bottom of the stairs, looking up at me. How long had she been waiting there? I raised my hand in a little wave as I reached her, and she pulled me into a hug. It was her way of trying to make everything better. A hug from Mum had fixed things when I was really little, but I hadn't felt safe like that in eleven years.

"Are you okay, honey? Jenna mentioned that you were both home early," she whispered, stroking my hair.

I pulled back to nod and convince her that I was all right.

"Are you sure? Did someone do or say something to you?" she asked, pressing further. Her eyes were full of worry. I was the reason she stressed so much. She was desperate to fix me.

But there was nothing anyone could do.

The damage had been done. It was now down to me to contain it—to stop the poison spreading any further.

I shook my head and rolled my eyes, successfully convincing her that I was all good. Sometimes I wondered how much she believed. Whether she trusted what I 'told' her or whether she just desperately wanted to believe it.

The tension in her eyes evaporated, but not completely. "Okay. You know you can come to me, though—for *anything*."

No.

I smiled again.

"Good. Now, let's eat, yeah?"

Mum tugged on my hand, pulling me through Cole's house. Sometimes—actually, most of the time—she still saw me as her little girl. It was as if, in her eyes, I'd stopped ageing the moment I stopped talking.

We stepped outside into the heat. It was a stuffy heat but their seating was under a large parasol so we had shade.

Taking a seat next to Cole, I watched David standing at the barbecue for a change. My brother Jasper was talking to Mia. Well, he was bickering with her, as usual. No doubt he was trying to convince Mia of one of his stupid theories. His last one was that 'sausages and bacon couldn't come from the same animal because they tasted nothing alike, and it was all part of some big conspiracy theory'.

Yeah, I was related to him.

Someone was missing from the table, though: my dad.

I glanced over my shoulder, looking around the large, landscaped back garden. He was nowhere to be seen, and anxiety curled in my stomach. Wasn't he supposed to be here, too?

I didn't want to be anywhere near him, but I also hated when I didn't know where he was. He could pop up from any direction.

Cole waved his hand in front of my face, bringing me back to reality. "Hello? You okay?"

I nodded and grabbed a can of Coke from the cool box by

the table just to have something to do—some distraction from worrying where Dad was.

"About school." My dad's voice finally cut through everyone else's.

Damn it, where the hell was he?

I jumped and spun my head around to find him walking towards me from inside the house. We'd just come from there and I hadn't seen him.

"You can't just walk out like that. If someone's bullying you then you need to let me know and I will contact the school."

I cracked open the can and nodded, looking down at the table, not yet able to meet his eye.

"I mean it, Oakley," he added sternly. His tone was harsh, but no one even looked up. To them, he was just a concerned father telling his daughter off because he was worried about her.

So that I wouldn't cause a scene or prolong the discussion, I nodded once more.

"Good girl. Now, grab a plate. I think the food's ready." He kissed the top of my head and went to take his seat next to Mum. I forced down acid rising up my throat.

Thankfully, Cole started talking to me about a class trip the sixth form students were taking to a theme park, and how he wished I was going, too. I threw myself into listening to him and not dwelling on Dad being angry, but I didn't feel hungry anymore. I knew I should eat, though. All I'd had today was ice cream, and Mum would start fussing if I didn't have a proper meal.

Despite the nap, I was *so* ready for bed.

David placed a plate of burgers and sausages on the table. I took a sausage and grabbed a bread roll, then I forced myself to take a bite of my ketchup-smothered, charred sausage.

"It's agreed? Two weeks in Italy!" Jenna exclaimed, clapping her hands together.

Italy? What had I missed?

"While you were off in Oakley Land, we just planned the holiday," Cole explained, reading my confused expression.

Oh! Okay, today was starting to look up. Every year, we would go away with Cole's family, and I loved every second of it.

"Italy," Mum confirmed, her face lighting up. "I've always wanted to visit the Vatican."

"That's why I suggested it, love," Dad said, kissing her cheek. It repulsed me when he touched her.

I turned my head away to see Cole wink at me.

My face was instantly on fire, and this time, I think he noticed. Last year in Spain, Cole and I were allowed to go off on our own. We'd only spent a short time with our parents. I wanted that again so badly.

Why do I have to turn into such an idiot when he does things like that?

We couldn't be together.

He deserved someone who could be normal with him.

Once we finished dinner, Cole and I went back up to his room so that I could watch *Hollyoaks*. We didn't have Sky TV because Dad complained that it was a rip-off, them charging so much, so Cole would record the next look episode for me every single day.

It was a trashy soap but watching other people's dramas and tragedies reminded me that I wasn't alone. Even if they were fictional.

Cole laid down on his bed first, his arm above his head. It was an invitation—one I didn't even need to think about. I shuffled down on the bed and laid my head on his chest, listening to the steady beat of his heart. My favourite sound.

"Whoa, bad move," Cole called out, shaking his head at the TV. He hated the programme so much that he would make a running commentary on everything that was going on.

I laughed at him, enjoying his stupid remarks. Secretly, he loved it, too.

"Oakley," he warned, glancing down.

I pressed my lips together. My mouth ached where I tried to keep a straight face.

Cole chuckled and moved fast. I gasped in surprise as he rolled us over and hovered above me.

Oh. Okay. What the hell is happening here?

His legs were either side of mine, and he pinned my hands over my head. I wasn't scared, not at all. For half a second, I waited for the panic, but it never came. Being alone with Cole had never scared me.

I should have shoved him off. But it felt... *right*. So right that my throat clogged with emotion so fierce I wasn't sure what to do with it.

Shouldn't I hate this?

"Are you sorry?" He half-smiled and raised a brow.

I shook my head to play along, but my mind was elsewhere. Like with the uncontrollable thumping of my heart and the heat that poured through my veins.

"All right, you asked for it," he said with a shrug. His blue eyes glistened, and his face became mischievous as it inched closer to mine.

What...?

Those eyes flicked to my lips and back up to my eyes.

Oh, God.

"Oakley, your parents said it's time to go!" Mia shouted as she burst into the room. "Whoa!" She gasped, and her eyes rounded as she spotted the position we were in.

It looked so, so bad.

Laughing, she backed up. "Actually, you know what? Why don't you two finish first? I'll just go tell them you'll be a minute."

Cole pushed himself up off me and reached down the side of the bed for something. He threw one of his trainers, but she managed to jump out of the way before it hit her.

"Shut the fuck up, Mia," he growled.

Mia cackled, delighted at what she'd seen, and stepped out of the room. I *really* hoped she wouldn't tell my parents about this. Not that we'd even been doing anything in the first place. I just didn't want them to think anything was going on with Cole because they probably wouldn't let us be alone together.

I *needed* Cole, and that wasn't an exaggeration.

Without looking him in the eyes because my face was flaming in embarrassment—something that had happened three times today—I quickly kissed his cheek and hopped off the bed.

Refusing to meet his eyes, I ran from his room like a little coward.

"Are you ready, sweetheart?" Mum asked, placing a protective arm around my waist when I made it back downstairs.

I didn't reply to her question because Dad stepped in front of me.

"Let's get you home. School tomorrow." He smiled and stroked his hand down the back of my head.

I pressed my lips together and slipped past them both, giving a wave to Cole's parents on my way to the front door.

"Thank you for tonight," Dad said to David and Jenna. "You'll have to come to ours soon."

"You're welcome, Max, and you know we'd love to," Jenna responded.

I took a deep breath and watched them exchange their good-byes. It looked so normal, just friends thanking each other, making plans, and saying goodbye.

Dad was a good man to the rest of the world.

I was the only one who could see through the facade.

The only one who knew the two versions of him.

And I hated them both.

"Why does it take them ten minutes to say bye?" Jasper moaned, appearing at my side. He shook his head and narrowed his blue eyes. His dirty blond hair whipped lightly with the movement.

Where had he come from?

I shrugged. They would say goodbye and then start another conversation. It would go on like that for a while. Made no sense to me.

"We're leaving!" Jasper called loudly.

Mum lifted her hand, telling us to go ahead, and went back to chatting about Dad's business. Judging by the recent hushed phone conversations and his stressed outbursts, I guessed it was in trouble.

I walked home with Jasper. He hung back at my slower pace. I could tell by the way he glanced over at me that he wanted me to hurry up, probably because he was keen to get home and play on his Xbox.

We crossed the road, almost home. It was getting late but still sweltering hot. The kind of heat that took your breath away and made you feel gross.

"Damn it," Jasper muttered. "You got a key?"

I sighed in exasperation and shook my head. My key was in my schoolbag in Cole's bedroom, and after him laying on top of me, I could never go back there again. Or at least not tonight.

We both turned and looked back towards Cole's house just as our parents were walking along the path. Mum had my schoolbag over her shoulder. Thank God I didn't have to go back and get it. I wasn't ready to see Cole again yet.

Dad unlocked the door and let us in. "Make sure you do any schoolwork you missed today, Oakley," he instructed, tipping his chin towards the bag that Mum let slip off her shoulder. There wouldn't be any missed work, it was the end of the year.

I nodded and took it from her. I was so drained from an extremely long day, and I just needed to be out of the way, so I went straight to my room.

Just as I snuggled under my thick, puffy covers, my mobile beeped with a text message. I knew it would be from Cole. Not only was he the one person to text me, apart from my parents and Jasper, but he'd also send a message *every* night.

My skin pebbled with goosebumps as I opened it. It said just one word. Every night, it would be just one word.

Cole: Night x

I hit reply and typed.

Oakley: Good night x

But, like every night, I didn't press send.

Chapter 5

Cole

I had no clue why I was sitting here waiting for a reply from Oakley. Every night, I'd wait like a moron, knowing full well a response wasn't coming. Most girls my age spend half of their lives and their parents' salaries texting. Not her.

Tomorrow was the last day of school. We would have six weeks off, and I planned to spend every one of them with her.

There were so many things we wanted to do, and now Italy. She was the only person I could be with constantly and never get bored. Oakley was so much more than my best friend.

"All right, loser," Mia said, leaning against my doorframe with a shit eating grin in place.

I leant against the wall and scowled at how much she was enjoying tormenting me over Oakley. I'd told her we're just friends a million times, but she never believed me. "What do you want?"

She arched her eyebrow, and I knew I wouldn't like what she was about to say. "So... what was going on earlier?"

"What do you mean?"

"Don't play dumb, Cole, it doesn't suit you." She moved into my room and closed the door. Folding her arms, she asked, "Is there something going on between you and Oakley?"

"No."

Not that I wasn't desperate to be there. Things were... complicated. I had to tread carefully because one minute I was sure she wanted more, and the next she would be so deep inside her own head, I didn't feel like I could ever reach her.

"Really? Because that's not what it looked like from where I was standing."

I gave Mia a look—one that told her to get lost. She obviously wouldn't be going anywhere, though.

"Don't be like that. I'm just worried about you two."

"Why?"

What could be so wrong about us being together?

I hated how people treated Oakley just because she was a bit different. Nothing between us was strained or ever felt weird because she didn't talk. Nothing.

She'd be my best friend—the person I shared things with, the one I laughed with, and made plans with—whether she spoke or not. I wanted to hear her voice—of course, I did—but it made no difference to me if that never happened.

I was crazy in love with her, silent or not.

People could piss off with their judgments.

"Because of how things are," Mia said, breaking me from my thoughts.

I gritted my teeth, and Mia seemed to notice how much that had angered me.

Her lips curved, and she held her hand up. "Don't. That's not how I meant it. I love Oakley, too. You know that. Probably not in the same way as you. The girl is like a sister to me."

She's so not like a sister to me.

"I'm talking about Max and Sarah, and how they see and treat her. I'm willing to bet *a lot* of money on them wanting you to be with her over everyone else on this planet, but I don't think they'd be okay with it straight off."

I frowned. "Why do you say that?"

"Er, well, for the how-they-see-her thing. I thought that was obvious."

They did treat Oakley like she was made of glass. I thought we were all guilty of that at some point. There were times when she'd look so lost, I'd just want to wrap her up.

We were all protective over her. I did it because I loved her. Mia was suggesting Max and Sarah were that way because of something else as well.

They still thought of Oakley as a little girl.

Damn.

That realisation was like having a hundred cold showers all at once.

And that was so *not* how I thought of her. One day maybe we would get to the bottom of Oakley's selective mutism, but at no point had I ever seen her as anything other than exactly who she was.

I blew out a breath and sat down on my bed.

"See why I'm worried now? I don't want you to get hurt, and I also don't want you two to be apart if you want to be together."

"But you don't think anything should happen between us until her parents realise she's not five anymore? How can they not see that?"

"I don't have to answer that, right? That was rhetorical?"

I scoffed. "You know it was. Look, it doesn't matter, anyway. I'm not sure Oakley is into me like that."

"You don't know how she feels because you two play best friends all the time. I mean, besides that *thing* I saw tonight." She pursed her lips, like she knew something I didn't.

"Yeah, I do. I don't really know how to explain our relation-ship, but even if she does want something to happen, I think she'd be wanting something in the future. I don't know if she's ready now. I can wait."

Really, I didn't know anything.

Mia's grin stretched across her whole face, and I groaned. I'd just admitted that I liked Oakley so she wasn't going to let this go.

Whatever, I could take it. Oakley was the most beautiful person in the world. We'd been friends since before we could walk, and it would always be her for me.

"I just want you to be happy, Cole. I know how much she means to you and how much you mean to her. I'd hate for anything to come between that. You know?"

"Are you telling me that you think it'd be a bad idea if we wanted more?"

Losing her as a friend because I fucked up as her boyfriend had been something I'd thought of hundreds of times before. It was always a risk, but I was determined not to fuck up.

"Not at all. I'm telling you, if you do, you need to handle it properly."

"Well, this chat's been nice... and a complete waste of time," I said. "I like her, I won't lie, but I'm happy with how things are right now."

She tilted her head like she thought I was full of crap. Accurate. "Then, I'm happy, too, I guess."

"Great."

Why wasn't she leaving?

She hesitated, on the edge of what looked like was going to be a confession. "Can I ask you something?"

"Sure."

"If another girl came along, someone you were physically attracted to..."

"Would I still go there even though I want Oakley?"

She nodded, wincing apologetically. I had a feeling there was more to this question.

"Now, no. I've liked Oakley for a while, in the sense that I felt something would eventually happen, but I still went out with a couple of girls. But the older Oakley gets, the closer to being done with high school she gets. And the more she plans for uni and the future, the less I've noticed other girls. I don't know."

Maybe that didn't make much sense. I wasn't sure what I was doing when it came to her. There was no plan—I was following my gut.

"No, I get it. An innocent friendship becoming more isn't always an overnight thing. Plus, she's still fifteen."

"Why ask that, though?"

Mia pursed her lips. "No reason. I just wondered."

Her dickhead ex was probably the reason. "You okay? Something on your mind?"

"Nah, I'm good. Night, idiot."

"Night."

She left my room, and I got undressed for bed. My phone sat on my bedside table in complete silence.

You're stupid if you think she's ever going to reply.

What was different about tonight? Nothing.

Groaning, I got into bed and forced myself to look away from my phone. I had to stop obsessing over it.

And I would.

But not today.

Chapter 6

Oakley

I woke up in the morning to the sunlight streaming through the crack in my curtains, and someone gently shaking my arm.

"Oakley, time to get up," Mum whispered. "Are you feeling okay? I don't normally have to wake you."

I rubbed my eyes and groaned. My body was heavy, tired, and I wanted nothing more than to get a few more hours sleep.

She watched me carefully as I sat up and turned to her. I smiled, letting her know that I was fine, though my head was pounding and all I wanted to do was stay in bed. But Dad worked from home on Thursdays and Fridays, and I knew he wouldn't be happy if I missed another day... even if this was the last one. He would worry about people finding out that I was skipping. It wouldn't look good for his perfect family image if his daughter was truant.

"Okay. Well, breakfast will be ready soon. I'm making scrambled eggs on toast. You need a good breakfast for your last day of school."

She patted my arm and left me to get ready.

Once she was gone, I wasted no time in packing my bag and

40

changing into my uniform for the very last time. It was far too hot for the school blazer, but the teachers didn't seem to care about students dropping like flies in the heat.

I took a deep breath before brushing my teeth. *Just this one last day to get through.*

When I got downstairs for breakfast, Cole was already sitting at the table, eating scrambled eggs. He wore shorts, a T-shirt, and an easy smile. My stomach clenched when he made eye contact. I felt like he saw so much more than everyone else... but only the good things.

"Morning, Oaks," he mumbled, chewing on his food.

I hated my name being shortened, and he knew that. *Arsehole.*

Chuckling, he pulled out the chair next to him.

He didn't seem any different after what almost happened the night before. I could feel a mild electric shock every time I looked at him.

I sat down next to him and dipped my chin at Mum, thanking her for the breakfast she'd placed in front of me.

"So, are you two doing anything after school?" Mum asked, grinning at both of us. I didn't think Mia would have told her what she walked in on, but Mum often got doe-eyed when she saw Cole and me together.

"Probably getting some ice cream or something, right?" He glanced at me and shovelled another forkful of eggs into his mouth.

I smiled in agreement. That sounded like the perfect way to end the year—unlike some of my classmates, who I'd heard were getting drunk at the park.

Mum made small talk with Cole, and I tried to force some food down. It was almost impossible with the butterflies Cole gave me every time his eyes slid to mine.

"Okay, come on. We're going to be late," Cole mumbled as

we finished breakfast. He grabbed my hand and pulled me off the chair.

I gasped in surprise but didn't pull my hand back. His touch always felt nice.

~

We parked outside the sixth form building, like we always did.

Our last day.

I could do this.

"Look, if anyone says anything to you today, come find me. You know what lessons I have, and if I have a free one, I'll be in the sixth form block."

The only reason I knew what lessons he had was because he constantly sent me screenshots of his timetable so I would know where to find him. It was sweet but completely unnecessary. I would never go running into his lesson to get him.

I could handle it.

"You could even... um, text me, you know. I'd come and find you straightaway," he added quietly, staring out of the window once he'd parked the car.

I dropped my gaze to my lap. That couldn't happen—ever.

It was a slippery slope from a casual text to 'why are you mute?'. It wasn't something I could risk. I wasn't allowed.

Cole sighed and flopped back into his seat. "Okay, just come and find me, then."

My stomach twisted with unease. Disappointing him felt awful every single time it happened. The atmosphere between us morphed into something else when he tried to hide his frustration.

"It's okay," he said as he ran a hand through his purposefully messy hair. "I'll see you later, yeah?"

Averting my eyes, I give him a short nod and got out of the

42

car. Cole sighed as he walked away from me, this time not looking back.

It's okay. He just needs a minute.

I'd make things better with him somehow. This wasn't the first time he'd needed some space from me after I'd turned him down.

Turned him down, as in not properly communicating. He could kiss me all he wanted.

My hope for an uneventful day was nearly crushed the second I pushed open the heavy green door. Julian was standing ahead of me in the middle of the corridor. He was messing around with his friends, shoving each other, and laughing. The corner of Julian's lip was swollen and bruised. He deserved it.

"Hi," Hannah said from behind me.

Startled, I spun around and held my hand over my heart.

I'd half-expected it to be Laura or one of her pathetic little friends.

I raised my hand in a wave, and we walked to our form room together.

"Sorry. Last day. I can't believe it. We made it, Oakley!"

Her excitement was infectious. Everywhere I looked, people were happy, chatting with animation and laughing.

I nudged her, and she beamed.

"No more high school!"

No more high school. Thank God!

The morning went by without incident and my music teacher let us go five minutes early for lunch. No one was doing anything now, anyway. Even the worksheets being handed out were being thrown in the bin without a mark on them. Mine included. Coursework was in, exams were done. The rest of it was just passing time. Craft and sport stuff, team games, and 'making memories'. There wasn't much I wanted to remember from high school.

I packed everything into my bag slowly so I would be the last one to leave.

"You coming to the canteen?" Hannah asked as she grabbed her bag and swung it over her shoulder.

I shook my head and smiled, grateful that she had at least invited me along.

"Okay, see you later." She waved over her shoulder as she walked out with her friends.

I quickly made my way along the corridor. After lunch, I only had two lessons to get through. The back corridor was deserted—everyone had already gone to buy food or gone outside since the sun was out—and less crazy than yesterday.

Someone grabbed me from behind. I gasped and clawed at their arm. He let go when he shoved me into a classroom.

I spun around, my heart almost leaping out of my chest. A wave of nausea almost drowned me.

"Hey, Oakley." Julian smirked, standing in front of the door, blocking my escape.

My clammy hands trembled as I clenched them together.

Gulping, I backed up a step. His hands on me made my stomach churn.

"I was hoping to find you on your own."

I swallowed down bile that worked its way up my throat.

"Come on, don't look so scared. I'm not going to hurt you." His breath smelt so strongly of tobacco that it made me gag. He'd been for a smoke right before grabbing me.

Julian leant towards me, and I recoiled in horror, not wanting this dickhead anywhere near me.

"I just want to talk," he whispered, tucking my hair behind my ear.

Violent images flashed through my mind so forcefully that I couldn't move for a second. They stole my breath and almost my sanity.

Don't be a victim again. Don't ever be a victim again.

I tapped into the anger buried deep—and there was *a lot*—and shoved his chest so hard that he slammed into the door behind him, his head bouncing off the square pane of glass.

I felt like screaming, like my blood was going to boil, and my teeth would snap under the pressure of gritting them together.

"Ah, fuck," he spat, rubbing the back of his head. "Why do you have to be such a little bitch, Oakley? What the hell makes you better than anyone else, huh?" he bellowed before punching the wall.

I jumped back, my eyes widening in shock. *What was that?*

Julian looked almost out of it. His eyes were dilated, and he was panting. I didn't think it was just tobacco he'd been smoking.

"Who the fuck do you think you are?" His lips curled, baring his teeth.

Oh, God, what's he going to do to me?

Nothing. He wasn't going to do anything. I *wouldn't* let him hurt me.

I stood taller, ignoring the dread and the desire to run away and hide.

The door swung open and Mrs Stains, one of the teaching assistants, stood in front of us. "What's going on? You shouldn't be in here."

Julian straightened up. "We were just talking about a project," he said with a cocky smirk.

"A project on the last day of school?" Mrs Stains asked, raising an eyebrow.

"Not a school one," Julian shot back.

She shook her head but knew there was nothing she could do, even though it was clear that Julian was lying.

"Out. Both of you."

I scurried past her and ran out of the building. It seemed like all I did at school was hide out. I hated myself for that, but it was easier.

So, I did what I did best and ran as fast as I could, putting some distance between me and the school. Screw it, I couldn't go back. I was *done*.

As soon as I reached the wooden shelter at the local park, I collapsed to the ground. Wrapping my arms around my legs, I took a deep breath to try to slow my pulse and stop myself from throwing up.

I squeezed my eyes closed as my phone started to vibrate in my pocket. It would be Cole looking for me. I really didn't want to see him. Well, I didn't want him to see me like this.

I counted in my head, reaching one hundred before I opened my eyes and looked up. The park was deserted... at least until tonight when it would be littered with empty bottles of cheap alcohol.

You're safe.

Trees around the perimeter blew softly in the warm breeze. I focused on those for a few minutes until my lungs didn't feel like they were made of lead.

Since I first sat on the ground, my phone had vibrated about ten more times with a few texts and a couple of missed calls.

I unlocked the phone and started reading.

Cole: Hey, where are you? I'm waiting near my car x

I sighed and scrolled down to read the next one.

Cole: Hurry up! I'm starving! x

The next two were similar, but after that, he must have started to worry.

Cole: Oakley, where are you???

Cole: Where the hell are you? Text me back! I just need to know you're okay.

No kiss on the last two messages. Cole was mad at me.

My heart sank at the fact that I'd upset him, but I wasn't in the mood to be around him or anyone. I had to get it together. One look into those pretty blue eyes and I'd crumble.

Switching the phone off, I lay down on the sun-scorched grass, feeling pathetic.

If the teacher hadn't opened the door when she did, what would Julian have done?

I wasn't sure if he would physically hurt me, but I didn't trust him. I didn't trust anyone besides my mum, brother, and Cole.

"Oakley?"

Cole's face came into view above me. I wasn't at all surprised to see him.

He sat down beside me and sighed. "What the fuck, Oakley? Do you have any idea how worried I've been?"

He looked as mad as he had been at Julian when he punched him.

I stared at him, trying to figure out how to deal with this situation. Cole watched me right back, his eyes sinking deeper into mine. I wanted to reach out and touch him, but I wasn't sure if he'd let me right now.

The air between us felt thicker, like I could choke on it, but that wasn't a bad thing.

"What happened?" he asked. His voice was tight, but he was trying to be calm. Hurt and confusion etched into his expression. I'd done that to him, and it felt horrible.

Still staring into his eyes, I gently shook my head.

"Nothing? You're telling me nothing happened?"

This time I nodded and hoped he would believe me.

"Why didn't you text back or wait for me before you took off like that? I was worried about you. You just walk off... like you don't even care."

I flinched at his words. I did care. *That* was the problem. I cared about him far too much to let him see me so vulnerable. To Cole, I didn't want to be 'poor Oakley'. I didn't want his pity, because then nothing could happen between us.

He scratched the back of his neck. "You should have at least replied. I didn't know what'd happened to you."

I looked away, not wanting to see disappointment in his eyes.

He hadn't mentioned me texting in a while, yet in the last two days, he'd brought it up multiple times.

His hands dragged through his hair. "Oakley! God, you have no idea, do you?"

His sudden outburst made me jump.

We had argued and annoyed each other before, but he had never been this angry. He looked wrecked.

Sucking in a sharp breath, he said, "Don't worry about it. You obviously don't give a shit about me, so just forget it. I'm done."

He stood up and quickly walked away, moving fast as if he couldn't be anywhere near me for another second.

What the hell?

I watched him walk away, leaving me completely numb besides the tears that rolled down my face. The ache in my chest grew stronger as I realised he was doing the right thing.

For him...

Chapter 7

Cole

Walking away from her felt so wrong but she made me so damn angry. No one else could get to me the way she did.

Most of the time, I liked it, but today, it *hurt*. I scratched at the annoying pinch in my chest as I put more distance between us.

I knew she hated school, and it killed me that I couldn't do more about it.

Oakley wasn't selfish, I knew that, but sometimes it seemed like she might be. She found it too easy to walk away from me and keep her secrets. It took everything I had to leave her back there.

There was no way I was going to go back to afternoon classes after that. I was too wound up. Besides, we wouldn't be doing anything, anyway.

Ben was leaning against my car, doing something on his phone when I got back. As I got closer, he looked up and pushed off. "What's going on, man? You took off without a word."

Yeah, that was a mistake. I shouldn't have bothered. She doesn't *care*.

"Nothing," I growled.

"Whoa," he said, raising his palms. "I was only asking."

I ran my hand over my face. "I know. Sorry."

"Oakley?" he asked, lifting his jet-black eyebrow. When I didn't answer, he nodded. "All right, what happened? Is she okay?"

"Who knows? She won't tell me."

"You guys have this telepathic thing going on, don't you?"

I looked at him, deadpan. "What?"

"You know what I mean. You get her and what she means when she doesn't talk and all that."

"Yeah, but usually I have something to go on. Right now, she's just pushing me away. I hate it, man. I know something happened at school today, but she won't admit it."

Sometimes, I felt so hopeless when it came to her. She was my best friend, and I knew when she wasn't happy. No one wanted to stop talking, no one wanted to have a shit time at school, and no one wanted to lock out the people closest to them.

Why couldn't she trust me enough with whatever was going on?

I'd told her a million times before that, whatever it was, I'd be there and help her, but that didn't change her decision to keep it locked away.

Nothing ever changed.

Even if it wasn't a decision—if she physically couldn't talk— she could at least admit it by text or a letter.

Why wouldn't she?

"It'll be cool, mate. You've fallen out before, right?"

"Kind of. I've never told her I was done before," I replied, wincing. That was a dick move, one I already regretted.

What the hell was I thinking? I couldn't even convince myself that I would ever be done. I was in far too deep.

I fucking loved her.

His eyes widened in surprise. Yeah, the whole time I'd known Ben, I'd always been fiercely protective of Oakley, so of course, me telling him I was done with her was a shock.

"You don't mean that," he said.

"You and I know that. Not sure she does."

"So... why are you still here? Maybe you should be, you know, telling her all of this. And while you're at it, just bloody kiss her. It's painfully obvious you want to."

"I need to go home," I said, digging into my jeans pocket for my keys.

"She at yours?"

"No."

"You're not going to fix it?"

"Don't, Ben. You've got no idea what it's like, so just don't."

"Right," he said, backing up. "Don't want to watch you make a huge mistake, but it's your life to screw up..."

"Thanks," I muttered sarcastically.

"Welcome," he replied, matching my tone. "Later, man."

"Yeah."

I got in my car and drove home the long way so I wouldn't have to go past the park. I wasn't in the mood to see her right now. Before I saw her again, I needed to calm down and figure out what to do next. Our summer was going to suck if I didn't handle this right.

No one was in when I got home, thankfully, and they wouldn't be until after five. I wanted to head straight for my dad's whiskey, but I knew dealing with Oakley on a hangover would only feel worse.

I slumped down on the sofa and gave in to the fact that I was going to stay there and obsess about her. If I hadn't brought up her messaging me, we wouldn't be in this situation right now.

But it's always bothered me. The stuff people hid were usually the worst things about themselves.

What happened to her? I would give *anything* to know so I could fix it.

Over the years, I'd become a master at getting on with it—at giving Oakley the space she needed to come to me in her own time.

Maybe that was wrong.

Maybe I should've taken a different approach.

Not that pleading, bribery, therapy, or getting angry has ever worked for her parents.

I knew that women were supposed to be inherently complicated, but Oakley gave a new meaning to the definition.

Pathetic thing was, I didn't care how complicated she was. I didn't care that she pushed me away—well, to an extent—and I didn't care that she gutted me every time she shut me out.

I was completely screwed.

It was only when Mia got home that I stopped moping about. I didn't have the energy for a full-on heart-to-heart with her. She walked into the kitchen and headed straight for the wine in the fridge. Her day must have been about as good as mine, then.

"What's up with you?" I asked, getting off my arse and following her.

"Ugh, nothing I want to discuss."

That meant Chris the Dick had done something—or someone.

"What about you? Why do you look like someone's just kicked your puppy?" she asked.

"Nothing I want to discuss," I said, using her words against her.

She smirked as she unscrewed the lid. "Touché. Well, how do you feel about drowning our sorrows?"

"I think Mum and Dad would have something to say about that when they got in."

Turning her nose up, she scoffed. "You're right, and I really don't need the third degree from them." Filling a large glass with white wine, she sat opposite me in the kitchen. "Question for you: why does the universe insist on throwing so much shit at you?"

I shrugged. Good question.

She took a long swig. "There has to be an easier way."

"Are we talking about Chris here? The guy's a bellend, Mia. It has nothing to do with the universe."

She froze mid-sip and glared at me. "It's not just him, though, is it?"

"Are you asking me why you're not strong enough to walk away?"

She narrowed her eyes. "Before you make me answer that, you need to ask yourself why you're sitting here looking like that over Oakley... *again*."

It wasn't the first time Oakley had unintentionally hurt me, and Mia knew it.

"It's not the same," I said, folding my arms.

"The situation, maybe."

Translation: Love sucks.

"Right. I get it," I said. "What do we do?"

"You won't like the answer."

"Tell me anyway."

"We just get on with it. We fight to be better people, more understanding, stronger. Ultimately, we've just got to ride it out until we're willing to change, and we've got to be okay with not being perfect human beings who are fully in control of their lives... despite what their stupid hearts want," she said.

"Yeah, you're right. I don't like that."

"And that, my little brother, is why they make alcohol."
Laughing, I shook my head on the way to the fridge.
Mia was right and beer was the answer.
Fuck love.

Chapter 8

Oakley

He was done.

Done.

I kept replaying his words over and over in my head like a masochist.

Each time they hurt as much as the last, until I'd doubled over.

I shouldn't have ever let myself fall for him. How did I think it was going to end?

You can't even talk to him!

I was sure I wasn't imagining last night when he looked like he wanted to kiss me. Tears flooded my eyes, making the world blur. Heartache and anger pulsed through my veins. This shouldn't be happening.

For the rest of the school day, which was only a few hours, I did nothing but sit inside the shack at the park and stare into space. Dad was at home so I couldn't go back early.

The park was peaceful so it wasn't so bad, but as I heard students walking by on their way home from school, I knew I needed to pull myself together and leave.

Walking slowly, I headed home, looking down at the ground.

Will Mum and Dad still be there? They were going to attend a charity dinner and would have to travel over a hundred miles to get there, so they were supposed to be leaving sometime in the early afternoon once Dad had finished work.

I prayed they had already left.

When I turned the corner, I saw an empty driveway, and I sighed in relief. I walked to the front door, feeling a little lighter. At least I wouldn't have their freak-outs to deal with... if they even knew I skipped school again. I'm sure if they'd received a call from school, they would've come looking for me.

When I pushed the door open, I saw my lazy brother sitting on the sofa, playing his Xbox. His university had finished for summer earlier than my high school, so his holiday started weeks ago.

One day, he would have to grow up and get a house and a job, but it was hard to imagine it after seeing him slob around here for so long.

"Hey," he grunted, not even looking up from the screen.

I dropped my bag and sank into the sofa beside him. School was over, but I couldn't even feel that happy about it. All I could think of was the fight with Cole and that pained look on his face.

Jasper took a double take of my face and paused his game. "What happened?"

I smiled and shook my head.

"Where's Cole?" Jasper's face hardened, his jaw clenched, and his eyes narrowed. "What did he do?" he demanded.

Why leap there?

Again, I shook my head and tried to make out that he was reacting over nothing.

"So, if Cole's not the reason you're upset, who is?" Jasper asked, frowning doubtfully.

Cole was the reason, sure, but it wasn't his fault.

"That idiot at school? The one I beat up last year?" he growled, referring to Julian.

Jasper was usually as soft as a pussycat but not when it came to me. He was overprotective and quick to lash out at anyone he thought was giving me a hard time.

I remembered the incident Jasper was referring to. How could I not? Jasper was still in sixth form. He had caught Julian saying some stuff about me. I still didn't know what, but it'd made Jasper punch him a few times. He'd been suspended from sixth form for a week and then given a week of lunchtime detentions for refusing to apologise to Julian.

It would seem Cole had fully taken over Jasper's role... as a brother. *Oh, God. Does Cole see me as a little sister?*

No, he couldn't. You don't almost kiss your sibling.

I shook my head in answer to Jasper's question, and he got up and walked into the kitchen. There was no way he'd dropped it just like that. I followed him, waiting at the door as he got his phone and started dialling.

Oh no! I knew what he was doing.

As he raised the phone to his ear, I leapt forward and grabbed it out of his hand. He'd started ringing Cole, but thankfully, the call hadn't gone through yet.

He narrowed his eyes. "Okay, I'm going to ask you one more time. Was. It. Cole?"

I sighed in frustration and shook my head for what seemed like the fifteenth time.

"Good. You're not going to tell me what it's about, are you?"

I raised an eyebrow and folded my arms.

"Yeah, didn't think so. You're too damn stubborn for your own good. You're okay, though, right?"

I dipped my head. Settling on changing the subject and getting my annoying, crazy brother back, I opened the fridge, grabbed two cans of Coke, and threw one at him.

That should fizz in his face.

"Thanks," he mumbled, aware that I was trying to end the conversation. He opened the can very carefully in case it exploded all over him.

Unfortunately, it did not.

"Mum and Dad left for that boring thing already. You'll need to cook tonight." He looked away, downing probably half the can at once.

I knew exactly what that meant. Mum had told him to cook, and he was trying to get out of it.

"What are you making?" Jasper asked casually, glancing at the oven.

I rolled my eyes, picked out two pepperoni pizzas from the freezer, and threw them at him before walking upstairs.

"Oakley?" he shouted after me. "Seriously, you're supposed to cook!"

No, I'm not.

I kept on walking, smiling to myself. He was *so* lazy. Christ, all he'd have to do was stick them in the oven for eighteen minutes. It wasn't difficult. I had no clue how he managed to stay alive now he wasn't living at home.

As soon as I closed my bedroom door, I practically ripped off my school uniform—one button popped off my shirt—and angrily chucked it into my laundry basket. I hated school, I hated Julian, but most of all, I hated myself.

From our fight earlier, it was clear that Cole and I were not going to go out for ice cream, so I got into my most comfortable pyjamas and prepared for a night of boring TV.

I should have practiced gymnastics. Dad had turned a spare room downstairs into a mini studio for me – guilt or bribery? – but I couldn't be bothered to do anything. I was going to embrace the mood I was in and sulk.

Sometimes you've got to, right?

Marcus, my gym coach, would not be happy if I didn't perfect the routine by next practice. I didn't care today, though. I'd been going to gymnastics since I was seven, and I loved it. Whenever I was there, it would take me away from my reality. I didn't think about anything or anyone.

It was as if all my problems disappeared.

I was just Oakley.

I was normal.

Until the end of class when Dad picked me up.

Lying back on my bed, I absentmindedly flicked through the TV channels and settled on re-watching yesterday's *Hollyoaks*.

Twenty minutes later, I heard Jasper stomping up the stairs. He pushed my door open. "Dinner! Come and get it. I'm not waiting on your arse!"

He wouldn't come serve me dinner because that would mean he was waiting on me, but he would walk up the stairs to tell me it's done. Idiot.

Grinning to myself, I followed him downstairs to get my probably burnt pizza.

"Ta-da," he said, gesturing to dinner.

He hadn't done too badly. Only the crust was a little darker than it should have been. I did turn my nose up when Jasper squirted mayonnaise all over his pizza. The only thing that belonged with pizza was ketchup.

"I spoke to Cole," he muttered, chewing his food, giving me a good view of the mashed-up dough in his mouth.

Nice. I looked away in response, not wanting to deal with that.

"You left school because of Julian, didn't you?"

That made me look at him. Was that just a good guess or had Cole told him?

I couldn't see Julian admitting to anything.

"Just tell me," Jasper demanded, sounding frustrated. "Was it Julian, Oakley?"

I nodded, feeling defeated. He was going to find out anyway.

Jasper jumped up, balling his hands into fists. "Little twat-faced bastard. I'm gonna kill him!"

Dropping my pizza, I grabbed his arm and shook my head. *What is it with the killing Julian thing?*

Jasper sighed after looking into my pleading eyes. I'd had enough of it all. It was the holiday, anyway, so it didn't matter anymore.

"Fine. But I swear, if he comes near you again, I *will* kill him."

I ignored that. It wasn't worth arguing over.

He muttered something under his breath and pointed to my plate, telling me to eat. "So...is Cole coming over tonight?"

I could tell he was dying to know what had happened between us. Jasper was a massive gossip.

I stood up and grabbed my plate, deciding to eat in my room since Dad wasn't here. I didn't want to have the Cole conversation with Jasper—or anyone, for that matter.

"I'll take that as a no," Jasper called after me.

My room was safe and cosy, decorated with fairy lights and posters of my favourite bands on the walls. I'd filled it with everything that made me happy. It was light and bright—everything I wanted to feel.

Half past eight was too early to go to bed, but I didn't want to go downstairs again and risk Jasper's questions, so I put on a film and curled up under the covers.

I laid in bed watching *Pretty Little Liars* on Jasper's Netflix account. Dad might hate too much TV, but my brother didn't.

As hard as I tried to focus and not think about... someone, I couldn't stop myself. My mind curled back around to Cole about every five seconds, making it hard to concentrate on anything else but him.

I should have gone over to his place and pleaded with him to forgive me, but I was too stubborn and too scared. Cole deserved so much better.

Groaning, I rolled onto my back and threw my arm over my head.

Forgetting him was impossible, even for a little while.

I was falling in love.

Chapter 9

Oakley

The next morning, I woke up to my brother's shouting.

"Oakley! Get up! We're going to Cole's for lunch!" he yelled much louder than necessary.

Jesus!

I rolled over and threw a pink stress ball at the door. Jasper laughed harder when he heard the bang. "You've got fifteen minutes!"

Cole's place for *lunch*.

Groaning, I sat up and checked the time. I didn't usually sleep in so late.

A day ago, I would've jumped at that. Now, I'd fake sickness, but Mum would want to stay with me then.

"We're booking the holiday today," Jasper called through the door. "Get up and get dressed."

My heart sank. This was going to be super awkward. What if Cole ignored me? Everyone would ask what was wrong.

But I missed him like crazy.

There was no way I could get out of it, though. Not without raising suspicion.

I didn't bother with a shower as I didn't have the energy to rush getting ready. After putting on a pair of shorts and a plain T-shirt, I brushed my blonde hair, and then I was done. I looked about as plain as I felt. My hair was almost down to my butt now. It was thick, like a cloak around my face.

When I was ready, I sat on my bed and chewed on my nail as I waited for someone to call me to leave. Maybe it wouldn't be so bad. I was fully prepared to do some grovelling.

Two short minutes later—minutes that felt like seconds—Mum shouted my name.

Butterflies swarmed in my stomach at the thought of seeing Cole again, but this time, they weren't the kind that made me feel stupidly happy.

I took the stairs slowly, prolonging the inevitable.

"You look nice, honey," Mum said, grinning wide, probably thinking the effort was all for Cole. It kind of was. I wanted him to want me, too.

Slipping on my flip flops, I followed my family across the road to Cole's.

Dad walked ahead with Mum—Jasper and I slightly behind.

"You okay?" he whispered when our parents were out of earshot.

I think I smiled at him, but he lifted a brow, so I guess it was more of a grimace. My energy had been zapped, I was unable to pretend I wasn't out of my mind over Cole.

Dad knocked on their door, and within seconds, Jenna greeted us with a hug each. Dad complimented her, smiling, and my stomach rolled.

I took every step as slowly as possible, delaying the inevitable, before I finally followed everyone through the kitchen and out into the garden.

When I made it out into the garden, I immediately sought Cole out. He was sitting at the end of the wooden table, staring into a glass of Coke. He looked sad... really, *really* sad. It took my breath away.

As we approached the table, he looked up and said a quick hello.

My heart went wild, slamming against my chest so hard, I felt lightheaded.

Where do I sit? Next to him in my usual seat seemed too awkward now.

I sat next to Mia instead, forcing Jasper to sit near Cole. It felt so wrong, but I picked up the Italy travel brochure in front of me to make it look like I'd just sat here to look at that.

Mia looked over my shoulder at the hotel we would be staying in. It looked amazing, but the excitement I felt yesterday just wasn't there now.

I felt Cole's eyes on me the entire time, burning holes into my skin. I squirmed at the attention, glanced to the side, and then, finally, into his eyes. My breath caught when I saw the pain behind them.

I gave him an apologetic smile and waited to see if he would respond. It took a few agonising seconds, but he smiled back, and his features softened.

Just when I thought he was about to talk to me, David placed a plate of charred chicken kebabs down on the table, which Cole immediately grabbed and started to eat. I picked at some charred peri peri chicken.

Please talk to me...

Ironic, really, me pleading with him to talk.

Throughout lunch, Cole and I exchanged glances, but he never uttered one word. It was easy to hide our fight when the conversation was full of holiday plans, but eventually Mum noticed.

She looked between us, and I prayed she wouldn't say anything. Faking sickness and going home sounded like a *very* good idea right now. I should've done that an hour ago and saved us all of this.

"Oakley?" Cole said as he stood up. He nodded, gesturing for me to follow him.

I didn't have to think twice. I got up and followed him inside. He'd made the first move, so there was no way I would pass up the chance to make things right again now.

The walk up to his room stayed completely silent, and the way my anxiety was raging, I thought I might start hyperventilating. His room was the last one along the hall, and it felt like a mile.

This had to be a 'clear the air' thing.

Sitting on the end of his bed, I hugged my legs and rested my chin on my knees. He sighed and sat down, facing me. The sun reflected off his face, lightening his ocean eyes. The smell of his aftershave wrapped around me, and I relaxed immediately.

I'm home.

In that moment, I knew one hundred percent that I couldn't be without him.

Not having Cole in my life wasn't an option.

He groaned as he stared into my eyes, making me feel like I could float away. It was as if he could see right through me and see the terrified, broken little girl lurking inside. I never, ever wanted him to see that.

"Look, I'm sorry about yesterday. I shouldn't have shouted at you, but you should've texted me to let me know you were okay."

I nodded and looked down at the bedcover. I *wished* I could have, more than he could ever know.

"Oakley," he whispered, gently lifting my chin so that I faced him.

His fingers lingered on my jaw, and my heart skipped a beat.

My eyes filled with tears, and my heart was full again.

Grabbing his hand, I squeezed gently in way of an apology.

His face lit up, and he nodded, knowing exactly what I meant.

Suddenly, he tugged my hand, making me fall forward. I gasped as I landed in his lap, but he just laughed.

"That's better," he muttered.

Yeah, it was. When did he get so bold?

It was too intimate, and I wasn't used to anything like this feeling natural or safe. The feeling was almost overwhelming. I wanted to run, but at the same time, I never wanted to leave.

I waited a minute, and he didn't do anything else. He just let me get used to this new moment. When my pulse slowed a fraction, I wound my arms around his neck.

With every passing second, I felt more and more at home.

His fingertips gently stroked my back, but he made no advance. He didn't try to kiss or touch me anywhere else, knowing we couldn't rush this. We'd been best friends our whole lives. I couldn't lose that.

"We don't fight again. *Ever* again, okay?" he said.

I nodded once. It was the easiest thing I'd ever agreed to.

He smiled again, flashing his perfect white teeth.

"Good. So, two weeks in Italy, hey? We have to hire a boat and do some water sports."

I raised my eyebrow, making him laugh and shake his head. *Hire a boat?* Neither of us could sail, and there was no way the first time we tried was going to be while we were alone in a foreign country.

"I guess you're going to go all girlie on me and want to sunbathe instead, huh?"

I nodded and smirked. I was pasty white, and I definitely needed to get a tan; even an off-white tan would be cool with me.

He laughed, holding me a little tighter on his lap.

"Fine, I'll make you a deal. I'll suffer through that if you go diving with me?"

He'd been trying to get me to go diving for years, but I hated the idea of it. I wasn't a fan of fish. Plus, everything in the sea was all slimy, and the sea itself was full of sewage and other crap.

I bit my lip, shook my head, trying not to smile. The deal didn't matter. He would sunbathe with me anyway. He always did.

Cole sighed sharply, pretending to be annoyed. "Fine, but two days sunbathing, max, and you have to buy the ice creams."

I pursed my lips and nodded. That part also didn't matter because as soon as we were there, he would go all gentlemanly and insist on paying.

"All right," he said, laying down and pulling me with him.

I nearly landed on top of him but managed to move to the side just in time. As natural as it was beginning to feel when we were closer, it was still something I had to get used to.

"We have to get your parents to let you go out at night this time."

That was another thing I loved about him. He was always on the same page as me.

But good luck getting that to happen.

The last time we had gone away, I'd had to be back at the hotel by nine, and I'd hung out there for the rest of the evening. We needed to think of some way to convince my parents I was more responsible now. I was almost sixteen.

"Okay, sunbathing, exploring, diving... don't give me that look, it's happening."

I nudged him, and he caught my hands, pinning them to his chest while we laid facing each other.

His fiery eyes settled on mine, and he inhaled sharply. It was as if he took all the air out of the room with that breath.

I felt it, too—the pull to get closer. To feel his body against mine. There was too much distance between us, and it felt so wrong. It was a feeling that could consume me. One I never wanted to end. I wanted to leap into it headfirst, and I didn't care about the consequences. That was scary... and exciting.

Cole's head inched towards mine a fraction at a time, giving me chance to stop him from... kissing me. *Oh my God.*

I spread my fingers as much as I could in his grasp and touched his chest. His breath quickened, and instead of making me ill, it made my body heat.

"You're beautiful," he whispered, closing his eyes.

The distance was gone, and his lips lightly brushed against mine. My brain must have short-circuited because I could no longer form thoughts.

None that didn't involve kissing him forever.

"Cole? Oakley?" Mia shouted up the stairs.

Cole pulled back and scowled towards his door. "What?"

He let go of my hands, and I sat up, running my fingers through my hair. The kiss was barely a graze, but it was *everything.*

Mia walked in seconds later, smiling wickedly. Her blue eyes shone with mischief. She tucked her brown hair behind her ears. "We're going in two weeks. Oakley, I'm holiday shopping on Monday, if you want to come?"

I nodded and finally got my thoughts back in order. My first one was imaging throwing something at her.

"I'm coming," Cole mumbled, still frowning at his sister.

Mia's jaw dropped. "*You* want to come shopping?"

"I need to get some stuff... but I'm not walking around every damn shop with you two. I'll go off on my own."

I rolled my eyes and sat back against the wall.

"All right, but we're going to be out *all* day."

He shrugged. "Yeah, whatever."

Mia clapped her hands together in excitement. "I need to go

and make a list!" She ran out of the room, slamming the door behind her.

Mia was organised. She had lists for absolutely everything and had yet to forget a single thing. I aspired to be like her, but I left too much to the last minute.

"How the hell are we related?" he muttered to himself, shaking his head at the door in disbelief. "So, you going to buy a tiny bikini?"

I tilted my head.

"I was joking." He laughed, but I didn't think he was joking.

Maybe I would get something nice. I wasn't sure about tiny, though.

Cole shifted up against the wall next to me. His side pressed against mine as he reached over and grabbed the TV remote.

My heart swelled when he pressed play on *Hollyoaks*. He'd recorded it even after our argument.

Still, there was something else I would rather be doing right now.

I laid my head on his shoulder and held on to his hand as we watched the show together in a comfortable silence.

"Well, that was shit," Cole mumbled under his breath as the credits rolled.

For a few minutes, Cole would alternate between stealing little glances at me and turning his attention back to the TV. It made me smile every time he did it, like he couldn't look away from me for long.

It was *very* mutual.

Something between us was changing. It made me nervous and terrified and thrilled all at once.

"Do you still want to go to Ben's party?" he asked after a while. "We should leave soon, if you do."

I'd forgotten all about Ben's party after our argument yesterday. I kind of did want to go, but I would have to get my parents' permission first.

Biting my lip, I nodded.

"I'll go speak to your parents."

He leapt off the bed and bounded out of his room. I smiled and lay back, mentally planning what to wear.

What the hell was I turning into? I never thought I'd be one of those girls who planned what to wear at a party. Maybe I *could* be normal.

Chapter 10

Oakley

"Cinderella, you shall go to the ball," Cole announced five minutes later, performing a little bow at his doorway.

No way!

I jumped up on his bed, making him laugh.

"I'll change quickly, then we can drop by yours so you can get ready." He pulled his top over his head.

What the...

Wow.

My scalp prickled with heat, and I was sure my cheeks turned red.

I hadn't seen his chest since... last year on holiday, I thought. He was quite sporty, and that showed on his toned stomach.

He didn't even seem to notice my ogling, thankfully. He continued to change, as if I were one of the guys. I didn't know where to look. What were the rules? I mean, I'd seen him shirtless before, but this was *way* more intimate than that. At least I thought so.

I turned my head away, knowing what was coming next. Something heavier than a T-shirt dropped on the floor, and I gulped.

Maybe I should've left, but he was blocking the way between the bed and the door. I was stuck.

It's fine, just don't look at him. Try to be calm.

Breathe.

I focused on the TV and kept perfectly still. On the inside, I was anything but calm. In fact, I seemed to grow a whole new bunch of hormones, which all wanted me to grab him and kiss him immediately.

Something jingled. When I realised it was his keys, I knew it was safe to look up.

"Ready?" he asked, swinging his keys on his finger.

I didn't acknowledge the question. I just got up and walked past him with my heart beating hard, and my lips wishing they were still against his. These feelings were growing stronger by the day.

We made our way downstairs and found our parents in the kitchen, drinking coffee around the island and laughing together.

"We're going," Cole told them.

"Okay. You both have a good time. Cole, please look after her and make sure she's home by eleven," Dad said, kissing my forehead.

I recoiled internally, swallowing my repulsion.

Wait. *Eleven?*

I usually had to be home much earlier than that. What had gotten into him?

Dad laughed when I glanced up at him with questions in my eyes. I didn't know if he saw that hatred, too. He ruffled my hair. "School holidays now. I guess I have to face up to the fact that you're not my little girl anymore." His frown deepened towards the end of his little speech.

I smiled and swallowed acid.

I'd never been so happy to grow up.

"You stay with Cole the whole time, and absolutely no alcohol," Mum added.

I backed up, nodded in agreement, and pulled on Cole's arm to get him to leave. No reason to hang around and give them chance to change their mind. They were normally cool when it came to Cole, knowing I was safe with him.

Just as we reached the front door, Jasper's hand flew out in front of us. "And where do you two think you're going?" he questioned, raising his eyebrows.

"We're eloping to Mexico," Cole muttered sarcastically, making me grin.

Jasper glared at Cole. "If you get her pregnant, I will kill you."

Where on earth had that come from?

Cole laughed and shook his head while I just wanted to disappear.

"What's wrong with you, Jasper?"

No one knew.

"Look, if you two want to start with kissing and naked time, I get it, and I support you. Just don't hurt her."

God, Jasper!

I pushed past my idiot brother and jogged to Cole's car.

"Good. Now... don't have her out too late, and for God's sake, wear a condom!" Jasper yelled after Cole.

Closing my eyes, I wished the ground would open up and swallow me whole. I couldn't stay around while they joked about that stuff.

I got in Cole's car and waited for him to follow. He dropped into the driver's seat and slammed the door.

"Are you okay? Ignore your brother. He's an idiot," he said, starting the engine.

Everyone knew Jasper was a man-child, but I wished he wouldn't joke about things like that. I just... couldn't.

Tapping the gear stick, I told Cole to get going.

"Well, all right," he replied, pulling out of his drive.

Ben only lived a few miles from us, so we arrived at his large house five minutes later. Music blasted out from what I assumed were huge speakers inside his home.

Outside looked like a car park for extremely bad drivers. Not one car was parked straight. Cole did as best as he could, adding to the abandoned feel of Ben's massive driveway.

"Ready?" Cole asked, sensing my hesitation.

I was nervous, my pulse thudding, but I was also determined to have a good night. This was the start of a long summer with him, so I unclicked my seatbelt and smiled.

"All right, let's go, beautiful," he said, winking and almost giving me a coronary.

Cole slung his arm over my shoulder as we walked inside. There were so many people crammed inside the house, and most of them were drinking in the lounge. Empty plastic cups and crumbled pieces of food were already scattered all over the floor. The place smelt of cheap beer and even cheaper perfume.

Ben was going to have a hell of a time cleaning it up the next morning.

Cole pulled me through the crowd, saying hello to some of his friends, and into the kitchen. No one really gave me a second look, so I felt instantly at home.

"*Cole!*" Ben shouted, throwing his hands up in the air. "Hey, Oakley, you came!" He almost stumbled on the spot but managed to grab on to the worktop to stop himself from falling.

He'd clearly gotten a head start on the drinking.

"Get yourselves some punch or beer or punch, and I think there's some JD left. I think I drank it, though. I don't know," he rambled, shrugging a shoulder.

"Okay, man." Cole laughed at his highly intoxicated friend.

He tightened his arm around me and guided me to the fridge, grabbing two Cokes and handing me one of them.

He wasn't going to have a beer?

Before the fridge door closed, I pointed to the bottles of Becks at the bottom.

"I have someone special to chauffeur home later."

I rolled my eyes at him. That was plain cheesy, but I couldn't deny that I liked it.

He chuckled and turned his attention to his friends as they approached. Sipping my Coke, I watched Cole joking and messing around with them. It was nice, seeing him play-fight with Ben and tease Ben's girlfriend, Kerry, about her awful taste in men.

However, as I watched Cole wrap his arm around Ben's neck, I couldn't help feeling a little stab of envy. We'd never be able to have the fun banter they did. That'd been stolen from me, and it made me burn with anger that I could never show.

But that didn't have to mean what we had was bad, right? It was just... different.

After wrestling Ben to the beer-stained floor—*yuck*—Cole got back to his feet.

"Want to dance?" Cole asked, running his hand though his hair and chewing on his lip.

As if I'd ever say no to that.

We'd danced together plenty of times before, so I didn't over-analyse the gesture. Well, I did... but not as much as usual. Throwing my empty can in the bin, which was much more than most people had bothered to do, I tilted my head towards the makeshift dance floor in the living room.

I held on to Cole's hand and pressed myself into his back as he pushed our way through the crowd. It was loud in here, the bass rattling my bones, but it meant no one could talk properly and that put me on their level.

How did Ben even know so many people? He must have just put an open invitation out because there had to be more people here than the entire bloody school held. No one seemed to even notice that Cole's 'mute friend'—something I had been called before—had come along with him, or they didn't care.

Cole finally came to a stop in a tiny bit of space near one of the speakers. He couldn't have found a worse spot to dance. There was barely room for one person, and it was *so* loud, but I loved it. Every second.

He pulled me close until my chest pressed flat against his. With my confidence soaring for the first time ever, I wrapped my arms around his neck and danced against him.

I could feel his breath on my face, and I wanted him to kiss me so much, I thought it was going to drive me insane.

All my insecurities of not being good enough for him vanished as his hand cupped my jaw. He wouldn't kiss me or be this close if he didn't want it as much as I did.

I could just about convince myself that I was worth his attention.

But he didn't know everything, and I wasn't sure if that would change how he felt.

Music vibrated through my body. I closed my eyes, feeling the beat and the thudding of my pulse.

I felt Cole's mouth press against mine for the second time. His lips were soft, coaxing mine and taking charge of the kiss. I was happy to let him lead. My fingers curled around his hair, and I felt him smile against my mouth.

He groaned and pulled me tighter against his chest. Elation bloomed in my chest, making me weightless. I wanted to hold on forever.

Before I knew what was happening, he was gone. My eyes flew open.

What was that? Had I done something wrong?

I followed where he was looking. A crowd had gathered around the stereo, which was now silent.

The music was off. What did that mean?

Biting my lip, I forced myself to be brave and look up at Cole. He was glaring at the stereo as if he wanted to murder it, which made me feel a whole lot better about the abrupt end to the kiss.

"What the hell, man!" Ben shouted from somewhere in the room.

Kurt, who was playing DJ, waved his hand at him. "I got it."

"Want to go outside for a bit?" Cole asked, his voice full of grit, and eyes on fire. I understood that feeling.

He didn't wait for a response; he took my hand and led me outside to Ben's massive garden. We left the stuffy air behind us, grateful to be out in the open.

The grass was littered with packets of crisps, bottles, cans of alcohol, and plastic cups. A couple guys were kicking a ball around and ripping each other to shreds with their words.

Spotting about the only clean space on the ground, I sat down, cross-legged by a tree, and waited for whatever was to come next. Cole lay on his side in front of me with his head perched on his hand.

He didn't say a single thing. Usually, that would be fine, but this was a different kind of silence. Inside, the music started up again. A few more people had drifted out—one of them to puke into Ben's parents' flowerbed.

I picked at the blades of grass to have something else to focus on. The awkwardness that fell over us was unbearable.

Laying down beside him, I bit my lip to refrain from saying something. It was the most I'd wanted to talk in a long time. I'd gotten used to being silent, unless you counted quietly testing my voice in the shower, but there was *so* much I wanted to say to Cole.

"Oakley?" he whispered softly as he reached over to stroke

my hair. His fingertips brushed over my cheek and travelled down along my jaw. My breath caught in my throat at the warm trail his fingertips left against my skin. "I can't wait to go on holiday with you."

I couldn't wait for that either. It was going to be perfect. But the direction Cole had taken the conversation confused me. He said nothing about the kiss at all.

"You're sitting with me on the plane, by the way. I'm stealing you every day."

Fine by me.

"You want to go back inside and get another drink?" he asked after a few more minutes.

What?

I was so confused. Why the hell had he brought me outside for five minutes if he didn't want to talk privately? Maybe he just needed fresh air.

Laughing, he stood up and offered his hand. I let him help me up and raised my brows. "I don't know, either, Oakley, but the music is back, and I want to dance with you again." Cole pulled me to his chest. "You cool with that?"

I couldn't bring myself to respond because my brain had done that thing where it had stopped working. He was so close, his scent dizzying.

He smirked and, my God, I had to think of a way to stay in control around him. The urge to be reckless scared the hell out of me.

"Cole!" Ben shrieked, stumbling towards us as we headed back inside. He must have sobered up slightly because he walked in a straight line, but the lopsided smile and glazed eyes showed he should give driving a miss tomorrow. "Want to do shots, guys?"

"Another time," Cole replied, pulling us into the living room. He wrapped his arms around me again. The song was slower this time, and that worked for me. "I just needed a minute outside, okay? You can stop thinking about all those questions. I can see your mind overthinking."

Well, that told me.

Would be nice if he'd told me why he needed a minute, though. I mean, he took me with him.

Cole's friend Kerry popped up from nowhere. "I hope I'm not interrupting. I've been waiting for Cole to bring you along, but he's obviously been trying to keep you all to himself."

I smiled at her, and that was it.

She was totally interrupting, but she was also the first girl to talk to me outside of school. And inside school, it was pretty much only Hannah.

Kerry waved her arm, shooing Cole away, and pulled me to the sofa. The second we were sitting, she launched into telling me stories of Cole and Ben doing stupid dares at school, and we were insta-friends.

Cole watched from a distance. I kept checking, and every time his eyes were on us—on me—but he didn't intervene, so I guessed that meant Kerry was cool. He wouldn't leave me alone otherwise.

She spoke *a lot*, but that was perfect because we spent ages together and it wasn't awkward. We balanced each other out, and I really hoped that she wasn't just being polite to me, because having a girlfriend was lovely. I only had Mia, but she was older so if she wasn't Cole's sister, I don't think we'd be friends.

"Oh, and I need to tell you about the time Cole and Ben got stuck in a lift and almost peed themselves."

I knew about that but I still grinned.

About every five seconds, Kerry's eyes would flick to Ben, so when another girl sat down on his lap, her eyes tensed a fraction. Over the years, I had gotten used to reading people's expressions more than most.

It was my sixth sense. Expression reading. I was rarely wrong.

Except with Cole. I couldn't always read him.

Once Kerry's attention was back on me, I raised my eyebrow. Her cheeks turned pink, knowing that I'd caught her staring. She definitely liked Ben, and from the hungry way he watched her when she wasn't looking, he clearly liked her, too.

"I'll get us another drink," she muttered, leaping off the sofa.

All right. I hadn't expected her to be shy about something like that. The girl was outgoing to the point that I envied her. She was beautiful with long chocolate hair, high cheekbones, and dark blue eyes. She also had the best personality.

What did she have to be shy about?

I caught Cole's attention. Wickedly looking between Kerry and Ben, I grinned. He moved through the crowd, ignoring everyone else.

My heart leapt when he stopped in front of me, his big blue eyes shining.

Damn it. I was totally in love with him.

Chapter 11

Oakley

"You okay?" Cole whispered in my ear, sitting next to me on the sofa, not leaving an inch of distance between us. Every inch of skin that was pressed against his was electric.

We were across the room from the speakers, but it was still hard to hear him. Not that it mattered. I was good at lip reading.

I swallowed hard as his breath tickled my skin, sending a shiver along my spine. A quick nod answered his question. Even if I could have talked, I wouldn't have been able to right then, my throat was bone dry.

Holding my finger up to tell him to wait for me, I got up to find the toilet. Cole relaxed back into the sofa.

I made my way along the hallway, performing a double take when someone mentioned my name. My heart stilled at the sneering tone.

"Cole only feels sorry for her."

"He can do way better than that freak, so don't worry."

"Yeah, you're prettier, and he knows it."

"Plus, you *talk*."

I slipped into the bathroom, locking the door to drown out

the laughter. Stumbling forward, I rested my hands against the sink and took a deep breath.

They won't get to me.

Wincing, I looked up and caught my reflection in the mirror. Tears stared back at me, proof that I wasn't as strong as I wanted to be. I breathed deeply through my nose.

I hated them all.

But Cole brought you here not them. He kissed you and not them.

Whichever girl liked him, it didn't matter. They were bitter and hateful. I didn't even know them and they didn't know me.

I swiped tears from my cheeks and went to the toilet. I'd survived way worse than a bit of jealously-induced bitchiness. They meant nothing.

Get yourself together.

I waited a few more minutes to give them time to move away, so I wouldn't have to pass them when I headed back to Cole. Then I unlocked the door and pushed it open.

This wasn't going to ruin my night.

Thankfully, there was no one around the corner. Well, there was but it was Ben and Kerry hiding in a corner looking very cosy. The cast of *Mean Girls* had gone.

Cole held his hand up, alerting me to his location now he was in the kitchen. I walked around a bunch of people taking shots and gagging after doing so. One spat it out over the floor and onto someone else's shoes.

I jumped to the side, avoiding the puke, and rolled my eyes as Cole laughed at me.

"Want one of those?" he asked, referring to the shots.

Shaking my head, I walked into his arms, craving his touch. Seemed like I didn't need alcohol to make me brave after all.

Cole grinned and kissed the side of my head.

"Jack's getting naked in the living room. I've seen that too many times, so I came in here." He laughed again. "Don't look so horrified. There's always one of them taking their clothes off... and it's usually him. I'm really glad you're here, it's much better with you." He scratched his jaw. "Are you having a good time?"

Was I? The part where he kissed me, I enjoyed. I liked Ben and Kerry. The sick I wasn't crazy about. And I definitely didn't want to see Jack naked.

I nodded and bumped his chest. He was excited to finally bring me along. He didn't need to know that, although I was enjoying it, I would rather be someplace alone with him.

His room. The moon. Wherever.

Narrowing his eyes, he said, "You want to leave."

It wasn't even a question because he could tell. Sometimes it was impossible to cover up how I felt.

As I was about to shake my head, he kissed me. Only for a second, but it was enough to make me lose my train of thought.

"Yes, you do. Come on."

We gave the group doing shots a wide berth and didn't bother to tell Ben we were leaving. Since he currently had his tongue down Kerry's throat, we didn't think he'd appreciate the interruption.

I tugged on Cole's hand as he led me across the road but not to his car.

"There's a park."

A park.

It wasn't the same one that I ran off to, but apparently, we were hanging out at a park now. We'd not done that since we were young.

"Humour me," Cole said. "It'll be fun."

I ducked through the fence rather than walking around to the gate. Cole took my hand and looked back at me over his shoulder. It was nine and the sun had just began to set, turning the sky orange.

"I'm going to push you on the swing."

My frown was a question.

"Remember going to the park when we were young? You loved the swings."

I did remember that, but we were no longer six and eight. Still, I wanted to see where this was going. We'd known each other forever but this was new.

Cole stopped at a swing and held the chains, waiting for me.

Grinning, I took a seat, facing away from him. Then, he began to push me. My hair blew in my face. I felt free... and three.

"Can I ask you something?" He walked around the swing, so he was in front of me.

The playful smile was gone, replaced with something more serious. He'd stopped pushing, and I kept still, letting myself slowly drift to a stop.

I didn't like the sound of this. His tone was the one people on TV used when they were about to break up with someone.

He waited patiently for me plant my feet on the floor, the swing now halted. "Okay. I don't want you to run off, so please stay," he said carefully.

Yeah, I'm not going to like this.

"Why don't you text me back?"

What... why is he asking that now?

Turning my head, I focused on the outline of a patch of mud in the wood chippings below me. That question wasn't a new one, but it hit a little differently since we'd grown closer.

I wished I could text him.

Sighing, he added, "Damn. Look, I'm sorry, but I don't get it. And, yeah, I'm sorry I'm bringing this up now, but I like you, Oakley, and I'm worried. Why don't you want to communicate with me? Please, Oakley. Is something really wrong? Because if there is, I promise you, it'll be okay. I'll help you. You just have to tell me."

Shut up. Just shut up!

I pressed my lips together to stop myself from blurting the truth out. The words were on the tip of my tongue, and I wanted nothing more than to open up to him—to believe that he held the power to make it right.

Nothing would ever do that.

It would rip my family apart. I was still legally a minor.

"Hey, you can tell me. You know that, don't you?"

I want to so bad it kills me.

I nodded once. Of course, I knew that. I could tell him anything, but it was the *after* that scared me the most.

He wouldn't be able to keep my secret—no way—and it wasn't something I could ever take back. Once it was out there, my life would implode. What it would do to my mum...

Smiling, I looked into his eyes, trying to convince him that everything was all right.

There are many different reasons people choose not to talk. Selective mutism was a recognised condition. I'd been asked every reason, and occasionally someone guessed right-ish, but I denied every possibility... even the ones close to the truth.

"Are you scared to talk again?"

Scared didn't even begin to cover it. I was petrified. Not talking was easier because then no one could make me tell the truth.

I was trapped in here, but it was safer for everyone.

I wouldn't hurt my mum or brother. I'd do anything to protect him.

Cole closed his eyes, pained, and he hung his head.

I'm sorry, I mouthed while he looked down at his feet, gutted that I was hurting him.

He slowly looked up and opened his eyes. For a second, the world stopped as I waited to see what he was going to do next.

He straightened and stroked my cheek. "It's okay, babe. Whenever you're ready, you can talk to me, okay? Or write."

My heart sank, and I looked away from him. Why did I need to speak or write things down? We'd managed to have a pretty great friendship for almost sixteen years now, and for almost eleven of them, I hadn't said a word.

Oh.

But this wasn't like before, was it? Things were different between us now. We were moving towards something *more*. Shit. Did he want me to speak before he'd consider *more*?

Tears prickled my eyes and blurred my vision before I could get myself under control. *Stop it.*

Cole groaned. "No, damn it. Hey, it doesn't bother me. I promise. I just want you to know that I'm here. I'll drop it now. I don't want to upset you."

I desperately wanted to ask him if he meant that... and *how much* he meant it, because I needed it.

Cole sighed and stood up. "Want me to take you home now?"

Frowning, I shook my head. That was the last place I wanted him to take me.

"All right. I'm getting hungry. Let's get my car and go to McDonald's for ice cream."

Just like that, we were okay again.

I stood. Who could turn down ice cream?

With a little smirk, he added, "And if you're good, I'll get you a milkshake, too."

Chapter 12

Oakley

I spent the first full day of summer at my aunt's, though my head was still with Cole. Ali was amazing and I loved her dearly, but she'd given birth to an entitled bitch, so I was never sad to leave.

My cousin Lizzie, one whole year older than me, was on top form, reminding me that I was different but should still be able to get a job. Ironic really since she didn't want to do anything that wasn't modelling and being famous.

She was going to be America's Next Top Model. From the UK.

If that failed, she planned to marry rich.

Jasper and I practically jumped into the car when Mum announced it was time to leave.

"She's exhausting," Jasper said.

"She's your cousin," Mum replied, making a sharp turn.

"Still exhausting. I need a nap."

Jasper was right, Lizzie was hard work. I had a love/hate relationship with her. Most of the time she was insufferable, but she was still family.

Mum pulled up in the drive, and Jasper laughed. "Cole have

a tracker on you or something?"

I rolled my eyes at him and then watched Cole cross the road, heading our way.

"Mind if I steal her?" he asked when we got out of the car.

"Back by eleven, Oakley," Mum said.

"I'll walk her home just before," he told her as he grabbed my hand.

My heart skipped a full beat at the feel of my hand in his. I'd not seen him yet today but that was now rectified.

I didn't even bother looking at Mum or Jasper. They would, no doubt, have *that look* on their faces.

"I have popcorn, sweets, and a movie. You look like you need to decompress after Lizzie."

Cole's parents and Mia were nowhere to be seen so they must have all been working still.

"Everything's upstairs, ready."

Frowning, I tapped his arm, and he pushed his bedroom door open for me. Maybe he was a stalker.

"Jasper texted me when you left," he said, guessing my question correctly. "I set up then. Go sit down... and no questioning the movie choice. It was your pick last time. And the time before that. And that."

Smirking, I sat back on his bed and grabbed a handful of popcorn. I'd watch whatever.

He hit play and climbed onto the bed, too. The title popped up on the screen, and I slapped his chest.

Are you kidding me?

He'd picked *The Hills Have Eyes*. I hated gory films. The sight of blood made me feel sick. Though I was fine with my own.

Cole laughed and popped a handful of M&M's in his mouth. "You'll be fine. I'll protect you from the actors on the screen."

The joke would be on him when I puked all over his bed.

I grabbed his pillow and wedged it between my chest and

legs where I could tuck my head into it. He was absolutely doing this on purpose.

"It's not even started yet, you big baby," he teased, shuffling closer so that our shoulders touched.

"So, was Lizzie her usual, charming self?".

Oh, yes. I pursed my lips, widening my eyes to tell him that she'd been on top form.

Cole knew what she was like. I thought, deep down, everyone did, but they never really said anything about her rude and entitled behaviour because she would probably freak out.

"She's jealous of you."

I almost snapped my neck looking up at him so quickly. That was the biggest load of crap I had ever heard... and I lived with Jasper.

"I'm serious, Oakley. You're smart and so damn beautiful, it's unreal," he whispered. "And I'm going to tell you that every day until you believe it."

My breath caught in my throat. No one had ever said anything like that to me before—well, besides my mum, and that wasn't the same.

Leaning closer, Cole slowly closed the distance between us, his eyes locked on my mouth with a hungry expression that made my belly ache for him. He tangled his fingers in my hair and parted his lips.

His woody scent made me lightheaded, like I was floating above my body.

I waited impatiently as he inched closer, and his lips gently brushed mine. A second later, he pulled away and stared into my eyes. I felt weightless, like gravity had been turned off and I could float away.

"You're perfect," he whispered against my mouth before he kissed me again.

His hand was in my hair, his lips driving me insane, and I

didn't quite understand how I could feel so hot and so... unsettled. I moved closer, pulling him flush against my body.

Cole moaned and rolled us down on his bed.

Curling my fingertips into his back, I pulled at him again like I was possessed. His teeth grazed my bottom lip, and I shuddered against him.

My body was overheating, and the need for more took me by surprise. His hand grazed down my side as he kissed me, and I shuddered at the sensation.

I slid my leg over his, and he dropped a fraction more of his weight on top of me. This was amazing.

Surrendering to these new feelings should've been scary, but for the first time, I felt in control of my body and our situation. He would stop immediately if I wanted him to. I curled my other leg around him, and he rewarded me with another moan.

His tongue grazed my bottom lip, and I froze for half a second. He wanted in. It was an intrusion, and no matter how good I felt, it was still a new step.

Cole pulled back, sensing my hesitation. "Are you all right? Is this too much?"

Yes, it's entirely too much... and still not enough.

My stomach flipped over again, and I squirmed at the intensity. I was more than okay, just trying to catch up with my body's reactions to him.

This is okay... perfect.

Grinning, I gripped the front of his T-shirt and pulled him back. His lips landed on mine, harder this time, and when his tongue touched my lip again, I opened up to him without hesitation.

I ran my hands up his back until I found his hair. My fingers knotted in the light-brown mess. Cole groaned in response, and my heart jumped. We kissed like it was the last thing we'd ever do, a tangle of lips and hands, exploring each other.

This was something I would never tire of doing. He made me feel pretty and desirable. I held him close, not wanting him to move yet.

A few seconds–or it could've been minutes, I wasn't counting–later, he pulled away and smiled. We were both breathless and in need of air. "You good?" he whispered, his voice husky.

Wow.

His lips were a little red and slightly swollen, but mine probably looked the same. I couldn't care less. I kissed him quickly in response.

Clearing his throat, he moved off me, kissing my forehead.

"So, do you want to watch something else? We can find one of those crappy chick flicks if you want. I don't mind."

We both knew he didn't want to watch anything, but I sensed that he was trying not to push me. He knew nothing of my past, but I was still fifteen, not legal until my sixteenth birthday, and he was seventeen.

I shook my head. Honestly, I couldn't care less what was playing on the TV anymore. His lips curled in a shy smile as he looked across at me. I did the same, a stupid grin on my face, and my heart flying in my chest.

A knock on his door interrupted us. I jumped up, pressing my back against the wall.

"What?" Cole called, laughing at my reaction.

Mia opened the door and walked in. Her smirk grew when she spotted me. Why did she have to come back so soon?

Do I look like I've just been kissing him?

"Hi," she said, folding her arms. "What are you guys up to?"

Yes, she definitely knows.

"Watching a film," Cole replied, and even though the movie was playing, he still sounded like he was lying.

"Mm-hmm. Of course, you were."

We both must have worn the same stupid grin on our

swollen lips.

Rather than leaving us, Mia sat down on the end of the bed. Cole took a deep breath as if her presence was taxing.

"Oh, I love this film, and since you were only watching TV…"

Cole's eyes narrowed, and if looks could have killed, he would've just murdered his sister.

"Great," he replied through gritted teeth.

I turned my attention to the awful film and tried to focus. It took every ounce of self-control to not glance at him and make it obvious what I'd rather us be doing.

A few minutes in, I felt his hand touch my hand, and he threaded his fingers through mine. The need to be closer to him weighed heavy in my stomach, a physical reminder of how desperately I wanted our relationship to evolve.

I watched the rest of the movie with a smile on my face, though I hated the horror.

By the time the credits rolled, I had to go home. Cole noticed it was almost eleven, too, and he glared at Mia for the thousandth time.

"I'd better walk you back, I guess," Cole said, sounding like he'd rather do anything else.

Mia looked over her shoulder. "I'll leave you guys to it. Bye, Oakley."

I watched her leave, and then I kissed Cole quickly.

"Come on, I'm not risking you getting grounded," he said, pressing his lips to mine one last time before he stood up. How quickly kissing him had become natural.

On our way out, I gave a quick goodbye wave to Cole's parents.

Cole wrapped his arm around my shoulder as we crossed the road. It was a friendly move—one that wouldn't make anyone think something was going on. Still, I liked that he was touching me.

"Home just in time, Miss Farrell," he said in a posh voice.

I nudged his shoulder.

He took the key, put it in the lock, and kissed me on the forehead before he opened the door. And stared into my eyes so intently, I thought my legs were going to give out. Dangling the key in front of me, he winked.

I took the key and pressed my lips together to stop myself from grinning like an absolute fool. It didn't work, I was gone.

"See you tomorrow, babe."

Sighing, I stepped inside the house and closed the front door.

"Well, well, well. What time do you call this, young lady?" Jasper said dramatically, resting a hand on the wall and crossing one ankle over the other.

I glanced from the clock to Jasper and raised a brow. I was technically two minutes early.

"You and I are going to have a little chat about you staying out all night with strange men."

He was definitely dropped as a baby.

I walked past him, shaking my head at his idiocy.

"Wait," he called after me when I made it to the bottom of the stairs. "Is everything okay?"

I turned around, nodding my head and shooing him away with my hand.

"You did use protection, didn't you?"

Gasping, I slapped his arm and ran up the stairs. I could still hear him laughing as I shut my bedroom door.

I didn't sleep with Cole, but if Mia hadn't interrupted us, I did wonder how far we would have taken it because I had wanted more. I didn't think we'd have slept together, not yet.

Cole's text came through just as I'd got into bed, and I fell asleep with a smile on my face and an unusually free heart.

Chapter 13

Oakley

I woke up to my phone alarm beeping loudly. Groaning, I quickly turned it off. All right, having an alarm in the summer was stupid, but I didn't want to sleep in. There was a certain blue-eyed boy I wanted to see.

After a long, hot shower, I got dressed and went downstairs for a much-needed hot chocolate. I wasn't big on tea or coffee so hot chocolate was the drink that turned me into a functioning human in the mornings.

"Good morning, sweetheart," Dad said, peering over his paper at the table.

I gave him a small wave and then grabbed the biggest mug I could find for my drink.

"Didn't sleep well?"

Sleep wasn't something I did much of, anyway. Last night, the dreams were good ones, though. I kept waking up, thinking I could feel Cole's lips on mine. I couldn't wait to go over there.

I shook my head and sat down opposite Dad, a table safely between us, and wrapped my hands around the boiling hot mug. Dad's eyes bored into me, but I pretended not to notice.

Where's Mum?

"Hey, Oaks," Cole sang as he walked into the kitchen.

My heart leapt at the sound of his voice. I looked over my shoulder and smiled as he approached. He was wearing a simple sage-coloured T-shirt and blue jeans.

"Morning, Cole," Dad said.

"Hey."

Cole sat beside me and took my hot chocolate out of my hand. I didn't do anything as I watched him sip and then wince at the boiling drink.

His eyes slid to mine, and I shrugged.

That's called karma.

"Hurry up and finish this. Mia said we're leaving in fifteen minutes."

What?

Oh, the holiday shopping.

"I can't believe you're taking this one shopping. You'll be there until closing," Dad joked.

Cole laughed. "Yeah, I think I'm going to regret it by midday."

Dad had never taken me shopping. He only bought me random things... and made me gym studios. One I hadn't stepped inside for ages.

Taking two large gulps of my drink, I handed the rest to Cole and went to get my shoes while he chatted with my dad.

My stomach churned when I heard them laughing together. I'd always wondered if Cole would believe me over my dad, or if everyone would think I was vindictive, lying about a man who busted his butt to provide for his family—the way he'd told me so many times.

It wasn't something I could risk. Besides, it was all over now. I could lose everything over something that happened in the past.

I didn't want to lose my family.

In a little over two years, I could leave home and move to uni.

I slid on my shoes and waited outside the kitchen door for Cole.

"Looks like you're off," Dad said, nodding towards me.

Cole looked over and drained the last of the hot chocolate. "Right. See you later, Max."

"Bye, kids. Have fun," Dad called after us.

I was already opening the door, but Cole raised his hand to my dad.

Mia was waiting for us in the car outside my house, impatiently tapping the steering wheel. I ran for the front seat.

"Really?" Cole said, chuckling.

Snooze you lose.

"Morning," Mia said, before shoving the shopping list on her phone at me.

I didn't realise she would need so many clothes for just two weeks. She could live there for a month and never have to wash anything.

I scrolled down on her phone three times, and there were still more things on it. She wanted sandals, flip flops, and two pairs of sliders. She had one suitcase for all this stuff to fit into.

Mia parked in the multi-storey car park, and eventually, we began to walk through to the shopping centre. She linked her arm through mine, leaving Cole to trail behind us, already bored, no doubt.

It wasn't going to take him until midday to regret coming along.

He moped around in the first two clothes shops, where Mia and I both picked up a couple of dresses. Unsurprisingly, as soon as we stopped by the swimwear section in the third shop, he brightened up.

"The little blue one," he whispered in my ear, discreetly pointing to a light-blue bikini that reminded me of his eyes.

I looked over my shoulder, almost level with his mouth.

"I really want to kiss you right now, Oakley. You have no idea."

Oh, I have a very good idea.

Leaning closer, I watched his eyes darken. He glanced up, I assumed to see where Mia had gone, and then he pressed his mouth to mine.

I bit my lip when he moved back and picked the bikini off the rail.

It wasn't something I would usually wear but this was my choice. I wanted to wear something nicer. A two-piece.

Dropping my gaze, I stepped to the side to pick out a pair of flip-flops. Cole chuckled and followed me to the next rail

"Oakley," Mia squealed, holding up two short halter neck dresses—one, salmon pink, and the other, yellow—with a look of indecision on her face.

I pointed to the yellow. Always yellow.

It was the colour of sunshine. It was happiness.

It was everything I wanted to be.

"Thanks!"

She was going all out. Cole rolled his eyes, looking like he just wanted out.

We shopped all morning and had almost everything we needed for the holiday. Throughout the day, Cole would stroke my hand or the small of my back, making it hard for me to concentrate on anything else. He'd gone off a couple of times on his own, but he'd come back not long after.

"Can we *please* eat now?" he whined for the hundredth time when we walked out of another shop with all our bags in hand.

Mia growled in frustration and pointed to KFC. "If we feed you, will you promise to stop whining?"

Cole grinned. "Yep."

He went off ahead to the counter to order while Mia and I found a table in the busy food hall.

"He's always thinking of his stomach."

We dumped our bags, and I could tell by the way she looked back up at him that she was going to say some stuff.

"So, what happened last night?"

There it was.

My throat turned dry.

Laughing, she said, "Don't look so worried. He hasn't said a word to me. He just seems *really* happy, so I figured something had happened between you two."

He's really happy.

And... I did that?

Squealing, she clapped her hands together. "He finally told you, then?"

Told me what?

I frowned, and she was about to say something else, but Cole put a tray down on the table.

"They're bringing your burger over, Mia, since your order's so awkward."

No, go away! I wanted, needed, Mia to keep talking.

Mia smirked and grabbed her chips.

Oh, come on!

Cole sat down next to me and immediately started stuffing food into his mouth. I picked at my chips and tried not to choke when he pressed his leg against mine.

"Kerry and Ben are going to watch a movie tonight. Do you want to go, too?" Cole asked, reading a message on his phone.

I nodded and kept my eyes clear of Mia who would probably make a face. One that screamed *you're going on a double date*. It was hard to tell if things between us were going too fast or not. We'd been best friends our whole lives, a gentle build up to what we were stepping into now. All I wanted was to leap in, it was too good to hold back.

Once we'd shopped for another hour, Mia drove us all home.

Cole helped me get my bags out of the boot and walk them to my house for me. The muscles in his forearms looked amazing under the weight of my stuff.

Dad laughed when he saw everything. "How long do you think we're going for?"

"You should see the amount of crap Mia got," Cole replied. "I thought I was going to die by the tenth shop."

"Women, eh?" Dad took the bags from Cole and turned to me. "Come on then, love. You need to spend some time with me and your mum if you're going out again tonight. We've barely seen you."

That's the point.

And how did he already know that I was going out?

Cole must have messaged him. I couldn't wait until the day when I didn't need to get Dad's permission to do anything. I couldn't wait to move away and only see him a couple times a year.

"See you later." Cole smiled and headed back to his house.

"Your mum's baking cakes and wants some help. I'll warn you now that she's planning your birthday party." He put the bags down on the sofa and gestured for me to go in the kitchen.

Reluctantly, I went in and sat down at the table. A birthday party was the *last* thing I wanted. All that attention on me? No, thanks.

"Oh, I've got so many ideas, honey. Did Dad tell you? Do you want to have it here, or we could maybe hire somewhere? How many people do you want to invite? What colour scheme?"

I frowned and looked down at the table.

Did she not know me at all?

"Come on, love, it's your sweet sixteen. We have to do something special. Please, please, let me organise this party." She looked at me with big hopeful eyes, wanting a normal daughter for once.

I'm sure this wasn't what she pictured when she found out she was having a girl. Weren't we supposed to go on spa days and spend hours talking?

We'd done none of that and never would.

Groaning internally, I nodded, giving her my blessing. She squealed and leapt forward to squeeze me. I couldn't say no to her. She deserved to throw me a party after all the hurt I'd caused her. Mum almost killed herself trying to help me when I stopped talking. The very least I could do was give her this.

"It'll be amazing."

Like hell it would.

Dad chuckled deeply. "You should hear some of her ideas. Chocolate fountains and candy floss machines. Just remember, it's a party for Oakley, not yourself, Sarah."

If that were true, we wouldn't be having one.

Mum dismissively waved her hand at him. "Hush. You're a man. The only part of this that concerns you is when it comes to the payment."

"As in most things," he countered, mixing the buttercream icing for the cupcakes.

They were happy... because she had no idea.

I took a handful of chocolate shavings and sprinkled them over the first batch of cakes.

"Aunt Ali and Lizzie will be coming. Unfortunately, Uncle Pete can't fly in from Australia."

I knew Mum missed her brother after he'd married and moved across the world. Mum, Ali, and Uncle Pete were close growing up. We'd only been out there once since he moved, and he came back every two years for a visit.

"We must plan a trip out there," Dad said. "Perhaps next year."

Mum beamed, placing her hand over her heart. "You can't take that back."

"I would never, love." He kissed her cheek, and I turned away.

After decorating twenty-four cupcakes and listening to Mum go on and on about my stupid birthday party, I went upstairs to get ready to go to the cinema.

This wasn't any trip, though. I couldn't wear my usual, casual clothes. This was a date. At least... it probably was. The four of us.

But Cole and I weren't together. Not officially.

I bit my lip, so out of my comfort zone. I had no clue what was going on or what to expect, but I'd dress nicely in case it was a date.

Swinging my wardrobe doors open, I frantically searched every hanger, instantly hating everything I owned. I had new clothes, but they hadn't been washed, and I didn't know who'd touched them or tried them on first.

I pulled everything out, hoping it would look better when I was facing it.

It didn't.

What the hell had I been dressing like for all these years? Everything I owned was plain and boring.... besides the bags of new stuff. Amazing what shopping while you're happy and having hope can do for you.

I did love my few band T-shirts... but on a date?

A 'maybe' date.

Lowering my standards by *a lot*, I grabbed a pair of black jeans and a black tank top. It could be dressed up with some nice jewellery. I had a few nice pieces, bought for me on birthdays and Christmases, though I didn't typically wear any.

When it was ten minutes to seven, I brushed my hair and swept on some lip gloss. My stomach fluttered as I waited in my room for Cole to pick me up.

Minutes later, my bedroom door opened, and Cole walked in. He'd changed into a black T-shirt but was otherwise the same.

His eyes roamed over my body, head to toe, and he said, "You look beautiful."

I didn't think I'd worn tight jeans and a tight top together before. Cole clearly approved, and for the first time ever, I liked my appearance, too.

He took a few short steps towards me to close the distance. Taking the heart shaped pendant of my necklace between his fingers, he whispered, "Your heart is my favourite thing about you."

That was good because it belonged to him.

There was so much I wanted to say but I couldn't. Literally, my throat felt thick, like my body was physically preventing me from talking.

He gently pressed his lips to mine, and I stopped breathing. The kiss soon turned harder, and his tongue tangled with mine as we explored each other. All the oxygen was sucked out of the room when his fingers found my hair.

He murmured against my mouth, "Let's go."

I groaned as he moved back, and he tilted his head, his eyes pained to have to stop.

We were both a little breathless but there was no need to make this more difficult than it already was. I took his hand and led him out of my room.

On the way out of the house, Mum smiled. Dad said and did nothing. He looked over from the sofa, and I couldn't read his expression at all.

I didn't care.

Cole opened his car door for me, and it was only when I sat down that I started to relax again. I was out of the house and with Cole. Everything was going to be fine now, as we drove away from my dad.

"It's Chinese food before the movie. I assumed that would be good with you since you believe spring rolls are a religion."

He pulled up outside Golden King, and I raised a brow.

Okay, Chinese food was the best, but I didn't quite pray to it.

Kerry and Ben were waiting by the entrance, smiling at each other. They only turned away as we approached. We walked over to them, and Cole took my hand in his.

Away from our families we seemed to act like a couple. I wasn't sure why we didn't when in front of them, though. It would complicate things, so I guess he wasn't ready for that. Honestly, neither was I.

"Hey," Kerry said, pulling me away from Cole. "So, how's it going? You two *actually* together yet? It's so sweet how he looks at you."

Not one word of that was quiet meaning Cole would have heard it all.

My cheeks heated, but thankfully I was ahead of him and he wouldn't see me blush.

Kerry requested a table in the corner so we could have some privacy, but it was pretty quiet tonight. The restaurant was tastefully decorated in red and gold. A stunning dragon painted onto the far wall that must've taken ages.

"You having sweet and sour chicken?" Cole asked, absentmindedly scanning the menu.

It was pointless looking at it since we always had the same things. There was nothing worse than being let down by a new dish.

He looked up to see my response, and I smiled. "Cool. I'm getting the beef chow mein. We can share."

"We need to go to the toilet, Oakley," Kerry said once we'd ordered. She jumped up so fast that she almost knocked her chair over and hit a server.

Cole and Ben laughed. I... didn't understand why I had to go to the bathroom, too. Who couldn't pee by themselves?

Kerry ushered me to the toilets, pushing me forward in a hurry and almost sending me flying. I wasn't naive enough to think we were actually going to the toilet. She wanted to talk.

Good Lord, she was persistent.

As soon as the door closed behind us, she turned to me. "Ben asked me to be his girlfriend! Can you believe that?"

I nodded because I could totally believe it. At his party, they barely came up for air.

"It was so sweet," she said before she launched into the story of how he'd bought her a rose and asked her to be his girlfriend right before we came out tonight.

Every word she spoke rolled into the next as she tried to get the whole story out as quickly as she could. Her excitement was infectious, and I couldn't help smiling with her.

"So..." She took a breath, letting her red face get some oxygen. "What the hell is taking Cole so long? I mean, it's not like he doesn't want to, duh. It's *so* obvious. Don't worry; he'll do it soon. I can tell."

It really didn't bother me—well, not too much, anyway. I was happy to take things at our own pace. I was only just getting used to these feelings and, at one point, I wasn't sure if I would ever want a boyfriend.

"We should get back. I'm starving, and they usually bring starters out quickly."

When we got back to the table, Cole and Ben were chatting about football—my least favourite subject.

"You survived, then," Cole whispered as I sat down, careful to turn his head so that Kerry wouldn't hear him.

I pursed my lips.

He draped his arm over the back of my chair and kissed the side of my head. His mouth against my hair made goosebumps scatter across my arms.

Don't grin too widely or you'll look like a psycho.

By the time we left the restaurant, my stomach was stretched, and I could easily have taken a nap. But we had a movie to get to... and I didn't want the night to end. We'd had the best time.

The cinema was small and old. Since the new chain cinema had opened in town, this one had become much quieter. I scrunched my nose at the scent of the musty fabric and old popcorn when we sat down. The chairs were threadbare, but the screen rooms were cosy.

"Scared yet?" Cole whispered in my ear three seconds after the film had started. Nothing had even happened. How much of a baby did he think I was?

I raised a brow, which made him chuckle quietly.

About twenty minutes into the film, *that* music started—the one where you *knew* something bad was going to happen, but not exactly when or what. I laid against his side, tucking my chin into my chest. I picked a spot just below the screen and concentrated on it while my heart pumped anxiety around my body.

Cole's chest rattled with laughter.

I was so going to make him watch chick flicks for the next week. Reaching over, I whacked him with the back of my hand, but it just made him laugh harder.

"Want to do something alone tomorrow?" he whispered in my ear during a slow part of the movie.

More than anything.

Then we both forgot all about the movie the moment he leant over and kissed me.

Chapter 14

Oakley

"That was *awesome*! I loved the part where she was drowned in the bath!" Kerry exclaimed as we made our way out of the cinema.

Yeah, that was precious...

"So, where to now, guys?" she asked.

Cole's eyebrows pulled together in a frown that might offend them if they could read it. He didn't want to do anything else as a group. "Erm..."

Ben smirked, catching on to Cole's reluctance. He turned to Kerry. "We're going back to mine, baby. I need some time alone with you," he said.

"Later," Cole replied. He let out a sigh of relief as we waved them off. "I know they're my friends, but I just want to be alone with you," he said, nuzzling my neck and making me laugh quietly. "Ice cream now, Miss Farrell?"

I nudged him in the direction of his car.

"Thought so."

Apparently, a big Chinese and half a box of popcorn wasn't enough. I still had enough room for ice cream. It was basically a drink.

It was too late for the café, so we went to McDonald's and sat in his car, sharing a McFlurry. Cole didn't make conversation as we ate because it was warm out and we needed to eat before the ice cream melted, but the silence was comfortable.

"You okay? We can go somewhere else if you're bored," he eventually said.

I shook my head, unable to recall one single moment when I was bored while spending time with him. God, if he could read my thoughts, he'd think I was a proper stalker.

He suddenly laughed at something. His gorgeous blue eyes turned mischievous, and I knew he was about to do something to me. I didn't have enough time to move before he heaped a spoonful of ice cream out of the tub and brought it towards me.

Ah, no. I watched his lips curled into the cutest smile that made my pulse thud under my skin.

My eyes widened, and I held my hands up in surrender.

I really didn't want to be all sticky and gross on my first date with the guy I was absolutely crazy about. Before I could blink, he flicked the spoon, sending the ice cream flying at me. It landed on my top with a soft thud before falling onto my lap. Gasping, I swung the passenger door open and hopped out of the car.

Oh, you're going down, Benson!

Cole's laughter blocked out the sound of a group of teens shouting and messing around outside McDonald's, as well as a couple arguing in their car nearby. After brushing the remains of the freezing cold ice cream from my clothes, I scooped up some of mine and flicked it at Cole through the door.

Despite being a rubbish aim, it landed on his chest. He stopped laughing immediately and looked down at the ice cream and chocolate sauce running down his T-shirt.

"You need to run," he warned, slowly placing the tub down on the dashboard.

With my heart flying in my chest, I sprinted off, desperate to get away before he got his revenge.

Cole's footsteps thudded behind me, getting louder by the second. He wouldn't be too far behind now. Adrenaline and excitement pumped through my body, making me grin like an idiot.

Pushing my legs harder, I managed to increase my speed, but it wasn't enough. I knew it wouldn't be. Cole's arm wound around my waist in no time, and we stumbled over each other's feet before falling to the ground.

"Too slow!" He laughed, rolled me over, and pinned me to the grass.

I couldn't move at all... not that I wanted to.

A couple years ago, Jasper landed on me while we were fighting over the remote. It was only a second because he leapt off, but it took me back. I was that terrified little girl being held down.

That had never happened with Cole.

I felt safest when I was with him.

My racing pulse showed no signs of slowing down, and the more I looked into Cole's eyes, the better that racing felt.

"What're you going to do now, huh?"

Gasping for breath, I tried to work that out for myself. My body pumped boiling hot blood through my veins, and I longed to pull him closer.

"Hey, are okay?" He let go of my wrists and sat up, forehead creasing.

Sitting up next to him, I smiled reassuringly. There was nothing wrong at all, but we were in a very public place. His eyes shone with excitement before they closed as his lips sealed over mine.

I was falling again.

His fingers stroked along my jaw and cupped the back of my

neck. He groaned and pressed his mouth to mine more firmly. I loved everything he did to me when we kissed. He gave me *everything* when he was this close.

I pulled away when I couldn't handle my crazy hormones anymore. Breathing as heavily as I was, Cole chuckled and murmured, "I need to get you home, but I don't want to let you go. This feels too good."

Yeah, it does.

Gripping his T-shirt, I pulled him in for one last kiss and then stood up.

"Well, all right." He jumped to his feet, and we walked back to his car. I used a napkin to clean the ice cream off my clothes.

Cole eventually and reluctantly dropped me off, and I let myself in the house. There was only one lamp on and the TV. Dad was alone in the living room, holding a glass of scotch.

He glanced up and quickly turned back to the screen. I had to go through the living room to get to the stairs, so there was no way to avoid him.

"Did you have a good time?" he asked, turning the TV off.

I folded my arms and nodded.

"Glad to hear it. Come on, it's bedtime."

Though he'd turned to me as he spoke, he hadn't actually looked me in the eye once. Not that I wanted him to but his reluctance turned my blood to ice.

Something's going on.

My stomach churned with nervous anticipation and dread, washing away the perfect evening I'd had. I wanted to turn around and run to Cole's.

Of course, I couldn't, so I followed Dad upstairs.

He stayed just one step behind me. I focused on the painting at the top of the stairs, wrapped my arms around myself harder, and held my breath.

What's happening?

At the top of the stairs, Dad cleared his throat. I turned to the side, so he could see some of my face, and I waited.

"Night, love," he said, kissing the top of my head before going into his room.

As soon as his door was shut, I dashed into my room and let out a deep breath. My nerves were fried. I put a book in front of my door so I'd hear if it was opened, and I got ready for bed with clumsy hands.

I'd gone from an incredible high to a terrified low within seconds.

But it was okay. I was in my room.

You're safe.

Cole's nightly text arrived as I slid under my covers, momentarily taking my mind off Dad.

I woke in the morning remembering that Cole and I were doing *something* alone today, and that thought was enough to forget how weird my dad had acted the night before. Well, almost.

As I skipped downstairs, my parents' muffled voices became louder until I could hear them clearly.

"I don't get why you're against this, Max! This might be the thing that works. She might be able to get through to our daughter!" Mum snapped.

My smile dropped, and I pressed my back against the wall.

"She won't go to the doctor, Sarah," Dad replied slowly. "You can't force her. We've tried that, and you saw what it did to her."

No.

Sliding down the wall, I wrapped my arms around my legs.

Mum was trying again. Another attempt to fix me.

Last time Mum took me to the doctor, I'd been *so* scared. I'd completely broken down, and I couldn't breathe. That was my first panic attack. I could still remember how tight my chest had felt right before I'd passed out. The fear of a doctor figuring it out was too much.

Mum sighed heavily. "I won't let her get like that again. Are you coming with me or not?"

Please say no. Please say no.

"I won't do that to her. I'm not tricking my daughter into this. You remember what the child psychologist said. We shouldn't push her. Oakley will ask for help whenever she is ready for it. When *she* is ready, Sarah, not you."

I hate him.

"Do you even want her to get better?" Mum snapped.

I flinched at how harsh she sounded. It was an accusation that he was about to pretend had offended him.

"How can you even ask me that? Of course, I do, but I will *not* force her into this. Whatever is going on with her, it will be all right. We'll deal with it, whatever happens. Whether she wants help to speak again or not, she's our daughter. If she's happy, that's all that matters to me."

God, he was such a liar.

I almost believed what he was saying, he was that good. Dad was smooth, charming, well liked, and well respected by everyone who knew him.

No one would ever believe you, Oakley. Not over me. You know that.

I did know that.

"I'm sorry." Mum sighed again, and everything went quiet for a few seconds. "I just want to find out what's wrong. I thought it would get easier, but it only gets harder."

What had brought this on? My sixteenth birthday coming up, maybe?

Her voice was muffled, as if she was speaking against something. Dad's shoulder, perhaps. He was comforting her, all while knowing he was the cause.

I curled my nails into my palms.

"I'm still going to take her..." Mum said. "Don't, Max. If she starts panicking like before, we'll turn around and come straight home. I can't just sit back and do nothing."

A tear spilled down my cheek, and my heart broke with hers. I wished she would do nothing. I wished she would give up.

Every time she'd tried to help me, it ended with her crying, and me feeling like crap. For everyone's sake, she needed to give it up.

Taking a deep breath, I wiped my face and pushed myself up off the floor with shaky legs. I swallowed the acid in my throat and ran my fingers through my hair.

You can do this. Act normal.

I walked into the kitchen, and they both smiled at me as if nothing had happened.

Mum discreetly dabbed a tear from under her eye and said, "Morning, sweetheart. Hot chocolate?"

For the first time, I wanted something stronger.

I was too scared to drink because I wouldn't be in full control.

I nodded and sat down at the table. Mum and Dad exchanged a glance before she turned away. Their discussion wasn't over.

"Croissants are in the oven. They shouldn't be long," she said, making me a drink.

"I'm going to have a shower," Dad muttered, shaking his head as he left the room.

"How was your date last night?" Mum asked, smiling at me a little too widely.

I frowned and shook my head. She went from needing to fix

me so desperately that it brought her to tears to asking about my night. At least she was okay with me and Cole getting closer.

Jasper came downstairs at the right moment, and Mum closed her mouth. I didn't want to talk about Cole right now. I didn't want him anywhere near a conversation about how I needed fixing still.

"Morning," Jasper muttered, rubbing his eyes. "I'm starving, Mum."

She rolled her eyes. "Sit down."

"You good?" he asked me, taking a seat opposite me.

I gave him my most reassuring smile and wondered how he would react if he knew the truth. Out of everyone, I thought Jasper would most likely be the one to believe me.

Although there was a three-year age gap between us and he annoyed the hell out of me, we were close. That also meant I didn't ever want him to find out. I didn't want him to look at me differently, to feel like he needed to tread carefully, and to not argue with me.

"So, what's everyone doing today?" Jasper asked. He stuffed a hot croissant, fresh from the oven, into his mouth.

I waited for him to react to the heat and spit it back onto his plate, but he didn't.

Was his mouth made of steel?

"I'm taking Oakley to gymnastics and then going food shopping," Mum replied, briefly smiling at Jasper while she busied herself with buttering the rest of the croissants. "What about you?"

I was so ready for a gym class. I needed it.

"Computer," he mumbled before stuffing more food into his mouth.

"You could look for a part-time job," Mum suggested. Jasper scrunched his nose up and she sighed. "Or not."

Lazy shit.

It was my parents' fault, though. They'd always said they'd support us while we were in full-time education. Jasper was going to string that out for as long as possible, no doubt.

"I was thinking we could go clothes shopping on Thursday. I need some final things for the holiday and thought it would be nice for us both to get our nails done," Mum said to me.

Ah, the doctor's appointment is on Thursday, then.

I nodded my head and picked at my food, no longer feeling hungry.

How was I going to get myself out of that one?

"Great." She beamed. "Now, eat up. We've got to leave in half an hour."

Once I'd managed to force down half a croissant, I went to get ready for gymnastics. I couldn't wait to get there and get lost in throwing my body around. Gymnastics was an escape that I longed for every day. I loved how all my thoughts would disappear, and all that was left would be the version of me I wished I could always be.

We left Jasper shouting at some game and drove to my gym class.

Mum dropped me off and had arranged for Cole to pick me up because we were going to do... something.

"Have a good time. I'll see you when you get home."

I waved over my shoulder as I made my way into the tired-looking building that smelt of trainers and sweat and air freshener.

It only took ten minutes for me to get a sweat on. Marcus worked us harder than usual, but after the morning I'd had, it was welcomed. By thirty minutes in, my muscles were burning. It was welcomed.

"That was great, Oakley!" Marcus said. "You nailed it! Now, go again."

Nodding breathlessly, I ran around to the other end of the

beam to start again. Adrenaline pumped through my body. I could do this all day. Or until I collapsed. The physical exhaustion was the best feeling... well, second to kissing Cole.

By the time my two hours were up, I was ready for bed, but I had something much better to do.

"All right, guys, see you next week!" Marcus shouted, dismissing us all.

I spun around and sprinted to the changing rooms to have a quick shower.

Cole didn't need to see me sweaty and gross. The girls stopped to gossip, but I didn't have time to socialise.

I showered, changed into some fresh clothes, and then frowned at my messy hair, stumped.

"Need a hairbrush?" Jade, a gym friend, offered, handing hers out.

I smiled gratefully and dragged it through the unruly blonde mass. When I finished, I placed it down in front of where she was applying her eyeliner, and I nodded once in thanks.

"You're welcome," she mumbled, looking in the mirror with intense concentration. Her bat wings had to be perfect. They always were. I wouldn't have the patience or the steady hand to do that.

Giving her a quick wave, I ran out the door, eager to meet up with Cole.

He was leaning against the wall in the entrance when I got out of the changing room.

The way his face changed when he saw me almost made me stumble.

His lips curled as he pushed off the wall. I moved towards him, still completely unprepared for the way he made me feel.

"Hey," he said and kissed my cheek. "I thought we could have lunch and go bowling. Then I'll take you home to get ready for tonight."

Tonight, too. All right.

I grinned up at him, no longer caring how crazy and eager I looked. It was hardly a secret that I was crazy about him.

"I'm not telling you where we're going tonight, though," he teased, bumping my shoulder with his. "Just wear something casual."

That was all I owned, so no issue there.

Cole grabbed my wrist and pulled me towards him. I bumped against his chest and gasped at the contact. Before I could think, his lips covered mine, and I was dizzy with happiness.

He laughed at my love-drunk expression when he pulled back. "I know how you feel. Come on, I'm hungry."

He was never not hungry.

Cole drove to the bowling alley and parked as close to the door as he could get so he wouldn't have to walk too far. Sometimes, he'd drive around a car park for a few minutes, looking for a better spot.

The restaurant attached to the alley allowed us to seat ourselves and place our order on an app. It was an easier way for me to order.

"Let me guess... you're having the chicken mayo burger," Cole said, raising his eyebrow in question.

I half-wanted to pick something else, but that was the best thing they did, so I dipped my chin instead.

"You're so predictable."

Right. Like he wasn't going to have a bacon burger.

Cole tapped away at the app. I watched over his shoulder as he added his bacon burger to the cart, and I smirked to myself.

I wasn't the only predictable one.

"Oakley..." He cleared his throat and put his phone down on the table.

My heart stilled at his tone.

"Your mum told me something yesterday. I'm not supposed to say anything, but I don't think I can stay quiet. She asked me how you were doing and, um..." He wrung his hands, looking lost.

He knew about the appointment with the doctor.

This was hard for him, and I was really glad that he was telling me. Cole and I didn't have secrets—besides my major one.

"Your mum is... she's taking you to a doctor."

I blinked twice and looked down.

"Hey, don't. It's fine. You don't have to go if you really don't want to."

That sounded like he wanted me to go.

"Maybe it would be a good idea to go, though," he added.

What?

I clamped my jaw shut in frustration and turned away from him. *We really don't have to talk about this.*

"Sorry. No, don't. I shouldn't have brought this up yet. Shit, I'm ruining this already, aren't I? I just want you to be okay. That's all." He took my hand and interlaced our fingers.

I melted a little as he stroked the back of my hand with his thumb. He wasn't ruining anything. He couldn't see it, but he was healing me, making me stronger, and giving me hope.

"I'm sorry, okay?"

Leaning in, I pressed a chaste kiss to his lips.

"You're perfect the way you are," he said, and pulled me closer. "I mean it."

Then, he kissed me until our food arrived.

Chapter 15

Oakley

Most of the week passed in a haze of Cole, Cole, and more Cole. We spent practically every minute together, hanging out and messing around. Our unofficial relationship was getting stronger with every date and every kiss.

But now it was Thursday morning, and I was on my bed, panicking about a stupid doctor's appointment. I'd managed to ignore it while I was distracted, but now I had no choice but to face it.

Mum still hadn't told me, so I assumed she was just going to spring it on me while we were shopping.

If we were even going shopping at all.

As I anxiously gazed out the window, my phone beeped, making me jump. It was a text message from Cole.

> Cole: Good luck today. Let me know if you want me to come x

Cole was the very last person I wanted there, but I *loved* that he offered, that he wanted to be there for me.

"Oakley, are you ready to go?" Mum called up the stairs.

My stomach turned to lead at the sound of her voice. As angry as I felt with her, and it was a lot, I couldn't help feeling sorry for her, too.

She was worried. I'd left school, was about to turn sixteen, and I still didn't speak. But what I could never understand was how some people were born mute and they coped. Why couldn't she accept that?

I mean, I understood that it was because I used to be able to and there was nothing medically wrong with me. But eleven years had passed.

With a heavy heart, I got off the bed and slowly walked downstairs. Dad was sitting in front of the TV, watching some construction show. He owned a building company, but it wasn't as big as he wanted it to be. That had always bothered him.

I didn't measure success by money and possessions. To me, it was all about family. In my eyes, Dad would never be successful. He didn't deserve it.

"Okay, honey," Mum started, blowing out a long breath. "I need to tell you something, and I need you to know that I'm only doing it because I love you so much."

Here we go...

I nodded for her to continue, knowing exactly what she was about to say.

"We're going to a doctor's appointment." She held her hand up. "Before you get angry, please remember, I'm only ever trying to do what's best for you."

Her eyes welled up with tears, making me feel sick.

That's what I'd done to her.

It was nothing compared to what the truth could do.

"Please, please, will you just go in there with me?" She swiped away a tear that rolled down her cheek.

Do it for her. You disappoint her in every other way.

Keeping my eyes fixed on the floor, I nodded.

"Thank you," she whispered. "I'll be with you every step of the way, I promise."

I didn't need to turn around to know that Dad would be staring daggers into me.

He didn't need to warn me anymore. I knew what I had to do.

For the entire drive, Mum couldn't look at me. I watched her grip the steering wheel hard and felt the anxiety radiating from her.

The closer we got to the doctor's surgery, the harder the knot in my stomach twisted.

It'll be okay.

No, it won't. It'll rip your whole world apart.

They won't believe you over him.

It'll kill Mum. You know it will.

I closed my eyes and begged my inner turmoil to stop. There was never anything I could do to put an end to the thoughts plaguing my mind, but it would be okay because I would never tell.

I could keep a secret.

Mum pulled into a parking space, and I pushed my fist into my churning stomach.

"I'll be with you the whole time, love. You have nothing to be afraid of."

As if that made it better.

I got out of the car and followed her to the front desk in a daze. Mum gave the receptionist my name. Wrapping my arms around myself, I kept my head down and counted my breaths.

"Okay, if you'd like to take a seat, the doctor will be with you shortly," the greying woman behind the desk told us.

Mum smiled. "Thank you."

We weren't in our normal doctor's surgery. This was a private medical centre. It was in the same complex but a completely different building. This one was painted a warm cream colour, and it smelled floral even though there were no flowers.

I looked around the room at notice boards and mental health flyers. Two other people sat in the waiting room; a lady around Mum's age and a young girl, probably a bit younger than me. She was super skinny and had dark circles around her eyes.

She was a patient here.

"Oakley Farrell?" a deep voice called.

I gulped and looked up. A plump man wearing black trousers and a smart black and white striped shirt smiled warmly. He had a kind, round face, and pale green eyes. Mum stood first, and I followed, knowing there was no way out.

"If you'd like to come with me."

My palms started to sweat as we walked along the short corridor and into a small room. I was shaking, desperately trying to breathe.

This man was trained to put the pieces of the puzzle together.

He's going to find out. He'll tell everyone, and you'll lose everything.

"Hello," Mum said, shaking his hand.

I slumped down beside her and counted.

In for five, out for three.

She'll never forgive you when she finds out.

Cole will think you're disgusting.

You'll take Jasper's dad away from him.

"Well, what can we do for you then, Oakley?" the doctor asked, bringing me back to reality.

I stared blankly at him. Did he expect me to answer?

That won't happen.

Mum squeezed my hand and started to explain my situation on my behalf. "Oakley stopped talking when she was just five years old. At first, we thought it was a joke. And then we thought it could be due to a minor choking incident—that maybe it'd damaged her throat somehow. We thought she could be afraid it would hurt too much if she spoke..."

As Mum reeled off a list of their theories, I found myself gradually shutting out her voice, building a wall as high as the stars. I wanted to vanish. I wished I was coming up to my eighteenth birthday so I could leave.

Suddenly, I felt my hand being squeezed again. It was a prompt, a plea.

"I don't know what to do anymore." Mum sniffed and tightened her grip on my hand.

The doctor nodded. "Hmm, I see. Well, fear of talking due to a previous injury is possible. However, this has been going on for a long time, so that seems unlikely."

He leant forward, resting his forearms on his mahogany desk. "Oakley, would it be okay with you if I examined your throat?"

My heart stopped. Fuck, no way was he touching me. I gasped for a breath, but my lungs were deflating.

No, no, no!

I didn't want any examinations. I hadn't had one in years, and if this doctor ruled out anything medical again, Mum's mind would drift... maybe to places she didn't want it to go.

I was confident she would never guess who'd hurt me, but it was a can of worms I wouldn't let anyone open.

"What kind of examination? What would that involve?" Mum questioned.

"Nothing too bad, I can assure you," he said. "For today, I'll just look down her throat to check if I can see anything—like scarring, for instance. If there is nothing visibly wrong—and I suspect there won't be—I'd like to perform a laryngoscopy. The procedure is usually performed under local anaesthetic, but we can do general if needed."

No chance.

My heart thudded too fast, and my head swam. I could see the destruction of my family in technicolour.

"We'll pass the laryngoscope down her throat, which will send pictures to a monitor. The procedure itself will take around twenty to thirty minutes."

My body turned cold from the inside out.

There was no way I was going to let him even look inside my mouth, let alone stick a camera down my throat.

I gasped again and tears sprung to my eyes, blurring my vision.

"Sweetheart," Mum said. "It's okay. I'm here. You're safe."

He's going to find out. Dad will find out. Watch your world crumble around you in five, four, three...

Shaking my head, I leapt up and yanked the door open. I sprinted to the surgery's exit and ignored the shocked look from the receptionist as Mum called after me.

I reached the car and slumped against the side. Closing my eyes, I let my tears fall. This was too much.

"Oakley!" Mum shouted. Within a heartbeat, she was in front of me as if she was scared I'd disappear. "Honey, please don't cry. It won't hurt. Please let him do the procedure. *Please*?" She sobbed and stroked my hair, the desperation she felt radiating from her body.

"Shh, it's okay. Breathe, darling. It's okay. It doesn't have to be today. You get in the car, and I'll go speak to the doctor. We can look into the procedure a little more and then decide. Come on, get in the car. It's okay."

I got up, opened the door, and squirmed out of her grip. I put my seatbelt on so she knew I was absolutely not getting back out, and held onto the seat.

By the time Mum came back, I'd calmed down and was thinking rationally.

She couldn't make me do anything. No one could force me to talk.

"Home?" she asked softly.

I nodded, staring out the window as I hugged my legs to my chest.

I'd never go back there.

Chapter 16

Oakley

"Hey," Cole greeted me with a questioning look on his face. I left Mum the second she pulled into our drive. She said nothing as I walked away, crossing the road to Cole's house.

He opened the door as I approached like he was waiting for me.

"I'd ask how it went, but I think I can guess..." he said, stepping aside so I could go in.

He nodded towards the stairs, gesturing for me to go up to his room. There was nowhere else I wanted to be, and I could feel the tension in my shoulders evaporating.

"So," he prompted, grabbing my hand, and making me turn to him once we were both inside his room.

He kicked his door shut with the back of his foot and pulled me into his arms.

Shaking my head, I swallowed the urge to cry again.

"That bad?"

Worse.

Ducking my head, I sank against him, and the fear of my

secret being exposed boiled over. The dam burst, and I sobbed into Cole's T-shirt, soaking it through in seconds.

"It's okay, I'm here," he whispered, moving us to his bed and tucking me against his chest.

As he stroked my hair, I let the tears flow. I was trying to forget and move on, but it was impossible to do so when Mum was constantly trying to fix everything.

No amount of doctors, specialists, or appointments could ever fix what had happened. When you were damaged like me, that was it—forever. It couldn't be erased, you had to just move forward. Mum was only making it harder.

Cole held me until I calmed down. When I was ready, I pulled my head away from his chest and grimaced at the mess I'd made of his T-shirt.

"You okay now?" he asked, his fingertips brushing along my jaw.

I was now. In Cole's house—his room—I was safe from the world.

"Did you go in?"

I nodded slowly. Last time Mum had tried to get me to go see a doctor about my condition, I hadn't even made it out of our front door.

"Did they examine you?"

I shook my head. *Never.*

"But you went into the room?"

I could tell what he was thinking—that I'd made it into the room, so maybe next time, I would allow them to do an examination. That the doctor could give me a pill and I would be magically healed.

"Are you supposed to go back?"

I nodded and then lifted a brow, telling him that I was but I wouldn't be going.

"I could come with you, if you wanted."

How important was this to him?

I wrapped my arms around myself.

"Don't do that." He pulled my arms apart and kept hold of my hands to prevent me from closing up again. "Oakley, hey, don't close yourself off to me. It doesn't matter if you never speak again. I've told you that a million times, so *please* believe me. I know you better than anyone else does. I know what every little facial expression means and how you'll react to a situation before it's even happened. All I want is for you to be happy. *I* just want to make you happy."

You do.

My eyes filled with tears again, but I wasn't scared anymore.

Could a person run out of tears? I hoped so.

"I mean it. If you're happy as you are, then that's all that matters to me. Are you happy?"

That was a loaded question. I had happy moments, most of them involving him, but I didn't think I would ever be able to work on true happiness until I was out of my parents' house.

I reached out and touched his cheek, running my finger across his lip.

Yes, right this second, I'm happy.

He grinned and kissed my finger. "Okay, I'll help you tell your mum to back off then."

That's it? I'd basically told him that there was no chance I would ever talk again, and he'd breezed past it, like I'd said I wanted to trim my hair.

I leant in and replaced my finger with my mouth.

Cole's hands slid up my waist, and I shuddered. His touch felt good, and I wanted to live in that moment forever. One where I could be normal. Have normal feelings without questioning if I should or not.

We broke apart when someone knocked on his door.

"Every fucking time," he muttered. "What do you want?"

Jenna pushed the door open and walked in with worry in her eyes. She looked back at a door that we had, technically, never been told to leave open.

"Everything okay?" she asked.

Cole didn't reply because she was addressing me, so I nodded.

"It's tacos tonight. I know that's one of your favourites." She smiled but I could see the worry behind her eyes. Jenna knew about the failed doctor appointment.

"Unfortunately, Chris is coming, too, but we'll still have a good night," she said, turning her nose up.

Jenna wasn't a fan of Chris, either. Mia could do so much better, she deserved the best.

Cole mumbled something under his breath. I couldn't quite make it out, but I could pretty much guess what it was. I think it rhymed with lucking and brick.

"You"—she pointed to Cole—"had better be on your best behaviour, for your sister's sake."

"I would be if he wasn't such a—"

I jabbed my elbow into his side before he finished that sentence.

"Why'd I get hit for that one? It's true!" he said, frowning at me.

Jenna looked like she was trying not to laugh. "So..." she said with a wide smile as she sat on the end of the bed. "Are you two okay?"

I side-eyed Cole while he stared deadpan at his mum.

"Not really. I can't get rid of her," he said sarcastically, tensing his body as if he was waiting to be slapped.

I decided not to since he was expecting it. Instead, I shrugged and stood up to leave.

He grabbed my wrist and pulled me back on the bed, making me fall onto the mattress. "I'm kidding. Sit down."

Jenna's smile grew. "If you two are together now, we should go over some ground rules."

"Mum," Cole groaned, and he pointed to the door.

Laughing, Jenna got up. "I'm going, I'm going. I think it's great. Not that we couldn't all see it coming or anything. But the door stays open from now on."

"Mum!" Cole snapped again, but he also laughed along with her.

Jenna half closed the door on her way out. We'd get no privacy now. Even with it like it was, you could still see most of his room from the hallway. His bed was on full view.

Cole trailed his fingers across my blushing cheek and down my neck. "Just ignore her."

Everywhere he touched was on fire.

I closed my eyes.

It's okay that this feels good.

"I'm going to close the door," he said.

I caught his arm as he went to get off the bed, and I shook my head.

"Come on, that's a stupid rule. Do they honestly think we're going to have sex while everyone's in the house?"

Tilting my head to the side, I told him that he was being dramatic.

"All right, but I want to be able kiss the crap out of you without the whole house parading past."

He made it sound like he lived with twenty other people.

I pushed on his chest, and his brows lifted. He was stronger and could stop me, but he let me push him down onto the mattress, anyway.

"I don't know what you're doing but I'm down for it."

Grinning, I swung my leg over and straddled him. It was a bold move, but I wanted to see what felt right—what I could handle—and right now, there was no way things could escalate.

Cole sucked in a sharp breath that made my heart flutter.

"I could get used to this," he said, running his hands along my thighs. He never went any higher than halfway up, and I wasn't sure if that was because we could be seen or if he knew that I wasn't quite ready for that yet.

But I felt more comfortable and confident with him than ever before.

I was totally in love and wanted every part of what that meant... eventually.

"As much as I want to stay here forever, and believe me, I do, we should go downstairs."

It looked like it hurt him to say those words, but I could hear his parents clattering around in the kitchen, so it was only a matter of time before we were called for dinner.

"Wait," he said as I went to get off him. "Kiss me first."

I didn't need to be asked twice, but I also wanted to tease him a little, so I pressed my lips to his and immediately rolled off him.

"Ah, come on," he groaned.

Smiling over my shoulder, I walked out of his room. He quickly caught up with me, though.

"That wasn't very nice, was it?"

But his expression didn't match his words, and I knew he was only playing.

Downstairs, his parents were cooking tacos and prepping everything that went with them.

"Where is *he*?" Cole asked.

Jenna replied, "Mia's room."

"That's the door that should stay open."

David laughed, and I did, too, under my breath.

"He's got you there. I trust those two more than him," David said, pointing to Mia's room above the kitchen.

"Oh, she'll realise soon enough. Besides, they're older."

What she meant was that they were older than me... Since I wasn't sixteen and legal yet. Not that I imagined them going easier on us when my birthday rolled around.

"Should we leave while you discuss this?" Cole asked.

I whacked his chest, and he grabbed me, wrapping me in his arm while laughing. His laughter was infectious—my favourite sound in the world.

"Hey," Mia said. "I didn't know you were already here, Oakley... though I should've guessed."

Cole's body tensed, still holding onto me. Chris stood behind Mia, smiling like he'd never messed her around or dumped her countless times. How he had the balls to come back into her house, I didn't know.

"Hey, man," Chris said, addressing Cole and ignoring me.

Don't get me wrong, I didn't want to acknowledge him ever, but Chris didn't know how to deal with me, so he just never bothered. It wasn't a loss.

"Chris," Cole said through gritted teeth. I nudged him again, knowing Mia wouldn't thank him if he made a scene. "I'll play nice," he whispered in my ear.

We sat down at the table, and Mia asked, "No Sarah, Max, and Jasper tonight?"

Jenna sipped her wine. "No, Max is meeting up with an old friend. Fred... or something like that, and Sarah's meeting up with her sister. I don't know about Jasper, but he wasn't home when I spoke to them."

I dropped my fork on the plate, but Cole was the only one to notice. My scalp prickled, burned.

It wasn't Fred.

Frank.

"You okay?" Cole asked.

Bile hit the back of my throat, and it took everything I possessed to turn and smile at him. I forced my hand to pick up the fork and scoop up the mince that I'd dropped from my taco. Somehow, I was managing to hold it together.

David said something I couldn't hear and Cole turned to reply.

Maybe Dad knew a Fred, too. I didn't know all of his friends.

My pulse throbbed in my ears.

While Cole was distracted, I placed the fork back down and focused on not passing out as my body boiled from the inside out.

I didn't know Dad still spoke to Frank. I hadn't seen him in years.

The rest of them chatted but it was all background noise to me. I couldn't hear a thing.

Please let there be a Fred. Please.

I could feel myself backing off, going to that faraway place in my mind where I could be safe until it was over.

That little pink castle on top of the hill was in sight. Daisies sprung up on the grass around it. The swing still hung from the tree, and the ducks swam in the moat.

It was an imaginary place I'd created when I was little, but I couldn't change it now. As childlike as the castle was, it had been my mental safe space for too many years. In there I'd been a princess, and I'd been safe.

I swallowed a tonne of anxiety that felt like sand, and I reached for my drink.

You're okay. You don't need the castle now. You have Cole.

Chapter 17

Oakley

The Italy holiday had finally rolled around. No Frank or Fred had been mentioned again.

I'd spent the first few days after that night on edge, wishing I could get conformation of who my dad had gone to meet.

But then I thought rationally and without fear. Surely if he was meeting up with *that* man, he wouldn't have told anyone. My mum didn't know Frank existed. Dad wouldn't risk that.

So, it *had* to be a man named Fred. He could be someone Dad worked with, maybe. After that realisation, it took another few days and a lot of inner lectures to let it go.

But I had. It was locked away again, where it would hopefully stay forever.

I was able to focus on the holiday.

"Can you sit still for two minutes?" Cole teased, laughing, and grabbing my hand.

His skin on mine did absolutely nothing to make me calm down. I couldn't because we were gliding across the sky toward Italy. Not even the turbulence that rattled my stomach could stop my smile. Things with Cole had been heating up but nothing *big* had happened.

My plastic cup of lemonade rippled like that scene in Jurassic Park.

Leaning over, I selected a new movie on Cole's iPad. He'd downloaded a few things to watch during our short plane ride. We were almost there, but I needed something to take my mind off the anticipation of being *alone* with him.

Jasper was on the other side of Cole, since I'd bagged the window seat.

"Bet I pull more girls than you!" Jasper said, wiggling his eyebrows at Cole.

Cole turned his head slowly towards my brother. "Are you talking to me?"

Sure, Cole and I weren't officially together, but everyone knew we were closer now... Including Jasper. Unless he really was that stupid.

Cole stroked my hand with his thumb. A tiny action of reassurance that made me stupidly happy.

"I have no wingman now," Jasper said.

"When have I ever been your wingman?" Cole asked.

I smirked at their exchange and squeezed Cole's hand. His touch was doing things to me. One brush of his thumb, and I wanted to be in his bed with his body against mine and his mouth driving me wild.

Something that had changed was I now stopped questioning whether I should be feeling what Cole made me feel. I stopped questioning whether it was okay for me to want to lose myself to those feelings.

Because it was okay.

Because it was my choice.

Jasper shrugged. "I don't need you, anyway."

My brother was disgusting. I couldn't stand how he went through women. His defence was that he was always upfront. Still, he could show some restraint.

"You're a pig, you know that?" Cole said.

Jasper laughed. "Yeah, but I'm not a sexually frustrated pig."

Cole and I stared blankly at Jasper. What did you even say to that? I had no clue.

Twenty-five minutes later, the plane began its descent, and I was so excited. We made it through the airport quickly and got a taxi to the hotel.

My room was small and connected to my parents', but it also had its own entrance, so I could come and go whenever I wanted. It was light, bright, and comfortable, and it had air-conditioning, as well as enough storage. Although it wasn't a huge suite, it had everything I needed.

I turned the lock on the adjoining door, only satisfied when I heard the click.

No one could get in.

I dumped my suitcase on my bed and opened the balcony door. It was small, just enough room for a table and two chairs. Stepping out into the warm air, I sighed. The view was beautiful. To my right were the mountains. At the top, they were covered with a dusting of thin white clouds. To my left was the ocean.

"Open up," Cole called through the door.

I was waiting for that. Opening up, I pulled on his wrist and dragged him into my room.

"Whoa, eager. I like it."

Chuckling, he kicked the door shut and cupped my jaw in his hands. "Why haven't you changed yet?"

I couldn't move once our eyes connected.

"Oakley?"

Nope.

I had nothing.

My gaze drifted down to his parted lips, his ragged breaths blowing across my face. I was momentarily stunned, my hormones turned me dumb.

Stepping back, he cleared his throat and said, "Get changed."

I could see how much he didn't want to go out, but we'd only just arrived and couldn't hide in my room without raising suspicion.

Backing up, I ripped the zip of my suitcase to open it, and I grabbed the first things I found. Denim shorts and a blue tank top. That'd do.

Holding a finger up, I twirled it around to tell him to look away.

Sighing sharply, he did as I asked. I could tell from the amusement on his face right before he'd spun that he wasn't bothered that I'd asked him not to look.

Cole kept his back to me and rifled through my suitcase while I quickly changed.

I'd just finished pulling on my shorts when Cole swung my bikini strap around his finger.

Jumping forward, I grabbed it out of his hand, making him laugh.

"Feel free to put that on."

I slapped his arm and then tugged, telling him I was ready.

"Sorry. Couldn't resist. You're perfect."

He didn't subscribe to the traditional definition of the word. Luckily for me.

My chest ached when he placed a chaste kiss on my lips.

"Got your key card?" he asked.

One time, I'd locked it in my room, and from then on, I apparently needed reminding for the rest of my life.

I held the card up as proof, and we headed out of the hotel.

The beach was a fifteen-minute walk away, and it was a beautiful sunny day.

Cole and I walked hand in hand, and I smiled as the golden sun made his eyes glow.

The sea was clear blue, with soft sands stretching out as far as the eye could see. There were people dotted around the beach, lying on colourful towels, and children were running around or building sandcastles. A few people were swimming in the sea and playing with large beach balls.

"Fucking sand is going to get everywhere," Cole grumbled as the sand sank beneath our toes.

He hated it in his clothes and hair and was never the one volunteering to be buried. Even as a kid.

I kicked some at him, and he arched a brow. "Oh, you want to go there?"

I do, as it goes.

Cole reached down and picked me up. I had to clamp my mouth together to stop from squealing. I only just about managed it. He'd heard me laugh quietly before. I wasn't always able to control every sound... and around him, I was wishing more and more that I didn't need to.

He laughed loudly when I slapped his back, but he didn't put me down until we reached a quiet spot. I kept my head down, avoiding looks from other holiday makers.

I straightened my hair the second I landed back on my feet, and I slapped his chest.

"Next time you kick sand at me, I'm pinning you to this beach towel," he said, laying his towel out.

Cole peeled his T-shirt off right as I was about to kick sand again.

I froze... again.

He did a double take, and his lips slowly curved at me staring. "You good?"

Oh, he was really enjoying this.

With a nod, I sat down on the towel, hotter than ever, and it had nothing to do with the sun.

I wasn't wearing a bikini, but I only had shorts and a tank top on. Cole sat beside me, one arm wrapping around my waist.

"We get to do this every day," he said, gazing into my eyes.

I curled my hand around the back of his neck and guided his mouth to mine. I was on fire instantly, my body craving more.

Cole moaned and pulled me flush against his bare chest.

This is it. This is how I die.

His hand cupped my jaw as his lips moulded to mine. I pushed my hands into his hair and tugged gently.

Cole pulled back, wide eyed and panting. He cleared his throat. "I need a minute."

I grinned and laid down, closing my eyes against the sun, I and wished I could stay here forever.

"There's a water sports hut up ahead. I'm going to book us in for diving."

Groaning, I reached out with my eyes still closed and slapped whatever my hand came into contact with.

"It's happening."

I pushed up on my elbows and watched him go book us into Hell.

It was getting pretty late by the time we'd had dinner and hung out by the bar with our families. Cole didn't want to go clubbing with Mia and Jasper, and I couldn't.

Both our parents were going to stay in the lounge and drink, so Cole and I told them we were going to explore the hotel. There were arcade type rooms and plenty of things to do.

As we walked through the hotel, I pulled him to a stop and pressed the button for the lift.

"Arcade is that way," he said, pointing ahead of us. "Your sense of direction is shit."

Wow, for someone so smart, he sure was being slow... but he

soon caught on when I pulled him into the lift and wrapped my arms around his waist.

His eyes brightened. "Oh, you couldn't care less about space invaders."

No, I could not.

"I like your plan, babe."

My smirk told him that I thought he would.

I let us into my room with the card that I still had tucked away safely in my bag. Cole turned to me and scratched the back of his neck when the door shut behind us.

Moving slowly, I kept my eyes on him as I sat on the bed and shuffled to sit against the wall.

"You think I could stay here tonight? I could sneak out early in the morning."

Biting my lip, I considered it. I wanted him to stay, but I was scared of getting caught. There was no way I could say no, though. My head and my heart weren't always on the same page, but I was only prepared to listen to my heart at this point.

I smiled and patted the bed.

Cole removed his top again but left his shorts on, and my mouth watered. He was so sexy, I couldn't believe he wanted to be in my bed, to kiss me, and hang out with me every day.

I'd hit the jackpot.

He climbed onto the bed and held his arms out for me.

Snuggling, I laid my head on his shoulder as he ran his fingers through my hair.

"You okay?" he whispered as the air in the room evaporated.

Gazing up at him, I contemplated how much to tell him.

"You look... scared. Of me? But why would—?" His mouth made an 'O' shape the moment he realised where me head was at. "Hey, nothing is going to happen between us until you want it to. I didn't ask to stay for any reason other than I *hate* being away from you."

Oh.

He leant over and pressed a kiss to my forehead. "You're tired, babe. Sleep."

My heavy eyes wanted to give in. It'd been a long day, getting up at three in the morning to get to the airport.

Cole shuffled us down so we were lying flat on the mattress. I curled around him, my leg slung over his, and my hand resting over his racing heart.

"Good night," I heard him mumble just before sleep pulled me under.

Chapter 18

Oakley

I woke up to the bed dipping, stirring me out of sleep. If we were making that a habit, I was on board.

"Sorry," Cole whispered. "It's almost six so I thought I should go. I'll come back in a couple of hours and we can go get breakfast."

He bent down to kiss me, his lips lingering on mine for a few seconds, driving my pulse wild. Then I watched him creep out of my room with the hope that he would stay again tonight. Waking up in the morning with him was the best feeling ever.

There was absolutely no way I could get back to sleep now—I was too eager to see him again. That one tiny kiss wasn't nearly enough.

I got up, took a long shower, and then I dressed. Opening the double doors, I stepped out onto the small balcony and sat down on the only seat that fit there. It was very peaceful, being so early in the morning. Only a few people were about in the resort.

My parents' balcony door slid open. We were separated by the railing, so they couldn't get to my room from here.

Dad stepped out dressed in shorts and a short-sleeved shirt.

He spotted me immediately. "Good morning. Did you and Cole have a nice time yesterday?"

I nodded and took a step back.

"Remember, I want you both back for dinner each night. No exceptions."

I lifted the corner of my mouth. Neither of us would skip on dinner, anyway. We knew if we did then that'd be the end of the freedom.

"Good. Ah, I think your mum's out of the bathroom. We'll see you for breakfast soon."

He went back inside, and I could breathe again.

Just after eight, almost right on time, Cole knocked on my door. "Hey." He stepped forward and planted a quick kiss on my lips. "Ready to go down?"

I nodded and stepped out of my room just as Mum and Dad walked out of theirs.

"Morning, honey, Cole," Mum said, giving me a hug.

"Hungry?" Dad asked.

"Starving," Cole replied. He nodded towards the lift at the end of the corridor. "You seen anyone else this morning?"

Dad shook his head. "Sarah just got a text from your mum, and they were on their way down. We'll meet them in the restaurant. I've not heard from Mia, and I'd imagine Jasper is... elsewhere."

Probably in some poor girl's room.

I stepped closer to Cole as we walked to the lift and waited for it to arrive.

"What do you have planned today? Your father and I are going shopping with David and Jenna," Mum asked me, even though she waited for the reply from Cole.

"We're diving this morning," he answered.

I raised my eyebrow at him.

"Is it safe?" Mum asked, frowning.

Dad chuckled. "Of course, it is, Sarah. There's a qualified instructor, isn't there?"

"Yeah, of course. I wouldn't let Oakley do anything dangerous," Cole said.

"See? They'll be in safe hands. There's plenty to do and, except for clubbing, we agreed that Oakley could do what she liked."

I often wondered if Dad was *cool* about things like this because he felt guilty... or, more likely, he wanted to keep up appearances.

"All right," Mum said, raising her hands.

In the end, it was only David, Jenna, and Mia who joined us for breakfast. Jasper, as we suspected, was nowhere to be seen. Not that it was much of a surprise. He now treated holidays—or any days, actually—as a chance to sleep with anything that moved all night, and then actually sleep all day.

Breakfast was an all-you-can-eat buffet, which Cole took full advantage of. I didn't eat much because I didn't want it to come back up while we were diving.

"Have fun and be careful," Jenna said as Cole and I got up to leave for the beach.

Fun was unlikely, but adrenaline was pumping through my veins at the mere thought of doing something so out of character.

I didn't take risks.

Cole grinned. "Oh, we will. Right, Oaks?"

I let that go, and we walked to the beach. I held Cole's hand so tightly, I was probably crushing his bones. Under my clothes was my bikini, but for diving, we'd be given a wet suit.

"Are you ready for this?" he asked when we arrived back at the sports shack.

I shook my head but grinned, unable to hide the smidge of excitement I felt.

That excitement ended thirty minutes later when I was in wet a suit and had an oxygen tank attached to me.

What kind of sick person wanted to pretend to be a fish?

People were supposed to stay on land.

Our instructor Kyle demonstrated how we'd dive down.

Cole and I sank to our knees and disappeared beneath the water.

My heart thudded, but I was still close to the surface, enough that I could stand. Right now, I was fine.

I sank down lower.

The instructor led us a little farther out, and then deeper.

Cole stayed right beside me, but after a minute, I didn't feel scared because it was beautiful down there... like another world.

I tried to gasp as fish swam around us without fear. Reaching out, I almost brushed one. But as much as I was enjoying it, I still didn't want to touch a gross fish.

Cole was going to be so smug when he saw how much I loved it. Bubbles from my oxygen tank rose in front of my face.

Spinning around, I came face to face with Cole. He took my hand, and through my mask I saw his eyes dance.

An hour earlier, diving had been my idea of hell. Now, I wanted to live down there with him. We'd be on our own, safe. I clung onto his hand, and we swam together, keeping up with Kyle and the others booked on with us.

Once our time was up, Kyle gestured for us to swim back to the surface.

"You so enjoyed that, didn't you?" Cole teased as we stripped out of our wetsuits. Somehow, he'd known that once I was under the water, I would love every second of it.

I shrugged nonchalantly, but my traitorous lips curling prevented me from pretending it was only 'okay'.

"I knew you would. Let's head back for a shower, then I'll

come to your room. Want to have lunch before we do something of your choice?"

I nodded and nudged him with my shoulder.

Back at the hotel we ate, and I found what I wanted us to do. There were leaflets about the hotel spa in reception—particularly the couple's massage.

"No, come on," Cole said. "Don't make me do that. You have the massage, and I'll wait outside for you."

I shook my head, lifting my brow. That was absolutely *not* going to happen.

He groaned. "Fine. But no more taking turns to do stuff. I don't want to have to get a bloody manicure next."

Cole walked me towards the spa. I playfully nudged his shoulder again, and he wrapped his arm around me, kissing my temple. It was harder to walk when we were clinging to each other, but neither of us cared.

"Welcome. I'm Luisa, how can I help you?" said a beautiful, dark-haired woman.

"Erm, hey. Do you have any appointments for a... couple's massage?" Cole asked.

She tapped away on her keyboard, her long nails loud against the keys. "Okay. If you want a thirty-minute massage, we can fit you in now. If you want the forty-five, I can book you in for tomorrow."

"Oh, the thirty. Definitely the thirty."

Why wouldn't he want some gorgeous Italian woman to massage him?

"Great. I just have something for you to fill in and then I'll take you through."

We're shown into a room with two white beds, the air filled with the scent of rose oil. There was a chest on the far wall with lots of little drawers, and a huge bunch of pink orchids in a white vase sat on top.

"There are towels on the beds. If you remove all of your clothing and cover yourself, your masseuse will be with you in five minutes."

My eyes widened.

Remove all of our clothes? Okay, I did not think this through.

I'd not been naked in front of Cole before.

There was a towel. We'd be covered.

Calm down!

She left the room, and I turned in Cole's direction and closed my eyes.

His laughter made me smile. "You can leave your underwear on. Just move your bra straps off your shoulders. I'll turn around, and I won't look. I promise."

Oh, God, I can't breathe.

With a deep breath, I opened my eyes and saw that Cole now had his back to me and was already down to his boxers.

I removed the dress I was wearing and tucked my bra straps under my arms. With my heart thudding in my chest, I slipped under the fluffy towel and placed my head in the hole.

The room felt about fifty degrees hotter than it did thirty seconds ago.

Cole waited until I'd stopped moving on the bed, knowing I'd be settled by then.

"You good?" he asked.

I glanced across at him and smiled. He'd turned my way, too, and was smiling at me in return just as we heard a knock at the door.

"We're ready," Cole called.

Thankfully, two women entered. There was no way a man who wasn't Cole was going to touch my body. They were only going to massage my back, scalp, and hands. I still had my underwear on.

My muscles gave as the masseuse worked them over,

allowing years of tension to be massaged away. The knots in my muscles uncurled in a painful way that didn't feel totally unpleasant.

"Okay, this was a good idea," Cole muttered.

Yeah, I bet he thought that with that stunning woman's hand all over him. I'd be jealous if that wasn't her job.

When our thirty minutes were up, Cole told me to get ready while he stayed laid down, his head in the hole, staring at the floor.

As I picked my dress up, I realised that I wouldn't have minded if he'd seen me, after all.

Impulsively, I touched his bare shoulder, and his head snapped up.

"What?" he croaked, his eyes widening when they landed on my half-naked body.

I was covered by my underwear, but it was still intimate.

With my heart flying in my chest, I bit my lip and dropped my arms that were covering stomach. Cole gulped audibly, his Adam's apple bobbing, and eyes dragging over every inch of my body.

"I... um... Jesus, babe, you're stunning. How are you real?"

He sat up and reached for me. My heart missed a beat as he took my hand and pulled me closer.

"And even more stunning when you're blushing."

Wrapping his arms around me, he closed the distance and pressed his lips to mine.

My fingers curled in his hair, and I kissed him back. This time was different. Heated. I wanted to crawl on top of him and get lost in the drag of his tongue.

And that was the exact moment I moved back, and Cole groaned out, "Don't go away."

I pointed to the clock on the wall above my head. We only had a few minutes.

"Fine." He jumped off the table and pulled on his shorts and T-shirt. I pulled my dress back on, and I ran my fingers through my hair. The scalp massage was amazing, but it'd messed my hair up.

We walked out of the room hand in hand with matching smiles.

"Tomorrow, can we do nothing but stay in the room?" he asked, kissing me in the middle of the lobby. "I've not had nearly enough opportunities to do that today."

Good with me.

~

Since our moment in the spa the day before, I'd grown even more comfortable around Cole. We changed in front of each other for bed last night, and then we did the same before the water park that morning.

Cole didn't get the full day alone like he'd wanted, but it was now mid-afternoon, and everyone had gone their separate ways.

We'd put one of the only English-speaking TV channels on in our room and were watching reruns of *Friends*. Neither of us could speak enough Italian to watch anything else.

So far, I hadn't taken anything in. Chandler's jokes went over my head. My body was humming. I couldn't lie still, not with Cole's bare chest beneath my cheek and his fingers drawing patterns on my arm.

The tension between us was so thick, I could choke on it. Cole laid far too still, like he was using all his restraint to keep his hands to himself, while I was desperate for him to roam them all over my skin.

Screw pretending to watch this.

I rolled over and hovered above him with my hands beside

his face, pinning him in... not that I thought he would try to make an escape.

A smile tugged on his lips as he wrapped his hand around the back of my head. He caught on fast and pulled me down.

His lips captured mine in a kiss that made my toes curl. Slowly, he rolled us over, so he was on top, in charge, making me feel like I was on the edge of combustion.

"Oakley?" His voice trembled when he said my name. "This is probably really late, considering everything, but... Mia said I was a pussy for not doing this." He sighed and shook his head. "Shit, I'm so bad at this. I shouldn't be. This is *you* and... Damn it, will you be my girl?"

My lips parted. I curled my hands around his neck and brought him back to my mouth, nodding into the kiss.

He pulled away, smiling, and dragged his lips down my neck, leaving featherlight kisses as he went. I arched my neck, giving him better access.

Cole moaned as he ran his hand down the side of my body and gripped the bottom of my top.

This was that defining moment where I had to decide if I was going to listen to what I actually wanted, which was Cole, or what I thought I should want, which was to never be touched again.

My body knew already, racing towards something big, and I was supposed to listen to my heart.

I loved how Cole made me feel and how natural being with him was. I loved every part of him, and I wanted this. I wanted this more than I ever thought possible.

When I didn't push him away, he pulled my top over my head and groaned. "So beautiful."

Everywhere he touched left a burning trail that stole the air from my lungs. I sucked in a breath when his finger trailed between my breasts and down my stomach.

"Do you want to stop?"

I ran my hands up his arms and across his shoulders, shaking my head, and Cole bit his lip.

"Are you sure, Oakley?"

His gravelly voice made my stomach clench. He wanted this as much as I did.

"Are you scared?"

Scared wasn't the right word. A little apprehensive. I shrugged a shoulder.

"Ah, you're nervous." He leant down and kissed my forehead. "Don't worry, I am, too."

Why would he be nervous?

"Don't look so confused. This isn't only *your* first time."

Cole was a virgin?

My eyes widened.

"Not sure if I should be insulted by your surprise or not."

I shook my head, trying to make sense of what he'd said. *How can he be a virgin?* He'd had a couple of girlfriends before. I mean, they hadn't lasted very long, but still...

He was seventeen, and so gorgeous, you couldn't help but stare at him.

"It took so long for me to even consider that there might be a tiny chance you liked me the same way I liked you. I've never slept with anyone because... because I've only ever wanted you," he whispered.

Oh.

Wow.

I couldn't quite believe what he was telling me. All this time and he wanted me, too.

A hot tear rolled down the side of my face, and Cole wiped it away with his thumb.

He murmured against my lips, "I love you, Oakley. It's always been you."

Closing my eyes, I took a deep breath as warmth spread through my chest.

I felt a harder pressure on my lips, and I kissed him back, showing him how much I loved him, too.

Cole moved to get me naked, fumbling as he removed my clothes and bra, his nerves now evident in his clumsy actions. He kissed me again and pushed off his shorts.

"Babe... you feel so good."

Sucking in a breath, I tilted my head and arched my hips into his, and pleasure exploded behind my eyes. God, that felt good. Cole hissed through his teeth, pressing his erection between my legs.

"I need to..." He sat up, his eyes roaming over my body, from my neck, down to my breasts, and then my stomach.

"I feel like I've died," he said with a tough chuckle before he grabbed something from his pocket. A condom. "You can stop looking at me like that. I was hoping, not expecting."

I smiled wide, and he shook his head, rolling the condom on his erection.

He leant down, and I thought he was going for my mouth, but he was too low. His lips parted, then he sucked a nipple into his mouth.

I felt like *I'd* died.

I gripped his arms and moaned. I wanted to say his name. I was desperate to do more, say more, feel more, on the edge of oblivion, and wishing he would hurry up and touch me.

His tongue grazed my skin, tasting me as he kissed and licked his way back up to my mouth.

Holding his shoulders, I prevented him from going anywhere ever again if I had my way.

Smiling against my lips, he ran his hand down my stomach and between my legs. I left the bed like I was possessed, arching to meet his finger that swirled around the little bud of nerves.

I kissed him harder, my tongue duelling with his. Groaning, he moved his hand and lined himself up with me.

"I don't want to hurt you," he bit out, slowly swiping his tongue over my bottom lip.

Curling my leg around his back, I pulled him down, making him groan again.

"Baby... push my chest if you want me to stop."

I nodded, claimed his mouth again, and then he slowly pushed into me. I felt my body stretch around him, but it was nothing more than a little pinch that was quickly replaced with an overwhelming burst of heaven.

"Babe," he breathed against my neck as he started to move.

This was the best thing we could ever do. Panting, I clawed at his back, my leg still tight around him, not letting him go as I climbed higher. My body moved against him of its own accord.

"I love you," he groaned, pressing his forehead to mine.

His words were almost my undoing. I was so close that I could feel the release within reach.

Tangling my hands in his hair, I cried out as he hit something inside of me that sent me flying over the edge. I clamped my mouth shut as my body convulsed, pleasure courting through my system.

"God," he rasped, his eyebrows pulled together. "Oakley."

My name was a prayer, and with closed eyes, he came, too.

Scooping me into his arms, he kissed me long and slow. His heart thumped to the same beat as mine as he squished me to his chest.

"You okay?"

For the first time in forever, I was absolutely okay.

Chapter 19

Cole

I lay perfectly still, so I wouldn't wake Oakley as she slept in my arms. She was so out of my league, I couldn't believe my luck that she wanted me.

If she saw herself the way I saw her...

She sighed in her sleep and rolled onto her back. A mass of blonde hair rested messily around her. Like a halo. She was a fucking angel, and she was *mine*.

Last night had been the best night of my life. The way she felt and tasted was forever etched into my soul—her gasps when I made her feel as good as she made me feel.

Sex was not at all underrated.

And I'd finally told her that I was in love with her.

I couldn't remember a time when I hadn't been.

I'd have loved to hear her say it back, but we didn't need words. I'd felt it.

When she'd first stopped talking, everyone had thought it was because of the choking incident. We'd waited patiently for a few days, and then it'd become obvious that something else was going on. At one point, Jasper had thought she was doing it for attention, but that wasn't like her at all.

I still wasn't sure what had caused her to stop speaking, but I think it turned into fear somewhere along the line.

She would have to come to us when she was ready. There had been so many times when I'd wanted to beg her, make her tell me, but I knew that would push her away.

I wasn't giving her an excuse to go anywhere.

But I wanted to hear her say my name again. I couldn't even remember the last time I heard it. We were little and her voice, now a distant memory, would've changed by now.

It was almost six in the morning, and I needed to sneak back to my room soon, but I was too comfortable, and she felt too good in my arms. I doubted anyone would be up at this time, but I couldn't risk getting caught.

We weren't supposed to have the door closed anymore, yet here we were, naked and locked in a hotel room.

After another ten minutes of staring at her like a stalker, I forced myself to get out of bed. She took a deep breath as I unwrapped her body from mine, but she quickly settled back into sleep.

Throwing on my clothes, I took one last look at her and left the room.

A couple in gym gear—on their fucking holiday—was there as I walked along the corridor. They paid me no attention as I passed them and let myself into my room.

I headed straight for the shower because I wouldn't be able to go back to sleep. I wasn't getting as many hours in since we'd arrived, thanks to the sneaking around, but I wasn't complaining.

It was only when I looked up at my reflection in the bathroom mirror that I realised I'd left Oakley alone the morning after we'd had sex.

She would wake up alone.

Shit.

Now it was almost seven, which was too late to sneak back. Besides, I didn't have a key. She was going to wake up alone whatever I did now.

I was such a dickhead.

Rushing around, I clumsily started to get dressed. If I knocked, I'd wake her, but at least I'd be there.

On my way back, I could hear signs of life, people talking in their rooms, and music drifting from somewhere. I raised my hand to knock on her door and felt my stomach tighten.

The door swung open a minute later. She was dressed in a big T-shirt and a beautiful smile. Raking her hand through her messy hair, she stepped to the side to let me in.

"Morning," I said. "I'm sorry I left; I didn't want to be caught. Then I realised this was not the morning to sneak out when—"

Her mouth landed on mine, and I smiled against the kiss, my hands roaming across her back, feeling every shudder as her body responded to my touch.

"Hey, are you okay? You're not sore or anything? I didn't hurt you?"

She stared into my eyes, tilting her head, and I had no idea what she was thinking.

"Oakley?"

Shaking her head, she sank into my embrace and laid her head against my chest.

"Are you sure? I mean, your first time is meant to hurt, and if you're sore, we can get you something," I rambled like an idiot. *What the hell would you even get for that?*

"I mean, I could run you a hot bath."

She pulled out of my arms, my least favourite thing she could do, and opened her wardrobe.

"Hey, what is it?"

Looking over her shoulder, she grinned and held up the blue bikini.

She was okay.

"Pool day it is." I caught her arm when she went to move past me. "I love you."

Rising on tiptoes, she planted a long kiss on my lips, showing me how she felt in return.

I sat on her bed when she went to get ready. I'd hoped that she would change in front of me now that we'd seen each other naked, but I wasn't going to push.

When she eventually came out of the bathroom sometime later, she wore a white dress over the blue bikini. I handed her the beach bag, and we went down to meet whoever was awake for breakfast.

"Damn, full house," I said, spotting everyone sitting around a table in the restaurant. Even Jasper.

"Morning," I said as we took our seats.

Jasper eyed me suspiciously, but that could just be his normal idiot face. When Oakley turned her head away, I knew that she was thinking the same thing.

We looked like we'd slept together, it was written in our smiles. I only hoped that no one else would notice.

"Water park, fuckers!" Jasper said, earning a glare from Max and Sarah.

It was going to be our second visit.

I moved my leg, brushing it against Oakley's under the table, and a blush crept into her cheeks. She was good at pretending nothing was happening while she ate breakfast, though.

"Mind if I come to the water park today?" Mia asked.

"Sure," I replied.

Mia had been hanging out with some girl she'd met, but she'd gone home this morning, so Mia was now at a loose end.

I'd hoped she would meet a new guy and forget about that prick back in England.

"Right," Max said as everyone stood up. "You four have a

lovely day. Oakley, you stay with Cole. Us old folks have a boat to catch, but we'll see you for dinner. Take care of her."

"I will."

He nodded and held his hand out for Sarah. He never told Jasper to look out for Oakley. Probably because he couldn't keep a fake plant alive.

"Let's go. Last time there were so many hotties there, I thought I'd died and gone to Heaven."

Oakley rolled her eyes and led the way to the lobby where we could get a taxi. I couldn't help but feel a little sorry for Jasper. Abby, his ex, had really screwed him over, and now he self-medicated with women.

I asked if he wanted to talk about Abby once. He got so mad that we didn't see him for two days. God knew how many people he'd slept with in that time.

No one had mentioned Abby since.

"There's a taxi. Let's go," Mia said. Jasper and I exchanged a glance. She shoved her phone into her bag. Something or someone on there had just pissed her off.

Oakley walked ahead with Mia.

"Bet you twenty quid that I score at least twice today," Jasper said.

I deadpanned. "When are you going to grow up?"

He smirked. "Cole, man, I'll do that shit when I'm in my forties. Why the hell would I want to settle down now?"

"Why are you bothering, Cole?" Mia said over her shoulder. "You know what Casanova is like."

"Isn't that the guy on *Titanic*?" Jasper asked.

Oakley snapped her head around and stared at her brother in disbelief.

I laughed at how dumb he was being and wondered how the hell he had ever got into university. "Jesus, man."

"What?" Jasper asked.

"Honestly, babe, it's a wonder you're able to dress yourself," Mia teased. "You're lucky you're good-looking, Jasper."

His lip curved. "You think I'm good-looking, sweetheart? You should see the parts of me that're covered."

"Yeah, no, thanks." Mia linked arms with Oakey and walked to a taxi waiting outside the hotel.

At the water park, we split up to go to the respective changing rooms and then met outside. Jasper was off immediately, without a goodbye, as soon as he saw a group of girls walking by. They were all beautiful and probably his age. None of them had anything on Oakley, though. That girl was buried deep under my skin, tattooed all over my heart.

With Jasper gone, I looked like a bloody pervert while waiting outside the ladies' changing room. I averted my eyes when a group of preteens walked out.

Awkward.

Mia eventually came out first, looking behind her. Oakley appeared next, and I lost the ability to breathe.

She was so beautiful, I couldn't take my eyes off her. That bikini looked like it had been custom-made for her, hugging her toned body to perfection.

"Swim and then slides?" Mia suggested.

My eye twitched.

No, go away.

I forced myself to look at my sister. "Sure."

Mia led the way to the largest pool with the rapids, and I followed with Oakley. She'd folded her arms over her chest, uncomfortable with the attention she was getting. There was nothing for her to worry about. I wouldn't let anyone touch her.

She stepped closer, her arm pressing against mine as we walked. I felt a twinge of jealousy every time I caught someone looking at her, but I couldn't blame them.

"Are you okay?" I asked.

She nodded, biting her lip.

"You look beautiful. If you could see yourself properly, you'd be the most confident person on Earth."

She looked away and took a deep breath, uneasy with compliments. It was my mission to change that.

Mia gave us some space, swimming lengths in a pool that people, including Oakley and me, were messing around in.

I held Oakley close as we disappeared behind a waterfall. "I don't want to be here anymore," I murmured against her lips.

She deepened the kiss, her hands tangling in my hair, telling me that she felt the same way.

"Can I take you back to the hotel? We don't have to do anything, babe, I just want to be with you only."

Gripping my hand, she tugged me towards the shallow end so we could get out.

We were going to spend the rest of our holiday getting lost in each other.

And we did, spending hours alone discovering each other's bodies, while our families and the rest of the world remained clueless to what was growing stronger between us.

Chapter 20

Oakley

Nausea rolled over me in big waves as the plane hurtled us back towards England. Our holiday was officially over but all I wanted was to be in my hotel room with Cole again.

He made me feel so special, and I was quickly becoming addicted to that.

So far, no one had mentioned us being together, other than Jenna when she told us to keep the door open. A rule we'd broken every day.

My dad hadn't spoken to me, and I hoped that continued. He'd already acknowledged that I was growing up and he was giving me more freedom. It'd been two years since it stopped.

It was over.

Cole stared out of the plane window with a small frown in place, no doubt feeling as disappointed to go home as I did. I sat back in my seat and tried to act as if my heart wasn't breaking.

"I hate the end of holidays," Mia grumbled, flopping down in Jasper's empty seat beside me. "The plane journey home is the most depressing thing ever."

I couldn't agree more. I longed to live in that holiday state where everything was perfect forever.

161

Nothing ever stayed perfect, though. I knew that.

Jasper sat in Mia's seat in the row beside ours, and Cole looked over his shoulder at him.

"Where were you?" he asked my brother.

I don't want to know.

"I just joined the Mile High Club," Jasper said, not bothering to keep his voice down.

Behind me, Mum scoffed.

Yep, I definitely didn't want to know that. I grimaced and looked past Cole to the plane wing. If I had to hear about it in detail, I was going to open that emergency door.

"Of course, you did," Mia said, fake vomiting.

Mia and Jasper argued like brother and sister. She hated his womanising but sympathised with the reason behind it. Jasper had given up on his cheating ex. Mia couldn't bring herself to do the same.

"Jealousy doesn't suit you, Mia," Jasper said.

"You think I'm jealous of you screwing some random in a stinky, dirty plane toilet? Wow, you really are up your own arse."

"Firstly, the toilet didn't smell, and secondly, I got her name first, so she wasn't random. It was one of the best experiences of my life. The girl could sure—"

"Thank you," Cole said. "We don't need your details, man."

I laced my fingers between his, thanking him for stopping my brother from talking anymore. Jasper didn't have a filter for when he was in the company of people who might not want to hear about his exploits.

And most people didn't want to hear.

The plane landed too soon, and I followed my family through the airport. All I wanted to do was get back on and fly back to Italy... or anywhere else in the world.

"It's going to be okay," Cole whispered in my ear, sensing my mood.

I gave him the best smile I could.

Once everyone had their bags, we walked to the long-stay car park where we'd left the cars.

"Are you coming with me, Oakley?" Mia asked as she unlocked her car.

I nodded and handed my suitcase to Dad's outstretched hand. All I had left was the car journey. Home was fast approaching, and I needed every last second with Cole before I got there.

Cole and I climbed into the back of the car, and Mia threw her keys to Jasper.

"You drive," she called.

My eyes widened in alarm. Jasper drove like he had a death wish, and I really didn't know how he hadn't wrecked his car or received a speeding fine yet.

"Buckle up, kids," Jasper chirped, smiling with exaggerated crazy eyes.

Although I knew he was only trying to scare us, I double-checked my belt. Then, I checked again. Whoever gave him his licence should have been fired. Gripping the door handle as Jasper revved the engine, I said a silent prayer and closed my eyes.

By the time we made it home in one piece, it was getting dark. The sky was a moody blue, the shade it usually turned before a storm. It made me miss Italy even more. While everyone fussed around, getting their suitcases out of the cars, I wrapped my jacket around myself, feeling all the anxieties and fears inside me resurface.

Back to normal.

My eyes stung with the threat of tears.

"Right, we'd better get inside," Dad ordered with what felt like a pointed look at me. Did the freedom he'd given me stop in Italy? "We could all do with an early night."

"Yes," Mum agreed.

Cole pulled me into his arms and held me close. "I'll see you in the morning. I love you," he whispered in my ear.

My heart skipped.

I love you, too.

We parted ways, my legs heavier with every step in the opposite direction I took. "You tired, love?" Mum asked.

I was exhausted. Physically and mentally.

I nodded, and she kissed my cheek.

"Okay, off to bed, then."

Dad didn't go to kiss me, thank God, so I gave him and Jasper a quick wave and legged it upstairs. I changed into my pyjamas, and I climbed straight into bed. Stretching out my arms and legs like a starfish, I suddenly wished Cole were with me. My bed was big and cold, and I didn't like it. I rolled over and stretched my arm over the empty space where he should be.

As soon as I pulled the cover up to my chin and wrapped it around me like a cocoon, my phone beeped.

> Cole: Being in separate beds doesn't work for me. Be ready at eight tomorrow. I love you x

I smiled in the dark and drafted a reply I would never send. Three simple words. I love you.

How bad could it be to send one text message?

No.

Clutching my chest, I dropped the phone on the bed with a soft thud and pressed my face into the pillow.

You can't. Not ever.

I *knew* how bad it would be.

Chapter 21

Oakley

I got up at seven because Cole wanted me to be ready for eight. I had no idea what we were doing, but that didn't matter.

Rubbing my eyes vigorously to clear the thoughts that had kept me awake all night, I took deep breaths. The need to reply to his message had been overwhelming.

It wasn't something I should have even been thinking about.

Startled, I spun towards my door just as it flew open.

Cole gripped the edge of the door and smirked. "And here I was thinking you'd be ready by now."

I had no clue how he could be so... *awake* after travelling.

"You're tired."

Clearly, I looked great this morning, then...

Cole reached out to tuck my hair behind my ear before he ran his thumb under my eye. "No, you look stressed. What's going on?"

I shook my head, hoping he would believe my nonchalance.

He stood still a minute, staring into my eyes, deciding what to do next. I couldn't let him start asking questions, so I grabbed a fistful of his T-shirt and tugged. His mouth landed on mine hard.

The kiss started slow with long strokes of our lips and the maddening flick of our tongues. He moaned, and his hands pushed into my hair.

We weren't alone so we had to be careful.

Cole pressed his forehead to mine. "Damn, what a welcome."

I pursed my lips and raised a brow.

"Do you still want to go out? We don't have to. We can hang around here or go to mine. I don't think we'll be alone anywhere." He whimpers theatrically. "I *really* need to be alone with you."

I really needed to be alone with him, too. But my parents were home. I wanted to be out of the house completely.

Holding my finger up, I told Cole to give me a minute, and I grabbed some clothes out of my wardrobe.

"Yeah, like you'll actually be ready in one minute."

Smiling, I locked myself in the bathroom and stripped.

I turned the shower temperature up too high and stepped under the water. The burn took me straight back, and I gasped.

Wincing, I placed my palms against the tiles as my skin turned pink.

What are you doing?

Stop.

You can scrub until your skin peels off. You'll never be clean.

No.

I scrunched my eyes shut, gripping the rough sponge as I scraped it over my legs.

Get off!

Get off!

Get off!

I cried silently for everything I'd gone through and everything I would continue to lose.

My hands trembled as I frantically rubbed my skin raw.

Tears streamed down my cheeks, mixing with the water and disappearing down the drain.

Calm down.

Crying didn't change anything, but at least it released some of the pressure that constantly built inside my chest.

Get it together. You're stronger than this.

Cole would have to wait because, as hard as I tried, I couldn't pull myself together. Sliding down the tiled wall of the shower, I curled my body into a ball and pressed my face into my knees.

That hadn't happened in a while. What was going on?

I took a deep breath. Then another. My heart began to steady, but it was replaced with repulsion and disappointment.

I was doing better. The best I'd been to date. The hot shower shouldn't have bothered me—shouldn't have taken me back to a time when I used to scrub that man off me with water you could boil an egg in.

If Cole knew the truth, would he regret having sex with me? Would he be disgusted?

My stomach flipped over, and I pressed my fist into my mouth as a wave of nausea rolled through my body.

Stop it. Stop it now.

None of it was your fault.

What Frank did was nothing *like what I've done with Cole.*

I practiced some breathing exercises I'd found online. Closing my eyes, I settled my pulse, refusing the castle. I could do this.

This was a blip. I didn't need to do anything other than get this, whatever it was, under control and go back to Cole.

Ignoring the fact that this would always be there, lurking

beneath the surface, ready to drag me under during a moment of weakness, I pushed myself up.

My legs held my weight, no longer made of jelly. I turned the shower off and stepped onto the cold tile.

Pink skin stared back at me in the mirror, but I knew it would fade soon enough. I gently patted my skin dry with a towel and changed into leggings and an oversized top, grateful that I didn't choose jeans before I went into the bathroom.

Cole was waiting for me in my bedroom, and there I was, having a meltdown on the shower floor.

You're a survivor, not a victim.

That couldn't happen again.

Digging in my wash bag, I found what I needed and dabbed a little under my eyes. I towel dried my hair as much as I could in two minutes and tied it up. It was already hot so it would dry quickly.

Wrapping my hand around the doorhandle, I took one last long breath and opened the door. Cole was on the other side, grinning at me. Gripping my thumping heart, I jumped back, startled.

Who just stood outside a room like that?

He laughed, tilting his head to the side, causing his brown hair to flop across his forehead, almost into his eyes. "I'd apologise, but that was funny."

I glared at him and folded my arms over my chest.

"I love you."

Every time he said that, I felt like I was going to come apart at the seams.

"Come on," he said, taking my hand. "We need to leave, and it'll take a while to get there."

A while to get where?

He smirked at my expression. I hated secrets and always wanted to know what was happening ahead of time. I was better with Cole springing things on me, but if it was going to take a while, I wanted to know.

"You don't want a surprise. How shocking. We're going to London."

I blinked hard. London? London, as in the capital? The one that was hours away from where we lived?

I'd always wanted to go there and do the touristy thing.

"I've seen your bucket list, Oakley," he told me.

Last year at school we had to make a list of all the things we wanted to do with our lives. I shoved it on my desk and assumed it was thrown out when I tidied.

I stared at him, my jaw slack.

"Thought we could tick some things off this summer. *Come on*," he said, laughing at my... silence, ironically.

I followed Cole downstairs where Mum told us to have a lovely time.

They were seriously letting us go? Unless he didn't tell them exactly where we were going. That would make most sense. My parents were happy to let me and Cole roam the hotel and beach, but driving two hours for a day out was pushing it.

We headed to the motorway, towards London, and that holiday feeling returned, once again. We were completely alone. I fell back into the seat and just watched him drive.

Cole glanced over, his eyes shifting between the road and me, sensing me staring. He smirked, and I felt my cheeks heat at being caught. It was hard to take my eyes off him.

The traffic wasn't too bad, so we made it to London in just over two hours. Cole parked, and I panicked, clutching my heart as cars whizzed around the city like they were playing bumper cars.

I was literally in a city full of Jasper-like drivers.

"We'll be fine," Cole said. "I'd never let anything happen to you."

I squeezed his hand and got out of the car.

"You need to relax, babe," Cole said as I roughly tugged him back from crossing a road. "We're not dying here."

How would he know that for certain? It was a miracle there weren't more hit and runs.

I grimaced and tucked myself into his side.

Cole eventually got us to the other side of the road safely, and we only had a short underground ride to our first stop: Madame Tussauds.

As soon as we were back up on normal ground level, I was fine. People still showed a shocking lack of self-preservation, but they were all used to dodging death each day, apparently.

In the museum, Cole paid the entry fee, and we went inside.

He was right when he'd said it was creepy. Hundreds of pairs of eyes followed my every move, kind of like when you were late to class. Cole stared at each wax celebrity like it was some big conspiracy waiting to come to life, and *Night at the Museum* was going to happen once the lights went off.

"It's just... why would you want to make wax people?" he muttered, looking at David Beckham in disgust. "This man is a legend, and they've made him out of wax. Do you not find that even a little bit—"

I covered his mouth with my hand and shook my head, grinning.

"Fine," he muttered against my palm. "Now, who else do you want to see? Kate and Wills?"

I curled my finger around the room, letting him know that we weren't leaving until we'd seen it all.

Groaning, he rested his forehead on my shoulder and awkwardly followed me to the next celebrity replica. I took his hand, stroking his thumb with my own as we made our way around the entire museum.

Then, because he'd only moaned seven thousand times and not more, I took Cole to get a massive burger and fries.

"London Eye next," he said, wrapping his arm around my waist and nuzzling my neck. "I need you, babe."

My heart thudded harder. Yeah, I was feeling that, too. We'd been so far apart for two days now, which wasn't a long time in the grand scheme of things, but I had become a little addict now, and Cole worshiping my body was my drug of choice. He made every touch feel like heaven.

Once we arrived at the London Eye, a man flicked his finger, beckoning us over as the line went down. He checked our tickets, which Cole had bought online over lunch, and our group stepped into a capsule.

I didn't even want to think about how high we were going. Cole wrapped his arms around me from behind, and I suddenly didn't care if we went right up to the bloody moon.

His warm breath cascaded down my neck. "Look," he said, pointing out Buckingham Palace and then Big Ben.

Leaning back against Cole's chest, I watched tiny people on the ground below us walking around.

"Enjoying it?" he asked when we reached the top.

I nodded and interlaced my fingers with his.

Loving it. I'm in love with everything we do together.

I floated into the house in a happy daze when Cole dropped me off at home, walking me to the door despite living a stone's throw away. We'd had to leave shortly after the London Eye, but it'd been a perfect day.

My little bubble burst the moment Jasper paused his computer game and raised his light eyebrow in my direction.

"I think we should have a chat about Cole."

Okay, I really don't think we should.

"Don't shoot daggers at me, lil sis. I know you're together."

Who didn't at this point?

"Don't try to hide it. I might not be Mensa"—*that's putting it mildly*—"but I'm not stupid. Do you think I can't see how you two look at each other? I know love when I see it, Oakley. I'm worried."

Worried about what?

Cole would never hurt me. Jasper knew that, too.

He took a deep breath and rolled his eyes. "Shit. Look, I know Cole's a good guy, but I just want you to know that I love you, and if he ever does anything to hurt you, I need you to tell me. I will cut his balls off. Clean off."

What a lovely picture he painted.

Pursing my lips, I nodded once. What was the appropriate response to that?

He laughed awkwardly. "I'm not kidding. I need you to promise me you'll be careful. Like... *careful.*"

I nodded quickly, not wanting him to elaborate any further because he would probably paint another picture I didn't want to see.

Jasper didn't know that Cole and I had slept together, and there was absolutely no reason in the world why he would need to.

I was still underage for a few more weeks. Though, technically, we hadn't broken any rules... laws. Sixteen in the UK but fourteen in Italy.

"By careful. Well, you know what I mean—"

I held my hand up and gave him a look of warning. Of course, I knew what it meant. He was rarely subtly. Cole and I had been careful every time.

"Okay. Well, I'm glad we got that straightened out. I've got a date with a new chick, Carly, so I'm going to do one."

He remembered her name. How refreshing.

Grabbing his leather jacket, he turned to me and said, "You do know that I love you, right?"

I smiled and nodded. *I love you, too.*

I wouldn't be living in my own personal Hell if I didn't.

Chapter 22

Oakley

"Honey!" Mum called.

Frowning, I pressed my face into my pillow. *Why can't she let me sleep?* I'd been up with Cole until eleven, then I couldn't drift off.

"Oakley, come on."

I felt like I'd only had three hours. Sighing in defeat, I rolled over and waited for whatever she needed me for at... ten. Ten!

All right, so it wasn't *that* early.

"Sorry to wake you—it looks like you needed that sleep—but I wanted to let you know that Auntie Ali's going away for the night, so Lizzie's staying with us. She'll be here soon. You need to make some room in your wardrobe, okay? Apparently, she's packed a lot, and she wants to hang a few things up."

I sat up and scowled.

Who needed hanging space for one night? Why would there be lots of stuff? I didn't want to share anything with her.

"Oh, come on, love. I know she can be a bit much but she's not that bad. It's only one night, you'll cope. Dad's making pancakes, so up you get."

I watched her walk away, and I scowled harder.

I flopped back in bed. *Lizzie for a whole twenty-four hours.* Groaning in frustration, I jumped up and stomped around in a mood.

This was not a good start to the day.

The second I got downstairs, Lizzie walked through the front door. What terrible timing. I'd not even had the chance to have a drink yet.

It was either hot chocolate or I could take a quick swig of Mum's gin.

"Oh, I can't wait for your birthday party, Oakley!" Lizzie gushed, pouting her lips, and fluffing her hair. She dropped a bag down on the floor, and I had no doubt that it'd be someone else who ended up picking it up for her.

Well, hello, Lizzie.

"Your mum's practically invited your whole year. She's so cool, you know. I would love a massive party like that."

No.

Cold dread slithered down my spine. Did that mean Julian had an invite, too? He was the only one I thought would still act like a dickhead, even with my family present.

"Pancakes, girls," Dad announced, poking his head around the kitchen door with a celebratory smile.

I wanted to slap it.

Dad was the self-proclaimed pancake king. Everyone raved about them, but they always tasted like cardboard to me.

I followed Lizzie to the kitchen table and sat down.

Twenty-four hours. I could do that.

I'd had worse for a lot longer.

"Hey, look who I found," Mum said as she walked into the room.

Cole trailed behind her, smiling. It quickly faded when his eyes landed on Lizzie.

I bet he wished he'd never come over now.

"Hi, Cole," Lizzie purred.

I think I threw up in my mouth.

I rolled my eyes. Cole frowned and sat beside me with a quick hello sent Lizzie's way just to be polite.

"I have something, sweetheart." Mum handed me a folder.

An A4 piece of paper was taped to the front with the typed letters, *Oakley's Sweet 16.*

God, please say this isn't happening.

My skin felt too tight around my bones.

I flipped the folder open and died a little inside. The first page was a list of guests. I slapped it shut, not wanting to know. It wouldn't change anything. This was Mum's desperate way of moulding me into a normal teenager, and I'd let her run with it.

"I was thinking we could get one of those chocolate fountains. What do you think?" Mum held up a magazine cut out of a giant white chocolate fountain.

I'd been warned about that one. Honestly, I was fine with chocolate, though.

I nodded along with her idea and dug my fork into my cherry pancakes.

I wondered if Dad remembered making these after his sick friend finished hurting me.

I remembered.

I couldn't forget.

Chewing, I fought the urge to bring it straight back up.

"Great," Mum said, pulling me out of the tunnel I was about to disappear down. She grabbed a pen and circled the phone number.

Picking at the pancakes, I glared at them like it was all their fault.

Why did he make cherry this morning?

"Ice cream?" Cole offered.

If no one were around, I would've kissed him. But then, if no one were around, we wouldn't need to escape. Nodding grate-fully, I stood up and took our plates to the countertop. I'd barely touched breakfast. Dad noticed, but he didn't say a word.

If I didn't love my family so much, I would have thrown them at him. The plate and all.

I had no idea if he thought about the past or if he was just better at blocking it out. It didn't matter either way, I supposed. Nothing could change it now.

"Take Lizzie with you," Mum ordered.

I narrowed my eyes at her, and Cole's expression mirrored mine.

It was then I realised that my mother hated me.

"Ooh, one minute," Lizzie sang as she ran off up the stairs, no doubt to change.

"Tell her we're in the car, please," Cole said to my mum.

Five minutes later, he sighed and slammed his head back on the headrest. "A minute? More like a fucking hour," he grumbled.

Well, that was Lizzie.

Finally, ten minutes later, she strutted out of the house wearing a very short denim dress.

"Jesus," he spat. "Where the hell does she think we're going?"

Hooters. Nightclub. Church. It didn't matter with her.

We drove in silence. Well, Cole and I did. Lizzie sang along to the radio. Her voice wasn't the worst in the world, but it certainly wasn't made for the higher notes.

I wanted to bash my head against the window repeatedly.

"We're here," Cole announced loudly, forcing her to stop singing.

He really was the perfect man.

"Here?" Lizzie scrunched her nose up as she looked at the quaint little diner-style café.

What did she expect? We were fifteen and seventeen, born without silver spoons in our mouths. I didn't work, and Cole did the odd job with his dad. This was about all we could afford.

I gritted my teeth and got out of the car. Lizzie followed behind, her heels clicking against the tiled floor.

"Do they do low-fat milkshakes?" she asked, briefly looking around in bewilderment at the quiet café.

"You could have strawberry or banana. Got fruit in them and all," Cole said sarcastically.

"Oh, banana, please."

"I guess I'll go order," he replied.

"Erm, aren't you going to ask Oakley what she wants? That's a bit rude."

Even his smile was sarcastic. I couldn't help smirking. "Yeah, I know what she wants."

Cole walked over to the counter to order, and the second he was gone, Lizzie didn't waste any time in digging for information on him.

"Is he seeing anyone?" she asked.

Yes. Back off.

I picked up a plastic coffee stirrer and debated on whether I could get away with ramming it into her eye, but I wasn't sure anyone would believe that I fell.

If I nodded, would she ask who? However, if I said no, she might try something with him. I couldn't sit there and watch her flirt with him.

I gave a quick nod, hoping that would make her stop looking at him as if she wanted to eat him.

"Ugh, of course he is," she grumbled as she slumped back in her chair.

Surely, Cole wasn't nearly rich enough for her.

He reappeared with a tray holding our milkshakes and ice creams.

"So, Cole, what's your girlfriend like?" Lizzie purred.

He froze, looking like a deer caught in the headlights. "Girlfriend?"

Shit.

"Yeah, Oakley said you were seeing someone."

I watched as a knowing smile swept across his face.

"Really?" he asked. "She did, huh?"

"Yep. What's she like?"

"She's all right," Cole replied, lifting a shoulder in a casual shrug. "But I will say one thing: she's incredible in bed."

I choked on my drink and slapped my hand over my mouth. *Why the hell would he joke about that?* I wasn't sure if I was burning in embarrassment, anger, or need.

"You okay, Oakley?" Cole asked innocently.

I nodded and forced myself to smile at him when all I wanted to do was chuck my ice cream all over him.

"Yeah? Really?" Lizzie asked, leaning towards him. "You're good, too, then?"

"Not had any complaints."

He was about to get one.

I concentrated on my ice cream, swirling the spoon around to soften it up.

He thinks you were a virgin.

I dropped my spoon, and it clinked loudly against the bowl.

"Whoa, careful, Oakley."

I mustered a smile and picked it back up, but the next mouthful of ice cream almost made me choke.

Out of the corner of my eye, I saw Julian and two of his friends walking past the window.

Please don't come in here. Please.

They laughed loudly, pushing each other as they walked through the door.

Of course.

Julian's smirk spread when he spotted us. Slapping his friend's shoulder, he strode to a table nearby. Cole's body tensed when he saw who had arrived.

"Fuck does this arsehole want?"

Not wanting him to cause a scene, I pressed my leg against his to tell him to stay calm. I wasn't sure if it would work, but I had to try.

"Hi, Oakley," Julian said, and there wasn't a hint of nastiness in his voice.

What was his game?

I smiled briefly and looked away just as Lizzie seductively fluffed her hair.

Oh no...

"Hi, I'm Lizzie, Oakley's cousin."

Julian's eyebrows shot up. "Really?"

She nodded and turned around to face him. "Yeah. So, are you going to her party on Saturday?"

He looked straight at me and replied, "Yep."

"Well, make other plans. You're not welcome," Cole growled.

"Actually, I am. Got an invitation to prove it, mate."

"Not your mate."

I hated my mum.

"Julian. Fuck. Off," Cole spat.

Lizzie watched them with wide eyes, her head flitting back and forth like she was watching a tennis match.

Perfect. Now, she was going to be grilling me about this.

I'd had enough, and I just wanted to get away, so I stood up and started walking out. I heard footsteps right behind me, and I knew it would be Cole. Then I heard Lizzie's heels clicking unevenly as she hurried after us.

"See you Saturday!" Julian called.

Cole turned around and gestured something, but I didn't look to see what. I got in the car and slammed the door.

"Don't worry," he said, stroking my hand. "We'll stay away from him. I won't let him come near you, I swear."

I looked up to the roof so the tears pooling in my eyes wouldn't fall. The summer holiday was supposed to be a break from everyone at school. The thought of seeing them all again had my stomach churning.

"What was that all about?" Lizzie squealed so loudly, it made me jump. She slammed the car door shut and huffed. "You were so mean to him, and he's lovely! He called me back and asked me to be his date to your party. Can you believe that?"

Yes, I could.

He was messing with me.

"I have no idea what to wear. Oh, God, we *have* to go shopping."

Could she be any more annoying?

"The party will be fine," Cole said.

No, it wouldn't be.

Chapter 23

Oakley

How could days feel like seconds?

Everyone was downstairs setting up the decorations and moving furniture around to make room for the DJ. My birthday wasn't until tomorrow, but my party was tonight.

Cole and I were the only ones not down there.

Don't suppose you can skip your own party...

I wasn't sure how much Mum and Dad knew about my relationship with Cole. They never mentioned it. The only ones who did were Mia and Jasper, apart from that one time when Jenna had told us to keep the door open.

Not sure if that counted as them knowing we were official, though.

I smoothed down my black dress and stared at my reflection. Cole was also staring at my reflection. He was lying on the bed with his hands on his stomach, his feet crossed at the ankles.

Casual but sexy as hell.

"Don't be nervous, I'll be there. If Julian even glances in your direction..."

I raised a brow, challenging him to tell me what he would do in front of my parents.

His lips curved at the corners. "I've got you. Don't worry. Kerry and Ben will be there, too. Mia and Jasper... but I don't know how much help he'll be."

I do. None.

He got up off the bed, and I watched his reflection move towards me. My heart responded in the usual way to him, by trying to break through my ribs.

His hands slid around my waist and settled low on my belly. "We're going to have fun tonight."

His touch took my breath away. Since we got home, we hadn't slept together. He offered no explanation as to why, but I knew it was because he was waiting for my birthday. Cole didn't want to sleep with me when I was underage, and I loved him so much more for that, even though it was completely different to what Frank had done to me.

I laid my head back against his shoulder and sighed. We'd have had a better night here alone. There was no way to get out of this party now, though. My mum had put a lot of effort into the planning, into seeing her daughter have one normal moment with her friends.

Only, I hated most of them.

Music drifted up the stairs, and Cole kissed my hair, whispering, "I think that's our cue... Fun, remember? How are you still so beautiful when you scowl?"

I nudged him with my elbow for being so ridiculous, and I turned in his arms. It was on the tip of my tongue to tell him how much I was in love with him. He deserved to hear those words; I just wasn't sure if I could risk everything to give that to him.

"Let's go," he said, kissing me softly before taking my hand.

Everyone at the party, besides Hannah, was doing it to see what my home life was like—to see how I interacted with my family when I didn't talk. None of them wanted to celebrate my birthday.

Hell, even I didn't want to.

Some of my family had already arrived and were standing around, drinking, laughing, and chatting. My grandparents from both sides of the family were sitting on the sofa with their too-full wine glasses. I didn't see Dad's parents often; they lived quite far away, so they only visited on birthdays and at Christmas.

What would they think about who Dad really was?

They wouldn't believe you, either.

The doorbell rang, and I took a deep breath, taking a peek at Cole to stop myself from freaking out. His eyes sank into my soul, knowing exactly what I needed. I didn't want to stop touching him, but we weren't alone now.

"Happy birthday, Oakley!" Julian shouted from across the room, throwing his arms out like an idiot.

I jumped and pressed into Cole's side.

Cole's eyes slid from me to Julian. His body tensed so hard, I thought his muscles might snap.

"Stay out of her way," Cole said, glaring daggers at him. "Come on, let's get a drink," he said to me, and we left Julian standing in the hallway with a cup I knew had more than Coke in it.

The whole house was decorated with pink and white balloons and decorations. While they were tasteful, it was so *not* me. Mum was throwing a party for every year I'd missed, refusing to go to the soft plays and magician shows.

My mouth dropped open when I saw what was on the kitchen counter. Oh, she had gone way too far. I stepped closer to the giant ice sculpture, hearing Cole laughing in the background. It was of a girl doing a cartwheel—of *me* doing a cartwheel.

Damn.

I wanted to ask Julian for some of whatever was in his cup.

"Honey, here." Mum handed me a plastic cup of punch.

Forcing my lips to twitch into a brief smile, I turned, pretending to look at something different so that she wouldn't see how much I hated all of it. She still saw me as a little girl.

My stomach buzzed with an uneasy feeling that I wanted to run from.

Just a few hours. For her. I could do that.

"Well, this is all very pink," Cole said, stating the bloody obvious. "She knows your favourite colour is yellow, right?"

I shrugged. Apparently not.

"Come on, I need some vodka in this before I throw up," he said, looking into the cup with a turned nose.

Yeah, it wasn't good. Far too sweet.

As we made a move, Kerry hopped in front of me and laughed when I jumped back. "Sorry. Happy birthday! This party's awesome, by the way. I mean, if you like pink, which I wouldn't have guessed you did..."

Cole wrapped his arm around me, holding me close. It was a protective action—one I hoped he would do all night.

"I'm guessing you like pink," Ben said, joining us and thumping Cole's arm.

I stared at him, deadpan.

"She doesn't like pink. Her mum organised everything," Cole said, though my expression was probably enough of an explanation.

Ben winced. "Ah. Ouch. Well, I've seen plenty of alcohol, so none of it will matter soon enough."

Kerry waved her hand. "Don't worry, Oakley. You have us to save you now." She pulled me to the side. Her grip was tight, and she strode confidently through the small crowd that had gathered by the doorway.

People glanced my way, and a few wished me a happy birthday, but no one stopped me to talk.

Thank God.

"Sit," Kerry ordered, pointing to the smaller sofa that had been pushed into the corner of the conservatory. The wall behind me shared with the living room vibrated with the beat of the music.

The party had already been split. My family, besides Jasper, was all in the kitchen, while everyone below twenty was in the living room, conservatory, and garden.

Cole and Ben joined us, both sitting on the arms of the chair.

"This is our corner. If anyone tries to take it, kill. Okay?" Kerry said.

"Erm, babe..." Ben muttered.

She shrugged. "I'm kidding."

We settled into a conversation—Cole and I flirting—and I was managing to have a good time.

Jasper knelt in front of me. "The blonde girl over there," he said, gesturing towards Jennifer. "Is she sixteen?"

I pointed up to the ceiling.

"Seventeen?" he asked, and I nodded.

He pushed up onto his feet and said, "All legal and fair game."

He made it sound like a joke, but we both knew he wasn't kidding.

My eyes drifted behind him to where Julian was dancing with Lizzie. I noticed how he'd move her closer to where we were sitting until they ended up right in my line of sight.

How the hell could Lizzie touch him?

After six cups of super sweet punch laced with a little vodka, my bladder was going to burst.

Cole watched as I got up. My head felt light. All of me felt light, actually, and I knew I had a bit of a buzz going on. I thought I would hate it, but it felt kind of nice.

I went upstairs to use the bathroom, and as I walked past my door; I heard giggling.

Oh, hell no! My room was off-limits, and I was ready to flip out on whoever was in there.

Did I want to see whatever was happening?

No, but I had to stop it.

Gritting my teeth, I pushed the door open.

Oh... God!

I wanted to bleach my eyes. Lizzie and Julian were all over each other on my bed, and now I was going to have to burn the sheets. And the bed. And fumigate the entire room.

I slammed my fist on the wall.

Lizzie gasped and looked up in shock.

Glaring at them, I pointed to the door.

Lizzie huffed and stomped out. "You're such a buzz kill, Oakley! Come on, Julian, let's go somewhere else."

She left without him, going down the hall and waiting for him to follow. I wanted to stop her from going into Jasper's room, but I would enjoy his reaction way too much.

Julian strolled towards me with a cocky grin. "Looks like we're alone now, huh?"

As if I was going to let this dickhead intimidate me in my own room.

I stood my ground as he slowly moved a couple of steps closer, and I met his stare. My stomach tightened, but I wouldn't let him see my anxiety.

"Sorry you had to see that, babe. She was all over me. Wasn't taking no for an answer."

He wasn't funny. I really couldn't care less what he did with Lizzie, I just didn't want it in my room. To be honest, they deserved each other.

He cocked his head to the side as he watched me with caution.

"Stop playing hard to get, Oakley."

Whoa. What the hell?

I wasn't playing anything. I would rather drink acid than go anywhere near him. He was gross.

"You think I don't see how you look at me?"

My eyes widened. He couldn't be serious. He was drunk. That was the only explanation that made any sense.

"Don't look at me like that," he growled. "I've had two years of you ignoring me and pretending like you don't give a shit. I have to fucking insult you just to get you to acknowledge me!" he shouted, stepping closer one more time, stopping when we came toe to toe.

Adrenaline coursed through my veins as he reached out to touch me. All I could think about was stopping him. As his hands grew closer, I balled my own hand into a fist and punched him as hard as I could. We both stumbled back in shock.

Whoa.

The sound—a dull, crunching thud—rang through my ears. Julian's hand shot to his mouth, and he groaned in pain. My hand immediately started throbbing. I shook it but that only made it hurt more.

Julian straightened his spine. His dark eyes were stone cold, and he sucked his bottom lip into his mouth as blood began seeping through a small cut.

I shouldn't enjoy that, but I did. It felt good to stand up to him.

"Stop being such a bitch," he spat.

I took a step backward, turned slowly, and walked out of my room. I half-expected him to follow me, but he didn't as I flew down the stairs.

"Bah," Cole cried as I slammed into him. "You okay?"

Yes, actually, I was okay. Screw Julian.

Cole glared, and I spun around to see what'd earned that look. Julian, of course, was standing at the top of the stairs. He ducked into Jasper's bedroom when he noticed Cole with me.

"What happened? Was that blood on his lip?"

I smiled and held up my fist. Cole's eyes widened in surprise and, I thought, awe. "Holy shit, did you punch him? What did he do?"

I waved his question off, telling him that it wasn't important. What was important was the fact that I'd punched him... and I still needed to pee.

"You're amazing," he said, lifting my hand to his lips. He kissed my pink knuckles. "Do you need me to talk to him? Murder him?"

Yeah, I could imagine how much talking Cole would do.

I shook my head.

"Have I told you how beautiful you look in that dress?"

The black number was tighter than I usually wore, but the bust wasn't cut low, and it sat on my knees.

I pretended to think and then shook my head.

"What an arsehole boyfriend I am," he teased. "Come dance with me so I can make it up to you."

I let him pull me into the living room and through the crowd that had gathered. Everyone was dancing. Some looked like they would be having sex if it wasn't for their clothes. People dry-humped beside the ornaments my parents had collected. That'd teach Mum for throwing a party *she* wanted me to have.

Dad was probably seething.

Good.

Cole wrapped me in his arms, holding me tightly against his body, and we began to move together. When he bent his head to kiss me, the rest of the world disappeared.

That was until someone tapped a microphone and Mum said, "Good evening."

My heart dropped into my stomach.

She was going to make a speech.

Chapter 24

Cole

I felt Oakley's body stiffen against me as soon as Sarah stopped the music.

Oh, no. What the hell was she thinking?

Embarrassment radiated off Oakley already, she hunched into me, trying to disappear. Over my shoulder, I noticed Jasper's horrified glare at his mum.

"Thank you for coming," Sarah said into the mic. "Sorry to interrupt and stop you from dancing, but I'll only keep you for a minute. I just want to say a few words about my beautiful daughter."

Oakley cringed harder. I felt awkward for her. If I didn't know that taking her away would make things worse, we'd be outside already.

My stomach burned at how little Sarah was thinking of Oakley in that moment. She wanted to make her life better, I understood that, but she was achieving the opposite.

"You've overcome so many obstacles, honey. Your dad and I are so proud of you."

Oakley tensed, and I wasn't sure she was still breathing.

"We know it hasn't been easy, but here you are, all finished with high school and turning sixteen."

Throughout Sarah's speech, Oakley never met her mum's eyes once. Nor did she look anywhere else.

Sarah raised her glass. "So, please say a very big happy sweet sixteenth to Oakley. Happy birthday, honey."

The crowd joined in, with the exception of Jasper and me.

"You okay?" I asked Oakley as soon as Sarah handed the microphone back to the DJ.

She nodded; her eyes still downcast and cheeks flushed deep pink. I groaned and grabbed her hand, pulling her through the kitchen and out to the back garden.

Everyone else went back to what they were doing without another thought. Hopefully they'd all be so drunk soon that they wouldn't remember Sarah's awkward speech. Most of them she'd never see again, anyway.

Oakley gripped my hand tightly as we moved outside. It was warm out, but the air was damp from the rain earlier.

"You hated that, right?"

Widening her eyes, she blew out a breath.

"If it helps, no one is going to remember that tomorrow."

She ran her fingers over some petals on a nearby rose bush.

"We can stay out here for a while. I don't want to be in there, either."

Her eyes flicked over to me, and she smiled. I took a seat on the outside bench and watched her slowly make her way over to me.

Sometimes she got so lost inside her head, I didn't know how to get her back.

The talk about her overcoming shit was playing on her mind, I guessed.

Finally, she sat down. I took her hand in my own and examined it. The redness had already faded. She had never hit anyone before in her life—well, apart from Jasper... and me, but that was playful.

"Julian tried something."

There was no other explanation for why he was so obsessed with her.

She peered at me like she didn't want to go there.

"Oakley?"

She sighed and half-nodded.

I wasn't prepared for the burning, insane jealously her admission brought on. "I hate that prick."

She flinched at my tone. I couldn't help it, though. He'd been a dick to her throughout high school, and now he was trying it on.

"Sorry. No fighting, I promise. Think I'll leave that up to you now."

She smirked and rolled her eyes.

"You okay to go back inside now?" I rubbed her arms, feeling the tiny bumps that had appeared on her skin.

Standing, she tugged at my hand, struggling since I didn't help in any way. I laughed and got to my feet, throwing an arm over her shoulders.

Back in the living room, I tensed at the sight in front of me. We'd come back too soon.

Julian now held the mic.

"Ladies and gentlemen," he slurred.

Shit.

"I would also like to say something about the birthday girl. Firstly, she isn't as sweet and innocent as you all think." He waved his arm around, spilling his drink on the floor.

Oakley gasped.

"She's a real little tease. Gets you all worked up and then runs away. Hey, Oakley?"

"What the hell is this?" Max boomed from somewhere in the crowd. "Get down!"

"Teasing me for years while screwing her friend!"

I was halfway across the room before I knew what I was doing, level with Jasper as we rushed to stop the prick.

Jasper launched himself at Julian and thumped him across the jaw.

I was about to join in when Mia grabbed my arm. "She needs you! Look!"

Turning my head, I saw Oakley standing in the middle of the living room, pale as a ghost, and looking like she was about to crumble.

I felt sick as I pushed my way back to her.

Max shouted, "You get out of my house and stay the hell away from my daughter!"

An eerie silence fell over the room, no one knew what to say or do.

"Time to leave. Everyone out!" Jasper said, but they already were.

I didn't think there was enough alcohol in the world to make everyone forget what happened here tonight. Thankfully it was all over so fast, I don't think anyone had enough time to record anything.

Honestly, I didn't give a shit about anyone else, though. They could talk and gossip, it didn't matter.

"Are you okay?" I asked, lifting Oakley's chin so she looked at me.

"Honey, it's okay. He's gone now. But is it true that you and Cole are... together?" Sarah asked. I'd not even seen her approach. She still saw Oakley as a five-year-old, so her shock didn't surprise me.

Letting my arm fall, I waited to see how Oakley was going to respond. I'd go along with whatever she thought was right.

Oakley's eyes flitted from me to her mum and then her dad. I wanted to wrap my arms around her and protect her from all of the questions that were about to come her way.

She gulped, and I felt her fear seep into my bones.

"No," I said. "We haven't..."

Oakley let out a deep breath as soon as I'd denied it.

"Why would he say that?" Max asked, raising his eyebrows, and folding his arms. He looked like he wanted to hit me.

"Because he's a *psycho*!" Jasper shouted *psycho* towards the door where Max had thrown Julian out. "He's the one who's been giving her a hard time. Cole and I have punched him a few times," he said with a shrug and a proud smile.

"He tried it on with her, and when she rejected him, he did that," I told Max.

Oakley appeared smaller, curling her folded arms into her chest. I hated that. I wasn't sure if she was protecting me or if she was just embarrassed.

Of course, her parents weren't going to like her having sex, but she'd been legal in Italy. We hadn't done anything wrong.

"Are you okay, sweetheart?" Sarah asked Oakley, brushing her hair out of her face.

Oakley nodded, backing up out of her mum's reach. Her jaw was tight, and I could tell that she was angry with Sarah for making her have the party in the first place.

So was I. She was supposed to go to sixth form in September, but how was she going to do that if everyone was gossiping about her.

"I'm sorry," Max said, reaching out to squeeze her shoulder. "Perhaps this wasn't a good idea."

Oakley cringed and stared down at her feet.

"Look, why don't you and Cole go upstairs and watch a movie? We'll sort everything out down here," Max suggested.

What? He was going to let us go upstairs alone. But no one

would expect us to do anything after this conversation, I supposed.

Jasper appeared just as shocked as I was, but then he knew more than anyone else.

"That went well," I said, exhaling when Oakley climbed on her bed, and we were away from the rest of the world again.

She ran her hands through her hair and dragged her cover over her bare legs.

"So, are we thinking that no one else apart from your mum and dad really believes that we've been angels?" I asked, getting onto the bed beside her, aware that the door had been left open.

Resting her head against my shoulder, she shrugged.

"I'm picking the movie," I said, grabbing the remote. She didn't respond like she usually would, and I couldn't breathe properly.

What the hell was I supposed to do now?

Her mum's words and then Julian's were bothering her more than I thought they could.

I signed into my Netflix account and put *She's the Man* on. Okay, not my choice, but I was so out of my depth, and I desperately didn't want Oakley to change her mind about us.

Arching a brow, she looked up at me with a big question mark in her eyes.

"It's your birthday... almost. You should choose the movie."

She watched me for a long heartbeat before finally resting her head back on my shoulder again, sighing the moment the movie started.

"Things will calm down, I promise. We stick together." I kissed the top of her head. "Okay?"

Her hand slid across my abdomen, and she nodded.

I breathed her in, and her hand splayed on my chest, making it hard to focus on anything other than the way she made me feel. I wanted her hand under my shirt, for us to be skin-to-skin.

Now was *not* the time.

"Hey, look," I said, flashing my phone in front of her. "Twelve-o-one. Happy birthday, babe."

She flashed me a smile.

"Can I give you your present now?"

She bolted up on the bed, making me jump at how fast she moved. Jesus.

I chuckled and reached for the bag I'd left in her room earlier.

I gave her the yellow gift bag and lay back down with my hands under my head. "Happy birthday."

Playfully narrowing her eyes, she reached into the bag and pulled out the card. Always the card first.

"So, what's going on in here, then?" Jasper asked, walking into her room without knocking. "You can't open them now!"

"Jasper, shut up. It's after midnight. It's her birthday."

Jasper leapt forward, cannonballing onto the bed. He grabbed her into a big bear hug. Oakley whacked him, pushing him away, and she grinned.

"Happy birthday, baby sis! You're so grown up now. I can still remember when you were little and carried that blanket around everywhere with you," he cooed, ruffling her hair.

Batting his hand away, she pointed to the door.

"Fine, fine. I'll go. I'll let you two get back to *unwrapping presents*," he said, making air quotes with his hands and laughing to himself.

Oakley bent her head and kissed me. I felt the fire consume me with the first touch of her lips. I wanted her *all* the time. She got under my skin. She was all I could think about. If Mum, Dad, and her parents weren't in the house, I'd take off that dress and show her just how fucking obsessed I really was.

She'd turned sixteen now, and I didn't want to waste any time.

After a few more seconds, I pulled away while I still had some self-control left. We couldn't risk someone walking in again. My body ached to be pressed up against her, though, and my jeans were getting uncomfortably tight.

"You need to open the presents," I whispered, breathing through the pounding lust.

She peered into the bag. Her lips were sexy as hell and slightly swollen from a kiss that'd driven me wild.

I'd bought her all of her favourite things: Haribo sweets, chocolate buttons, some biography of a gymnast she had looked at when we were shopping once, and a crazy bright purple nail polish that she liked that had made me look like an idiot when I bought it.

And, finally, she pulled out the box that had a white gold necklace with a little heart pendant and a diamond set into it.

I held my breath as she opened the box.

Her jaw dropped open the moment she saw the necklace, and her eyes filled with tears. That was exactly the reaction I'd wanted.

Unless, of course, it was disgusted shock.

She pulled it out of the box and ran her hand over the heart. It was similar to the necklace she already wore but the new one was me giving her *my* heart.

She removed the one she was wearing and replaced it with mine.

"You like it, then?" I whispered, smiling at her rosy-pink cheeks as I ran my fingers along her jaw.

There were no words she was about to say, but she didn't need to, anyway. The way she looked at me, like I was some grand prize, was everything I needed.

She covered my mouth with her own, and I was lost again.

Before we could get too worked up, she went to get changed for bed. I knew I wouldn't be able to stay the night, and there was no way I could get into bed. So, I stayed on top of the cover while she slowly fell asleep on her pillow.

"She's had quite the night," Max said, leaning against her bedroom door.

I was very grateful that I'd taken my eyes off her for a minute, so all Max had seen was me sitting beside his sleeping daughter, watching TV.

"Yeah, I know."

"So, about tonight..." He walked to her desk across the room and took a seat. "You would tell me if anything had happened between you two, wouldn't you?"

Absolutely fucking not.

"She's just turned sixteen," I said. "Nothing has happened."

The lie slipped from my mouth too easily, but I would lie to everyone to protect the things she wanted to keep private.

"Okay," he replied, clearing his throat. "We knew she would get a boyfriend eventually. She's a beautiful girl. We're glad it's you."

"Thanks, Max. You know I wouldn't hurt her."

He blinked heavily. "Yes, I know."

He hadn't given me that talk yet, so I wanted it out of the way.

Jasper had already threatened me.

"Your mum and dad are about to head off. Birthday breakfast in the morning," he said, standing up and leaving her room.

That was my cue to leave, too.

"I love you," I whispered against her hair, and a part of me I couldn't switch off wished I would get to hear her say those words back to me one day.

Chapter 25

Cole

The summer passed by in a blur of dates with Oakley, and school—sixth form—would start again on Monday.

This year would be a lot different. Oakley and I were together, and she was going to start her first year at sixth form. There would be no more searching her out in the school adjoined. We would share the common room when we weren't in lessons.

It was the first time I didn't dread the end of summer.

The next thing to stress over was uni. Oakley was a year behind me at school, and there was no fucking way I was moving too far away from her.

"Cole, will you hurry up? You take longer to get ready than my sister!" Jasper shouted.

I winced at his loud fucking voice cutting right through me.

"Jesus, Jasper! I'm standing right next to you! I'm ready." I grabbed my wallet and slipped it into my pocket.

Tonight, I was going out with Jasper and Ben. Oakley was having a girls' night in with Sarah, Mia, my mum, and Kerry. She seemed pretty excited to spend the evening pampering herself with that muddy-looking crap they put on their faces.

She'd slowly come back out of her shell after party-gate. It took about a week before she was normal with me again. That was a *slow* week. But we were better than ever now, and when both our parents were at work...

"Cole," Jasper whined, breaking me from my thoughts. "Why are you so slow?"

I raised my palms. "Five minutes ago, I was in the shower, and now I'm ready. Why are you so anxious?"

"And why were you in the shower just two minutes ago?"

He'd just come over here, literally passing Oakley as she left to go home.

"We're going out," I said as a terrible cover for the fact that I'd spent the afternoon in bed with his sister.

We'd both needed to be that close again after the last few weeks.

He saw my expression and laughed. "You're so whipped. But I'm glad you are. She's going to really need you one day."

"What's that mean?" I asked, frowning at how serious he'd gotten.

He tilted his head, looking at me like I'd just asked something dumb. "You know what that means. Whatever made her quit talking to us is bound to catch up with her eventually. I've been prepared to drop everything since it happened, but she won't want me now."

My stomach turned to steel.

"I'll do anything for her. You know that."

"I do, bro, and that's why your face is still pretty. Now, hurry up because you're wasting valuable drinking time."

I pushed my feet into my shoes, but I was distracted by his words. He was right. One day, she'd have to face whatever had gone down, right? I had absolutely no idea what that was, but I knew it terrified me. I also knew there was nothing that could scare me away from her, no matter how hard things got, no matter how much it hurt.

"Cole!"

"Yeah, you can see I'm ready, for fuck's sake."

Jasper chuckled. "You need a drink."

I shoved past him, rolling my eyes.

"All right, man, I'm going to bet you right now that I get more phone numbers tonight," he said, slapping me on the back as we walked outside for the taxi.

"I'm not getting any phone numbers tonight. I'm with your sister, remember?"

"So, you fold? I win?"

I pinched the bridge of my nose. "Yes, Jasper, you win."

The Uber pulled up outside my house, and I'd never been so grateful to see a stranger before.

Jasper stopped and looked at his reflection in the window, messing his hair up. "Do I look okay?"

"What?"

"Hey, I have insecurities the same as everyone else. I might be so close to perfect that it's scary, but—"

"You look fine, Jasper. Get in the car," I said, cutting him off. It was generally much easier to agree with him and just go along with it.

"You don't think I should have gone with the blue shirt?"

I shook my head, taking a deep breath. "Are we really doing this?"

He nodded, deadly serious.

This was going to be a very long night.

"No, you shouldn't have gone with the blue shirt." I shoved him into the back of the car. "What you're wearing looks good. So does your hair."

That should cover it.

He laughed and scooted over to let me in beside him. I gave the driver Ben's address.

"I'm flattered, man. I really am. But you're with my *sister*, and if I'm honest, man bits just don't do it for me."

Why didn't I drink before I left the house? A whole evening with Jasper on top form... I must have been mad.

He'd be going back to uni soon, and we wouldn't see him until Christmas.

Ben walked out of his front door as we pulled up. He looked like a kid on Christmas morning. Since he'd gotten together with Kerry, his nights out had dwindled.

"Hey," he greeted us with an excited smile as he got in the front. "Ready to get shitfaced?"

I laughed. "Oh, yeah."

It had been a while since I'd had a night out with the lads, too, and I was looking forward to it. Most of my time was spent with Oakley now. I was more than happy with that, but I needed this, too.

The queue into the club was short, and we barely had to wait two minutes before making it to the front.

That probably meant the inside was shit.

The built-to-hell bouncer shot his muscular arm out, stopping us just as we were about to go in. He must have eaten ten pounds of steak and raw eggs every day. The veins in his neck poked through his skin, and the material of his black top was stretched around his bulky shape.

Jasper tried that diet once and threw up all over the kitchen.

"ID," he demanded of Jasper.

I watched with a smile as Jasper's face fell, and he pulled his driving licence out of his wallet. The bouncer studied it for a second and handed it back, nodding for us to go inside. We made our way through the crowd of barely-dressed girls to the bar.

"I'm fucking older than you!" Jasper exclaimed, waving his hand in my and Ben's direction. "What the fuck!"

Ben and I laughed, pushing him towards the bar. If we'd been asked for ID, we'd have shown our fakes.

"Well, clearly, you don't look your age."

He grumbled something under his breath and walked to the bar to get the drinks. Jasper turned to get the bartender's attention, but as she got to us, he turned away, noticing a group of girls.

Here we go.

"Well, hello, ladies," he said, using that smile that seemed to get him whatever and whoever he wanted.

Since he was now otherwise engaged, I ordered three JD and Cokes, and three shots of tequila. Ben and I sat down on stools and got comfortable, ready to watch Jasper make a twat out of himself all night.

"You want to dance?" he asked a blonde that was touching his arm.

It was a miracle he didn't get slapped more. Watching him chat up women was like watching a car crash.

Ben and I exchanged a glance. "Beer. Lots of beer," he said, walking off.

"I have a boyfriend," the girl replied to Jasper, raising her eyebrows but not actually looking too bothered that she did.

That wasn't going to impress Jasper. Not one bit.

His eyes narrowed, and I knew his head was back with Abby, telling her they were over after he found out she was sleeping with another guy.

Without saying a word, Jasper turned away from her, like she didn't exist anymore. Her eyebrows shot up and she stormed off.

"Want to dance?" he asked another girl who was standing right next to her friend.

Ben laughed, and I watched, open-mouthed.

The blonde's friend snorted. "Are you serious? Do I look like a backup or something?"

Jasper's face turned thoughtful.

Oh, shit. He was taking far too long to say no.

Shrugging unapologetically, he replied, "Sorry. She's hot, and I saw her first."

The girl's face reddened. She slapped his cheek, and the sound made me flinch. That had to hurt. It didn't seem to faze Jasper, though, and I had a feeling that wasn't the first time he'd been slapped.

I really hoped it would happen again.

"No need to be all touchy, love. I was only being honest! I thought women liked that," he called after her as she stormed off with her friends.

"We've only been in here for five minutes and you've been slapped already. That must be some sort of a record," Ben praised, slapping him on the back.

Jasper smiled proudly and downed his shot.

Halfway through the night, Jasper ditched us for a group of women here from Thailand. He was in his own little idea of Heaven.

I sat back at the sticky bar with Ben, downing drinks. The place stunk of beer and sweat.

"Never? It's never awkward with her or anything?" Ben asked.

"No, not ever." Well, not always, and never because she wouldn't speak. "I know what she's thinking pretty much all the time. It's written all over her face, I don't need her to say it."

He nodded along. "Wow. I have no idea what Kerry thinks, and she doesn't shut up!"

They were different ends of the extreme, one never talking and one always talking. They balanced each other out perfectly.

"But do you ever wish she would talk? I mean, doesn't it

bother you that you'll never hear her say she loves you? And what about the future? When you get married? She won't be able to say the vows and shit. How would that work?"

I swallowed a big gulp of JD. That one hadn't crossed my mind, but marriage wasn't something I'd thought of.

There was nothing stopping her from signing, but she didn't currently know sign language. She didn't do anything to really communicate. I tried hard not to dwell on that.

"Fuck, mate. I shouldn't have brought that up. You'll figure it out."

"Yeah," I said, shaking the uneasy thoughts from my mind. "I'm not worried."

I was, of course, always worried. Not about being with her but about *her*.

Jasper slumped in front of us. "Hey!" Standing up, he reached for a redhead. "You are beautiful," he told her.

"This should be good," Ben muttered.

I moved slightly closer.

"Hotel room," Jasper said.

It was like watching a 'what not to do'. Still, it provided me with a lot of entertainment.

The next thing I heard out of his mouth over the thumping music was, "Hitler."

I looked at Ben in horror. What the hell was Jasper doing? Why, oh why, was he talking about *Hitler*?

The girl frowned and started to look a little scared.

What possible reason would anyone have to bring up a dictator responsible for the most hideous crimes to a girl they were trying to chat up?

It must've been a dare, picking random, awful topics to see if I could still make it work.

I wanted to make a quick exit, but there was something

about the train wreck I just couldn't look away from. I should have recorded it for Oakley.

Sure enough, she threw her drink in his face and then slapped his cheek before storming off. I stood, frozen. He raised his hands in celebration, looking around the club. It was a game.

Between him and who?

"Cole! Man, did you see that?" he asked, stepping back to us.

The front of his shirt was soaking wet.

"I really wish I'd taken Oakley out tonight," I told him.

"Please, I'm way more fun."

No, no he wasn't.

"Drink up, we're leaving," I told them.

I took my phone out and messaged Oakley.

Like a fucking idiot, I waited for a reply.

I wasn't sure I would ever get anything.

Chapter 26

Oakley

On a sigh, I picked out my outfit and started getting dressed. Today was the first day of sixth form. Not only was it going to be a bad day, but in the evening, Mum's friend was coming over for dinner.

A friend who just so happened to be a psychiatric doctor.

Apparently, they met at Mum's new Pilates class last week. I bet she thought she hit the jackpot. I could refuse to go to a doctor—or run away from it—but it was harder to refuse when I was in my own home.

She was still trying to fix me.

I was terrified that this woman might see more than a girl refusing to talk. Selective Mutism was what everyone kept telling us. I guess it was true because I could talk and chose not to.

But it wasn't really my choice.

I brushed my hair and put on lip gloss. At least this year I would get to spend much more time with Cole. The classes were small as the sixth from wasn't huge. Most people had moved on to college for their A-Levels or courses.

Hannah was at college, so I wouldn't have her anymore.

Mum smiled when I got downstairs. She was perky, sipping from a coffee mug and pointing to a plate of pancakes. "Eat up, I'm just going to do my hair."

Someone thinks their daughter is going to be cured.

"You ready for today?" Cole asked, startling me at how close he was.

I slapped his chest, and he jumped back, laughing. "I'm sorry."

Oh, he was not.

"It's going to be okay, you know? We'll be together a lot, and if Julian says or does *anything*, I'll flush his head down the toilet."

I tilted my head to the side. After getting punched by me and my brother and having my dad throw him out, I didn't think Julian would be coming anywhere near me.

"Think about it... every free period we have together, we can go for a walk. I'll buy you ice cream," Cole stepped up to me and pressed his forehead to mine. "We can hide behind the bike shed, and I can kiss you until we can't breathe."

So, there were going to be perks to returning to school.

With a nod, I leaned closer and kissed him.

He groaned, sending that familiar shiver right through me. It felt like ages since we'd been alone together. I was craving that feeling of being complete that only he could provide.

Cole and I sat to eat, and Jasper strolled in a few minutes after we finished.

Wait... he was wearing that yesterday.

"Well, good morning, baby sister," he chirped, ruffling my hair as he walked past. I slapped his hand.

"Good night?" Cole asked.

My brother turned around, flashing us a smile, and picking up a pancake. "A gentleman never tells."

"Right. So, good night?"

Grinning at Cole's joke, I glanced up at Jasper and shrugged. He had him there. Jasper was no gentleman.

"Man, she was a firecracker."

Cole checked his phone. "Good for you. Unfortunately, we don't have time for the details. Come on, Oakley."

I was only too happy to not hear all the ways in which my brother pleased a woman. I'd been there before and almost thrown up.

Instead of a wave, I playfully slapped the back of Jasper's head.

"Hey! You'll miss me when I'm gone."

He sounded dramatic, but I knew he meant when he went back to uni.

On the way to school, I watched the time pass on the screen in Cole's car. I'd already changed the radio station twice and cranked the A/C up.

"You don't need to be nervous."

At no point had being told not to be nervous ever worked.

But I smiled at him because the last thing he needed was to be worrying about me. This was A-Level year for him, his grades determining if he could go to uni.

That wasn't a conversation we'd had and, to be honest, it was one I wanted to avoid for as long as possible. He'd already have been gone a year before I turned eighteen, so I couldn't do anything but watch him go and hope long-distance would be enough.

"There's a bunch of change in the car. You're going to want some for the vending machine," he told me.

I reached out and grabbed a pound. Then another. Then another.

Cole chuckled. "Well, I do like it when you've got a sugar rush."

Before I knew it, Cole was reversing the car into a space outside the sixth form block.

"I would give you the whole speech about today being fine and me being here if you need me, but my arm's starting to bruise! You're violent... and I don't hate it. Does that make me weird?"

I nodded, leaning my head back on the seat.

"You like my weird, though. Don't even try to pretend you don't."

Shrugging, I trailed my fingers up his arm, feeling his skin pebble beneath my touch.

"Oakley." My name was a ragged warning. We were in a carpark, on school grounds, and this was not the time to for things to get heated. He shook his head. "Don't look at me like that. I have to get through a whole day."

I grabbed my bag and got out of the car with a stupid grin on my face. Cole jogged around the car and threw his arm over my shoulder.

"This is going to be the best year ever, babe, I know it."

A few people looked at us as we walked towards the sixth form block, but not as many as last year. There were fewer people here than in the high school.

Someone behind us gagged loudly.

I didn't need to look back to know who it was. Cole rolled his eyes, and said over his shoulder, "Fuck off, Julian."

I was glad Julian decided to come here instead of going anywhere else... not.

"We'll go out at lunch. Get ice cream," Cole said, placing a kiss to my temple.

Ice cream and hot chocolate were my weaknesses. I had a massive sweet tooth.

I grabbed a fistful of his T-shirt and pulled him closer, so there was absolutely no space between us. He teasingly brushed his lips against mine. Usually, I wouldn't be comfortable with kissing him in front of so many people, but in that moment, I didn't care. I crushed my lips to his, feeding off the energy between us.

I felt Cole jolt as someone slapped him. "Nice show!"

Moving back, I smiled at Ben and Kerry.

Cole narrowed his eyes. "Thanks for ending it, dickhead."

"You were seconds from a personal space lecture from Mr Phelps. I did you a favour."

I left Cole, Ben, and Kerry once the bell rang. I had my timetable, starting with double Sociology. I was also taking Psychology, History, and English Literature.

I made my way to the classroom and took an empty seat next to a new kid. He had dark hair, pale skin, and looked painfully shy. Meeting new people was always hard. It didn't take them long to realise that I didn't talk, and the expression was always the same confused pull of their brows once new people found out.

I smiled at him, which he returned without saying a word. I pointed to my name written neatly at the top of my notepad. By tomorrow, everything I wrote would be back to my usual messy scrawl.

"I'm Kyle," he whispered. "Oakley's a weird name." His eyes widened. "Not *weird*. I didn't mean weird. I meant... unusual. Sorry."

My smile widened at his rambling. I held my hand up, letting him know it was okay. I didn't think it really suited me, either. I should have had a more common name—one that no one would bat an eyelid at.

As the lesson began, I flicked open my textbook and followed where the teacher was reading.

It was then that Julian walked in late, grunting a half-hearted apology.

Great, he's taking this class as well.

"Julian, I saved you a seat," Leanne said, looking at him through her eyelashes.

"Continue reading through the questions and answer what you can. Julian, take a seat and start reading from the top of page seven."

Julian ignored Leanne and sat down on the other side of me. I was now between him and Kyle.

"Who's the new kid?" Julian asked. "Ah, you won't tell me."

I rolled my eyes.

"I'm Julian. Who're you," he asked Kyle, leaning across me.

Kyle scowled, hearing our exchange. "Kyle," he said.

I kept my head down and worked on the questions related to the text in front of me, determined to nail this class and become that CEO.

"Oakley," Julian whispered in my ear.

I stiffened and bit back the urge to punch him again.

He sighed and actually sounded... sad. I wasn't aware that he felt regular, human emotion.

"Hey, Oakley... please?"

I took a deep breath and forced myself to look at him. His thin lips pulled up at the sides into a real smile. Hell must have been mighty cold right now.

"Hi." He shook his head at himself. "Look, I'm sorry, okay? Sorry about your party and everything else. And I mean everything." He nervously shifted in his seat. He didn't make apologies often. That much was clear from how uncomfortable he looked. I kind of liked it. "I know I've been a dick to you, and I don't deserve anything, but I'd like to be friends... if you can forgive me."

If I had been standing up, I would've fainted.

"Don't look so shocked. I never hated you."

What the hell happened to him over the summer? This was

probably a joke. But why would he mess with me again? He knew that Cole barely needed a reason to hurt him. One wrong look and Cole would be on him.

I wasn't sure if I could trust Julian, or if I even wanted him as a friend in the first place.

He grimaced. "So, can you forget—"

"Enough, Julian. First day, first lesson. These are your A-Level years, so buckle down," Mr Phelps said. "Are we clear?"

"Crystal," Julian replied, putting his head down.

I managed to write three more words when he whispered, "Can we talk after class?"

I jumped at the sound of Mr Phelps slamming his hand down on the desk. "There will be plenty of time for discussion. Right now, I have asked you to read and answer the questions. Both of you can come see me at lunchtime."

What the hell? My jaw went slack.

Did I... Did I just get detention for *talking*?

There was absolutely nothing funny about my silence or the reason for it... but still, I felt a bubble of laugher sitting in my throat.

Julian mumbled a string of swear words under his breath and started his work. This sucked so much.

Julian was such an idiot.

After a couple of seconds, he nudged me and tapped on the paper in front of him.

I ground my teeth. Hadn't he done enough already? Reluctantly, I looked down to see what he'd written. One word.

Sorry.

How about stop doing things to be sorry for?

I smiled half-heartedly to get him to leave me alone.

Which he did for the rest of the lesson.

At lunch, I made my way to the detention room. I didn't even have enough time to see Cole first, so he was probably waiting for me in the sixth form block.

Scowling, I sank down on the closest seat and pulled a book out of my bag.

Out of the corner of my eye, I saw Julian smile sheepishly from across the room. I ignored him and started to read.

Ten minutes into our twenty-minute detention, I saw Cole's face peek through the door, his eyes filled with amusement. He walked off, but I knew he wouldn't go far.

Oh, yeah, this is hilarious!

"I've just got to pop to the office for one minute. Do not move," Mr Phelps ordered before leaving the room.

The second the door closed, Julian got up and walked over to me. I sighed as he sat on the chair beside me.

"Leanne's having a party on Friday. You want to go?" he asked, kicking one leg up on the desk.

No.

He knew I was with Cole, so either he was delusional, or he just didn't care.

Maybe a bit of both.

"I'm trying here, Oakley."

That was true, and I couldn't fault him for that. It did seem like he was trying, but he'd spent too long making my life hell. I could believe that he didn't want to fight anymore, but I couldn't trust him.

The door swung open, making us both jump.

"Get away from her," Cole growled, glaring at Julian as he slipped into the room. He put a cheese sandwich on my desk that he must've bought from the canteen.

Julian glared back and flipped Cole off before returning to his seat.

"What?" Cole said innocently, surprised at my look of reproach.

I rolled my eyes, smiling, and shook my head.

"So, detention, huh?"

"We got it for *talking*," Julian interrupted.

Cole angrily frowned at Julian. "Are you trying to be funny?"

I grabbed his hand and shook my head.

No, that's exactly what happened.

"Wait, you really got detention for talking?" he asked.

I grinned, amused, and that seemed to give him permission. He barked a laugh and reached for my face, running his thumb across my lip. "Sorry."

Without warning, Cole leant over the table and pressed his lips to mine. Every kiss from him made me melt and my pulse thump.

He pulled away just a few seconds later and walked out of the room with the biggest, cheekiest grin I had ever seen on his face. I couldn't help smiling to myself.

Julian didn't try talking to me again for the remaining few minutes we had to serve.

When detention was over, I made my way to the bench outside the front of the school to quickly eat my sandwich before afternoon classes started.

"Oakley?" a female voice called.

I looked up to see Abby jogging towards me.

Oh, this bitch could do one.

The last I'd heard, she was studying at a uni forty-five minutes away. I never wanted the witch to come back.

I wasn't sure if Jasper knew she was back.

"Hey." She smiled warmly as she sat down. "Isn't this great? I managed to get my work placement here. I'm so glad I get to see you again. I'll be helping out in some of your English Lit lessons, so we can catch up," she said.

Today was the day for arseholes to make ridiculous requests, apparently.

I smiled sarcastically. Did she really expect me to be happy about the situation?

She was the reason my brother had *cried*. She was the reason he couldn't trust women anymore and slept with everything with a pulse.

I hated her.

"Anyway, I just wanted to say hi before I meet with the principal. Look, I'm going to talk to Jasper. I miss him. And I miss you. You look good. Happy."

She stood, and I fought the urge to trip her up as she walked off.

"That who I think it is?" Cole asked, joining me on the bench. "Jasper isn't going to like this."

No, it might crush him all over again.

Chapter 27

Oakley

I sat awkwardly at the dinner table with Jasper beside me as I glared at Mum's doctor friend, Sadie. I was bordering on being rude now but no one else had noticed, even though the atmosphere around the table was sombre.

We all knew why she was really here, though no one admitted it out loud.

"So, Oakley, how is gymnastics? Your mum told me your instructor thinks you could be Olympics material."

I blinked twice, leaving Sadie's question hanging. Marcus had said that years ago, but I would have to put in a lot more time and effort, and I didn't want to.

Gymnastics wasn't about winning trophies. I just needed the escape.

Mum set her wine glass down and smiled. "Don't be shy, sweetheart. You're so talented."

Shut up!

"Why is it called cottage pie, anyway? I mean, I get the shepherd's one for the lamb, but what's cottage and beef got in common?" Jasper mused, staring at the large oven dish in the middle of the table.

Grinning in amusement, I poked at my carrots. He was trying to take the heat off me.

Sadie smiled at him and launched into asking more questions.

"What A-Levels are you taking?"

"Did you have a nice time on holiday?"

"Do you like any other sport?"

"What university are you looking at?"

"What do you want to do after graduation?"

At no point did she ever ask me anything directly, but I knew what she was doing. I ignored every question.

It wouldn't work.

I'd never tell.

When the conversation turned to my childhood, I knew I didn't have long before the really personal questions began.

"What age did you start gymnastics?"

"Who was your first friend?"

After we finished eating, Mum plucked her photo albums from the bookshelf. She had a separate one for every year of our lives.

"You remember this, Oakley?" Mum asked, pointing to a picture of me on my fourth birthday.

I was wearing a hideous pink dress, eating chocolate cake. There was pink icing all over my face and hair from having had a cake fight with Jasper, Cole, and Mia. Once we'd finished the food fight, they'd crammed us all into the same bath and sprayed us clean with the shower head. The water was gross and pink with little bits of wet cake floating around in it.

I nodded and looked away, not wanting to dwell on it too much. That part of my life had ended a long time ago.

"And what did you do for your fifth birthday?" Sadie casually asked me, flicking through the photos.

I died.

I gave her a flat look and pushed the photo album labelled *Oakley – five* towards her. She forced a smiled and started looking through it even though I could tell she had no interest in seeing the pictures at all. I got the impression that she didn't like failing at her job of getting me to talk.

I was a challenge. A puzzle she wanted to figure out.

She had no idea how much I wasn't going to let that happen. She was career-driven. I had to save my family.

I was going to win.

Sadie sat up straight, flicked her straggly hair behind her shoulder, and asked, "Which birthday was your favourite?"

Every one before my fifth.

I shrugged, and she pursed her lips. The night was going to be a constant battle with her.

Dad scowled at Mum, unhappy that this woman was interfering. To her face, he'd be nothing but charming. I wondered if he was sitting there stressing, too, wondering what Sadie could see.

But everyone made the mistake of looking at me rather than Dad.

After Mum and Dad cleared the placemats from the table, we moved into the lounge. Mum made it clear that I was to sit downstairs with them all, even though Jasper was allowed to sneak off.

Sadie's questions were relentless, but she'd switched back to asking things that mostly required a yes or no answer, which meant I was winning.

The whole time, I could feel Dad's eyes burning into the side of my head, his silent demands booming in my mind. He played along, following Mum's lead with questions to Sadie.

Not even the highly paid specialist could see through him.

Men like him were disgusting, lying, hypocrites, and I hoped every one of them would die an agonising death.

I didn't care if he was my dad. I *hated* him.

And a tiny part of me, one that I hated myself, wished he would be normal—wished we could rewind time and have everything happen differently.

I wanted, more than anything, to have a dad who protected me.

But life wasn't a fairy tale.

Mum and Sadie started to get a little frustrated. They were both still kind, but I could tell by the tightness in both their eyes that they knew this wasn't going anywhere.

I left the room to get a glass of water, not at all surprised when Sadie followed me into the kitchen. Turning off the tap, I placed the glass on the counter and waited.

"Can we talk?"

I sighed heavily and nodded.

"So, you were five when you stopped talking?"

I furrowed my eyebrows.

"And you didn't have any problems with talking before that?"

Problems?

"Any anxiety about speaking to people?"

I gritted my teeth.

Back the fuck off.

"Did you say something wrong or overhear something you shouldn't have? Anyone tease you for saying something they thought was silly?"

My stomach churned and bile hit the back of my throat. I wished she would understand that I didn't want to talk to anyone about it.

"Is everything okay?" Dad asked as he walked into the room.

For the first time ever, I was happy he'd interrupted, as much as I didn't want him anywhere near me.

"Everything's fine," Sadie replied. "I just thought Oakley

would be more comfortable with talking to me alone. Most patients I have are one-to-one."

I'm not your patient, I wanted to scream.

"Hmm," Dad said. "Perhaps another time when Oakley doesn't have to get to bed for school."

I faked a yawn on time, adding to Dad's excuse, and grabbed my glass.

"You're tired, darling. Go to bed," Dad said.

Sadie watched me, so I stopped as I went to pass Dad. I let him kiss me on the forehead. My skin crawled, but it was necessary.

I forced away any unwanted thoughts and walked out of the room with frayed nerves.

There was going to be a discussion about me, that was obvious, so instead of going into my room, I stopped at the top of the stairs. Sitting down against the wall, I wrapped my arms around myself.

For a minute, they talked about Sadie's job, but the conversation soon turned to me.

"So... do you know what's wrong with her?" Mum asked, and I could hear the anxiety in her voice.

Blood whooshed in my ears.

"It's psychological," Sadie said. "I'm almost certain of it. Oakley *can* talk but, for some reason, she chooses not to."

"How do you know?" Dad asked, sounding like the concerned father.

I bit my lip until it hurt.

"I don't. Yet."

"But what does that mean? How can we help her? I don't even know what's wrong with my baby," Mum said, taking a shaky breath.

I pressed against the knot in my stomach.

"She's strong-willed. I don't think you'll be able to *just find out*. There is no quick fix with conditions like this. The only way to get her through this is therapy. It will be a long process, and it won't work unless Oakley wants it to. I'm sorry, Sarah, but I don't think, for whatever reason, she's ready."

"But..." Mum trailed off.

I heard silence and then strangled sobs as Mum broke down.

No.

Hugging my knees to my chest, I closed my eyes as pain cut through my chest.

I'm sorry, Mum. I'm so, so sorry.

"I know it's distressing, but you have to remain positive and let her come to you," Sadie said. "I would suggest that you don't keep pushing her. Treat her as if nothing's out of the ordinary. The more pressure you put her under, the more she'll shut you out. Therapy *will* help. Oakley can get better but only when the time is right for her."

"So, you're saying we do nothing?" Dad cut in, his voice laced with fake frustration.

"I think, for now, that's all you *can* do. It's never taken me longer than two hours to get someone to give me something. Oakley's given me *nothing*. I think you should offer her therapy but make it clear that it will start when she is ready. She needs to be the one in control."

A metallic taste filled my mouth, and I realised I had pierced my lip with my teeth. Pressing my fingertips to my mouth, I looked down at the blood.

I couldn't hear much more because they'd moved now, but I heard the front door close, which meant Sadie must've left.

"God, I need to speak to her," Mum said.

I scrambled to my feet, wiping a tear that was running down my cheek.

"No, wait!" Dad called. "You need to calm down first. If you go up there in the state you're in, you'll push her further away.

You heard what Sadie said. We need to do this properly, Sarah. We should've done this a long time ago. Pushing her isn't the answer. We've probably made the problem worse through trying."

He should get an Oscar.

"Okay," Mum whispered, backing down and bursting into tears.

I let out a big breath and leaned my head against the wall.

"Something bad happened to her, didn't it?"

My heart shattered with despair, and my stomach turned over. I wanted to step into a boiling shower or run off to an imaginary castle again.

You're stronger than that.

I swiped angrily at the tears streaming down my face, and I headed to my room. I turned and jumped when I came face-to-face with Jasper, quickly dropping my gaze to the floor.

"Whatever's wrong, I'm here," he whispered. He looked scared for me. His jacket was on, and his keys were in his hand.

I shrugged it off like it was nothing, all while dying inside, and I pointed to his keys. Where was he off to?

"Erm... I'm going to see Abby," he mumbled. "Do you think I'm crazy?"

Yeah.

I wiped my face with my hands and shook my head. They hadn't properly spoken about what had happened and they needed to. He needed to. Hopefully, he would be able to move on to something better rather than meaningless one-night stands.

"Want me to stay here? I can meet up with her another time. You come first." He wiped away a tear that I'd missed.

I shook my head and gave him a little shove towards the stairs.

"Okay. I'll see you later." He kissed the top of my head and walked downstairs.

As soon as I was in bed, I curled up in a ball and buried my head in my pillow.

What was I going to do now?

It felt like hours that I'd been lying in bed, silently sobbing into my pillow when I heard his voice.

"Oakley."

I shot up at the sound of my name, and Cole chuckled quietly.

He slipped under my covers and wrapped me in his arms. "Jasper called. He said you were upset and gave me his back door key so I could sneak in. Your parents are in bed, don't worry."

With him here, I could hold on. My shattered heart mended a little. I clung to him like my life depended on it.

"Are you okay?" he murmured against my forehead.

I wasn't but I knew how I could feel better.

I tilted my head and claimed his mouth, getting lost in something good.

Chapter 28

Oakley

I'd made it through the first week at school, and Jasper had just arrived back home for the weekend from uni. He wasn't supposed to, and it wasn't because he'd missed us. It was because Abby had moved back.

Jasper, Cole, and I were in my bedroom after our families had got together for dinner. We hadn't had the chance to talk about Abby because Jasper had left for uni straight from visiting her. I'd had other things on my mind.

Jasper glanced my way and chuckled. He kicked his legs up on the bed. "You're dying to know what happened between me and Abby, aren't you?"

I scoffed, trying to pretend that it hadn't been driving me crazy. When they broke up, he was a mess, not eating or sleeping properly. He was angry all the time and refused to talk.

It took a while for him to open up again, but when he did, he did it with every girl he could find. The last thing I wanted was for that to happen again.

"He's got you there," Cole said. "You look like you're about to explode."

Maybe that was because Cole's fingers were tracing random shapes on a small, exposed part of my hip.

I raised my palms to say *What the hell?* Seemed a bit weird that he picked now to stop talking about his love life when a week ago he told me about a woman he slept with in a toilet cubicle.

Jasper sighed, looking down at his hands. The cocky smirk was gone. "She told me she wants to get back together—that the other guy was a mistake." Tramp. "And that she's sorry. But I don't know if I can trust her again."

How would he? Every time she went out with her friends, every time she didn't pick up his call, he would wonder.

Trust was so easy to break and almost impossible to rebuild.

"Did she give you an explanation this time?" Cole asked.

One of the things that drove Jasper insane, besides the obvious, was the fact that Abby never told him *why* she cheated. She just kept telling him it was a mistake.

He deserved to have all his questions answered.

His gaze slid from his hands to me and back. "She did. She opened up, cried a lot, and apologised. I want to believe her."

I nudged Cole to ask for me.

"Ah," he said, rubbing his arm, though there was no way that hurt. "You don't need to know everything, babe."

My jaw dropped at how little he knew me.

"If you promise me you'll be nice to her at school, I'll tell you," Jasper said.

Nodding, I sat up straighter, facing him.

"You're such a gossip," Cole teased.

"She told me that, after our argument, she went to a party and drank too much. She was hurt and angry, and she just wanted to get wasted with her friends. She ended up in his room. They... well, you know the rest."

So, it was revenge sex.

She ruined everything because she was angry.

I couldn't understand that.

Jasper looked down, his face twisted in pain as he remembered back to that time. I hadn't seen him so vulnerable in a long time. "I keep thinking that maybe we can try again, but is there really any point if I'm constantly thinking that she's screwing someone else?"

No, there wasn't. I shook my head. Jasper's happiness meant so much to me, but she'd hurt him a lot, and I wasn't convinced they'd work now.

"You just hate her," Jasper said.

I hated her less than I had since she'd given him answers, but I couldn't forget how heartbroken he'd been. I'd never forgive her for hurting him like that.

"She's worried about you," Cole said.

"Doesn't matter, anyway. In the end, we decided to try and be friends. We'll see if anything can happen in the future. I don't even know if we'll even be able to do the friends thing or not, but I don't want to be angry anymore. You know what I mean?"

I knew exactly what he meant. That was why I wasn't walking straight away from Julian every time he talked to me. He only ever tried when I was away from Cole, but he was trying. I didn't have the energy to keep fighting him, and I didn't want sixth form to be the same as high school. I was over it.

"I'm not sitting around here reminiscing about the shittiest time in my life any longer. I have a date with a cute little brunette tonight. Later," Jasper said, getting off the bed and leaving my room.

Cole and I exchanged a look. My brother was back.

"He's so weird, babe."

Jasper was weird, but he was still one of the best.

I gasped at the sudden jolt as Cole rolled over and pushed me down on the bed. Closing my eyes, I curled my hands in his hair as he peppered featherlight kisses across my cheek and along my jaw. My body responded to him, heating unbearably until I thought I was going to pass out.

I curled my legs around his waist and felt his smile against my skin. "You're getting carried away, and it's going to make me get carried away. We're not alone, remember?"

With his mouth on my skin and his scent filling my lungs, I honestly didn't care. This meant the world.

He groaned when I tightened my legs around him, his erection pressed between my legs. "Oakley..." On a ragged breath, he pulled his head away from my neck. "I'm going to sit an arm's length away, and we're going to watch TV." I didn't move. "Babe," he prompted.

Dropping my legs from around him, he scuffled away and sat at the other side of my bed. Smirking, I sat up and turned towards a TV that neither of us were interested in watching.

Cole rubbed his lips with his fist and took a deep breath. I would never get tired of making him feel like that. We wanted each other... equally.

For the rest of the evening, Cole was a perfect gentleman and only held my hand, stroking his thumb over my knuckles.

"How are you, sweetheart? Okay?" Dad asked, walking into my room once Cole and his family had left.

My stomach tightened, but I nodded.

"Good." He cleared his throat and sat on my bed.

Over the past year, he'd aged so much. Grey hairs dominated the previously light-brown one on the sides of his head. The lines around his eyes had multiplied and deepened. Every day, he looked more and more like a middle-aged man. I wondered if he felt that, too.

He was losing his good looks, and I hoped his charm went with it.

If people guessed, then it wouldn't be my fault. But who

randomly guessed that kind of thing? Mum wasn't going to wake up one morning and think that her husband, the man she had spent most of her life with, was a sick bastard who liked hurting children and sharing them with his sick friend.

"Sweetheart, I know that in the past we've had our difficulties."

My heart stopped. *Difficulties.*

"But I want to make it up to you, to have the relationship we once had."

I felt the blood drain from my face. Those trips stopped when I was thirteen.

Why? Why now?

I sucked in a ragged breath and mentally punched myself when my eyes began to sting with unshed tears.

If I could move, I would run.

He raised a palm. "No, sweetheart. No, no. I want *us* to go. To reconnect, for me to make this right."

The blood in my veins froze.

Nothing would ever make this right. Not this trip, not a hundred trips. But this was the closest to an apology he'd *ever* offered. Could he really want to heal our relationship? It wouldn't ever happen, but he might want to try. I wasn't a little kid or underage anymore. Why would he want to take me away?

I wish I knew what he was thinking.

"Do you remember when you were younger and you would ride around on my back, laughing as I bucked you off onto the sofa? Or when I would come home from work, and you would run out the front door to greet me?"

Yeah, but that was another life. That was before. Everything now is after.

Slowly nodding my head, I forced myself to take deep, even breaths. Thoughts of Frank and his overbearing frame looming over me filled my head. I could still smell his scotch-tainted breath and feel his rough stubble scratching against my skin.

My lungs screamed for oxygen. I curled my arms around my legs.

Breathe. You're fine. It's over. You're fine.

"I know things have been hard, but I want to change that."

Hard? He used words like difficult and hard to describe years of abuse and forced silence.

Clenching my jaw, I watched him try to untangle the choices he had made. Now he wanted to start again and for us to be the perfect family.

Why?

What... wait... could this be the start of allowing me to talk? Mum wasn't giving up, despite him telling her over and over that I shouldn't be pushed. There were only so many more years he could get away with that before she questioned why he wasn't trying harder to fix me, too.

I'd be going to uni in two years.

He could be doing this now, 'fixing' our relationship, so that I wouldn't want to tell anyone when I finally decided to use my voice. We could use therapy as the reason I started talking again.

But he had to know that I wouldn't tell anyway. I wouldn't do that to Mum and Jasper.

Maybe he couldn't count on that alone.

"Oakley, I want that relationship back. I want us to do things together, watch a movie or go for a bike ride. I want us to do normal father-daughter things, whatever you want... I'd take your lead. Most of all, I want my little girl back." He rubbed his jaw, his eyes filling with tears.

It was impossible to tell if he was genuine, but I knew I couldn't trust him

But I wanted to. As much as I shouldn't, I wanted all of those things, too. I wanted us to be a normal family more than anything.

I didn't want my dad to be a monster.

If I didn't try like he wanted me to, there might not be any chance that I would talk again. I would never be able to tell Cole that I loved him, too.

Peering up into Dad's eyes, I saw how broken he appeared.

He was the master of deception, so I didn't know how much of that tortured expression he'd practiced in the mirror.

"Oakley, my business isn't doing well at the minute. I'm afraid it will fail. I don't want to fail at another thing in my life. I don't want to look at us as a failure anymore. Let me make it up to you. Let's draw a line in the sand, put the past behind us, and be a proper family. You, me, your mother, and Jasper. I'll never be able to fix the past, but I can change going forward. I want us to be a happy family again. Like when you used to sit on my shoulders at firework displays."

I could remember two years of doing that. It was all in the before.

Do it. For everyone's sake, do it.

More than anything, I wanted to talk.

"Please, give this a chance. Let us get to know each other again. Let me be your daddy again."

I sucked in a deep breath and nodded my head.

Maybe it wasn't the right choice, but I *had* to know.

My voice was worth fighting for.

"Thank you," he whispered. "Thank you for trusting me to repair what I broke. Now, get some sleep. It's late."

As he walked out of my room and closed the door, I ducked under my cover.

Confused by my own conflicting feelings for my dad, I curled into a ball. In the past, I'd loved and hated him.

I could forgive him, I thought, if he gave me my voice back.

Chapter 29

Cole

By the time the weekend rolled around, I was more than ready for a chance to be alone with Oakley, but a trip with her dad was going to ruin that. We'd had parents around us the whole week long, and it wasn't like we could do anything at school.

Well, we could but I didn't think she would.

Now she was going to be away until Sunday, and I was seriously losing my mind. I was going to miss her like mad.

Mia walked into my room and shoved the door shut.

"Do come in..."

"I need to talk to you, and you can't get mad. You have to let me finish, okay?" she said, pacing.

"Sounds like something I'll get mad over."

She stopped and turned to me. "Please, Cole."

"All right, I promise. Sit down and tell me what's going on."

Taking a seat on the edge of my bed, she wrung her hands together. She looked like she'd had a rough night, and it was late afternoon now. Her brown hair was tied messily on the top of her head, and she had circles under her eyes, proof that she'd been worrying about whatever she was about to tell me.

"Chris and I broke up."

That wasn't something to lose sleep over.

"Well, halle-fucking-lujah," I said, throwing my arms up in celebration.

"And I'm having a baby," she added.

My jaw hit the floor. "I'm sorry. You're *what*?"

"Pregnant. With child. Knocked-up. Bun in the oven. All of those are me."

Grinding my teeth together, I growled, "That bastard got you pregnant and ditched you?" I was going to kill him. It was exactly the shitty thing that arsehole would do.

"Wait!" she snapped, grabbing my arm. "You need to let me finish. And keep your voice down because I've not told Mum and Dad yet."

As soon as she was finished, I was going to go to his house. Mia might be a fool for taking him back so many times, but she didn't deserve this.

Neither did her baby.

Shit, she was going to be a mum.

She took a calming deep breath, threaded her hands together, and continued. "I found out a couple of days ago that I'm pregnant. It's made me look at everything differently, you know. My relationship with Chris is... well, let's face it, it's shit. I don't think we've ever gone a few days without arguing, and then there are the other women. I don't want my baby growing up around all that."

She uncoupled her hands and tenderly touched her flat stomach.

Jesus, there was a human growing in there.

"This baby is the most important thing now. I know I have to be away from Chris to be the best mum I can be."

It took a new life to make her realise how bad Chris was for her. But she would never be free of him. He was the kid's dad.

"That's great, Mia. You and the baby deserve so much more than him. What did he say?"

"He said I'll go back to him soon enough. He shouted a bit, said I'd tricked him into getting pregnant, as if he's some trophy. I don't care what he thinks, though. I didn't get pregnant on my own, and I certainly didn't plan it. Not sure how much involvement he'll want, but I won't stop him from seeing her if he wants."

"Her? How can you know?"

Mia shrugged and, despite her appearance, she'd never looked happier. "I don't mind what it is, but I have a feeling it's a girl."

Fuck. A niece that would grow up and need protecting from men like her own father. If Chris didn't step up, I sure as hell would.

"I hope Chris does the right thing by the baby, but if not, you know you won't be alone, right?"

Mia threw her arms around me, almost knocking me back, and squeezed the life out of me.

"Whoa." What the hell was this? "All right, but you know you're probably squishing the baby right now," I teased breathlessly as she squeezed my rib cage.

"Thank you, Cole," she whispered. "And she'll have her Auntie Oakley."

"Yeah."

"Cole." Mia laughed at me. "You've got that sappy look on your face."

I shook my head, clearing my thoughts. "Sorry."

"It's cute."

"Don't call it cute."

"You love her."

"Yeah."

She reached out to pinch my cheeks, but I whacked her hand away. "Adorable, Cole."

"When are you telling Mum and Dad? They'll be pissed. You know that, right?"

Mia's face dropped. She was almost twenty, but Dad still thought of her as his little girl. He would definitely *not* be happy —well, not at first, at least. I knew he'd love that little baby to death once he'd gotten his head around it.

"They won't be pissed at you."

"I'm telling them in a minute actually. I am *not* looking forward to it, and thanks for your overwhelming words of encouragement, by the way."

"You're welcome. It'll be fine."

"Seriously, thanks for being supportive. It means a lot." She stood up to go tell our parents. "Oh, and if you hear shouting, come save me."

"Yeah, good luck, Mia. It was nice knowing you."

She rolled her eyes and slowly walked out of my room, groaning to herself.

I stripped out of my clothes and slipped into bed, noticing how silent the house was. I wasn't sure if that was a good thing or not.

Suddenly, Dad erupted, calling Chris every bad name under the sun.

He'd come around quickly though. I was sure of it.

"I'll miss you this weekend," I whispered in Oakley's ear as she pressed her body into mine, driving me wild minutes before I had to say goodbye.

I didn't think she really wanted to go on this trip. I didn't want her to, either.

Max was excited, packing the last few things into the car when I arrived. It'd been a while since they'd gone away. I think he wanted to get her away for a while since Sarah had recently been back at making appointments and offering therapy.

It wasn't something I objected to, but I didn't like how Sarah pushed.

Oakley and I were alone in her room, and I had her pinned to the back of her door, kissing her enough for the whole weekend.

Her fingertips slid under my T-shirt and clawed at my back, making me shudder. I wanted to strip her clothes off and lay her down on the bed, but we didn't have time... or a free house.

Groaning into the kiss as her tongue danced with mine, I hooked her leg around my waist and arched my hips into her, my self-control slipping.

She kissed me like she wanted to disappear into me.

"Hey, you okay?" I asked when she let me come up for breath. I wasn't complaining but I'd never seen her so frantic in her attempt to lose herself to us.

Was she just going to miss me, or was there more to it? I could tell from the subtle tightness around her eyes that every time Sarah mentioned a doctor or therapist, Oakley hated it.

I pressed my forehead against hers. "You'll have a good time, and I'll see you in thirty-two and a half hours."

The corner of her lip turned up as she tried to hide a grin.

With a sigh, she took my hand, and we walked outside.

I watched her drive away and wondered just how slow the weekend would pass.

For the entire morning, I was unintentionally annoying my parents and Mia. Apparently, I was intolerable when I missed Oakley.

Mia had entertained me for a couple of hours, talking about the baby and her plans, but she quickly got bored of my moping.

In the afternoon, I grabbed a couple of snacks and set my PlayStation up. Tonight, I'd arranged to go out with Ben, but I still had a few hours until I needed to meet him.

Just as I started playing *Fallout 4*, my phone started ringing.

I stared down at the name with my heart in my throat.

Oakley.

What?

I had *never* seen her name flash up on my screen before.

Reaching out with a shaky hand, I grabbed the phone and answered.

The first thing I heard were muffled sobs and each one cut through me like a knife to butter.

"Cole," she breathed. "Help me."

Chapter 30

Cole

I swallowed hard, my heart hammering against my ribcage.

"Help," she repeated.

Her plea snapped me back to reality.

"Oakley?" I mumbled, the blood draining from my face. "What... baby. You're... What's going on?"

"Cole." She sobbed harder. Her broken voice was everything I wanted to hear, but her words were not.

"I... I need help."

"What's wrong? Where are you?" I questioned as I frantically searched for my keys while my head was all over the place, still trying to catch up to the fact that she was *speaking*. Fuck. "Oakley, you need to tell me where you are right now."

Something was very wrong. Where the hell was Max? Had they gotten into an accident?

"Do you need the emergency services?"

"You," she replied roughly.

What? That meant Max was okay.

"Where?"

"Um," she whispered, trying to catch her breath. Her voice sounded painful, like every syllable was pure agony.

239

I listened hard, my hand around my keys, frozen in the middle of my room as I tried to catch every raspy word. It took a minute for her to explain where she was, but as soon as I got it, I was sprinting downstairs and out to my car.

I had no clue what was going on, but I needed to get to her. She was on her own near a lay-by off the motorway, and I still had no idea why because she cried too hard and just told me to hurry.

My body was numb as I sprinted past Mum and Dad on the sofa, ignoring their questions. I'd never felt so cold and hopeless before.

I should probably have stopped to tell them, but I was too desperate to get to her.

A journey that should have taken thirty minutes took me less than twenty. My foot, flat to the floor in the car, raced me towards her. It still took far too long.

My phone was ringing but it was Dad, so I ignored it.

Slamming my brakes on when I spotted the lay-by, I swung in and shoved my door open.

Jumping out, I shouted, "Oakley! *Oakley!*"

The sky had turned grey, and a few drops of rain splatted on the ground around me. What the hell was she doing out here alone?

"It's me, where are you?" I moved towards the trees where she must've been hiding. Why? From what? Who?

Seconds later, she appeared from behind one, stumbling on uneven ground as she made her way to me.

Gasping at the sight of her tearstained face and the pain in her red eyes, I ran forward and caught her as her knees buckled.

"What's wrong?" I mumbled against the side of her head, and she burst into uncontrollable sobs again, her body trembling against mine. "Okay, baby, you're fucking scaring me. What's wrong?"

She mumbled my name, not yet ready to talk, so I held her together until her breathing evened out. I was so tense I thought my muscles might snap.

Stroking her hair with dread slithering down my spine, I asked, "What happened? I'm here, you're safe, but I need you to tell me what's wrong. Please."

She nodded against my shoulder. I gripped her upper arms and tried to pull back to see her, but she clung to me tighter and whimpered, burying her head in my chest.

"What is it?"

"I-I don't want you to lo-look at me," she whispered, her voice cracking.

I wasn't sure what I expected her to sound like, but I loved it. I just didn't love what she was saying.

"Why don't you want me to look at you, baby?"

She was quiet for a minute, and with each passing second, I waited, my heart dropping lower. "I can't... I can't do it again."

"What can't you do?"

She shook her head and dug her fingers in my back so hard, it scared me. What did she need to hold on so tightly for?

"You can tell me anything. I'm on your side, always." I pushed my hand through her hair and kissed the top of her head. "Oakley, please, what can't you do?" I was getting desperate, and I just needed to know what was wrong so I could fix it. "Why are you alone?"

"I thought it'd st-stopped." She took a ragged breath and cleared her throat. "It stopped when I was thirteen, but he's... he's back."

"Who's back? What stopped?" I shook my head, trying to make sense of what she was saying.

Something stopped when she was thirteen. And someone's back? Who?

241

It didn't make sense. No one had left when she was thirteen —not that I could remember, anyway. Where the hell was Max?

"Fr-Frank," she said, and her body shuddered. Her legs gave way again, but I held her up.

"Who's Frank? I don't know anyone called Frank. Shh, it's okay," I whispered. "Talk to me."

"He's the man who... hurt me." Her voice so quiet I barely heard her.

"Hurt you," I repeated. "How did he hurt—" I froze mid-sentence as I realised what she was trying to tell me.

No.

I hunched forward, her words a physical blow.

"Hurt you. He... touched you?"

She didn't need to confirm it. Her reaction did. She burst into fresh tears, her sobs punching holes in my heart over and over.

I had no strength left. Her confession knocked everything out of me. We both fell to the ground, and she landed in my lap. I gripped hold of her and buried my face in her hair. My lungs burned. I squeezed my eyes, seeing white dots dance behind the lids.

No.

This bastard Frank had abused her, and I wanted to slaughter him in cold blood. But I couldn't move. I couldn't think straight. I couldn't stop my heart shattering along with hers.

I wanted her to tell me that I'd got it wrong, that I didn't understand what she was saying, but that wasn't going to happen. She'd been hurt so badly, it made me want to hurl.

"Where is he?" I asked through clenched teeth.

"At our ca-camp," she murmured against my neck, stuttering and sobbing.

"But your dad's..."

Her body turned to stone.

Oh my God.

"Oakley?" Max knew. He fucking *knew*.

I swallowed the bile that hit the back of my throat.

Her *dad* let this happen.

He knew some sick pervert had hurt her, and he was sitting around a fucking campfire with the bastard. It didn't make sense for Max to do this, but Oakley wouldn't lie. Rage like I'd never felt before set fire in my stomach.

I pulled back to look at her, but she lowered her head, staring at the ground and refusing to meet my eye.

Fuck that.

"Hey," I said, lifting her chin. "Look at me. Don't do that. You have nothing to be ashamed of, you hear me."

She shook her head and met my gaze. I'd never seen anyone so broken, haunted, and it made me want to rip Frank and Max apart, limb from limb.

"I'm going to take care of you. No one will *ever* hurt you again."

She pressed her palm to my chest, over my heart. With the other hand she wiped tears from my face. "You've saved my life more times than I can count."

"I always will. *Always.* Oakley, I need to ask you something right now. Did Max... did he hurt you, too?"

"No, he didn't. He never touched me, he just let *him*."

My hands trembled with anger around her, and I blinked away tears.

"Where is your camp?" I asked slowly, trying to keep the anger out of my voice. It didn't work. I was breathing rage.

"N-no. You can't, Cole." Her breathing hitched. "Please. I-I can't. My mum. Please, don't."

"Shh," I whispered, wiping fresh tears from her cheeks, trying to get a hold on my own emotions. They could wait. I shoved them deep down. All that mattered was her. "It's okay, you're with me. But... Why did you mention your mum?" I asked.

There was no way, absolutely no way, that Sarah knew about this.

"It'll break her heart. I can't. I don't want to hurt her. I don't want her to hate me. They'll hate me or tell my I'm lying. Everyone will believe him. He's the perfect husband, son, father, friend. Who would believe me over that?"

She sucked in a breath, her voice wavering, breaking all over the place.

"Is that what he told you?" My voice was cold and dangerously calm.

Dipping her head in a quick nod, she said, "I wanted to tell her. I tried to when it first started, but Dad... walked in. He shouted at me when she left. I was so scared. I didn't want to hurt Mum. He said that if I did, it would kill her... I took it literally." She coughed to clear her throat. "He told me not to talk."

If she wasn't wrapped up in my arms right now, I would be off looking for blood.

"*That's* why you haven't spoken for eleven years?" I said between gritted teeth.

Her dad was the reason. Hate and rage wrapped around my throat, squeezing so hard I could choke.

"Oakley, where is he?" I asked again.

Her eyes widened in panic. "You can't. Please, Cole. I need you with me. Please don't leave me."

"I... I'm not," I said, holding her tighter, willing her to keep me together, too. "I'm never leaving you again."

She'd been going on trips with her dad ever since I could remember.

She fucking stopped talking when she was *five*.

No.

"We're going to the police. They need to rot in prison for the rest of their lives."

She gasped and pulled back, tucking her chin into her chest. "No. Mum will—"

"No," I said cutting her off. I wasn't having that. I had to get it through to her that they had to pay. No one was going to blame her. "No. Oakley, your mum's not going to hate you. She couldn't. What happened wasn't your fault. Those sick bastards... Your mum will believe you, just like I do. She loves you. She could never hate you," I said, begging her with my eyes to believe me. "Look at me."

She raised her head, and the second her eyes met mine, tears fell—hers and mine.

Stroking her cheek, I said, "Everything's going to be okay, *I promise*. But we need to go to the police. We can't pretend."

I couldn't pretend. If I saw Max's face, I was going to cave it in.

"I can't."

"Let me get you out of here and we'll talk about it in the car."

We were still on the ground on the edge of a motorway. She'd cut herself open and spilled her deepest secret, and I needed to get her out of there.

I got to my feet first, helping her up.

"Cole, thank you," she whispered.

"For what?"

"For coming to get me... For believing me."

"Always. I love you so much." As we drove back towards home, I broke the silence with a question. "Please will you let me take you to the police? I swear to you, your mum and Jasper will believe you. My parents, too. Everyone."

Her breathing hitched, and she grabbed hold of the side of the seat.

"Baby, I'll be with you the entire time."

"Okay," her voice was barely a whisper, but I was so damn proud of her.

She didn't say much on the way to the station, and I didn't push it. She was lost to her thoughts and needed a minute.

We walked into the building, hand in hand, and I asked for someone to report child abuse, trying not to lose what little control I was holding onto.

The officer at the reception desk looked from Oakley to me and nodded. "I'll be one minute."

A lady with soft features and a calming voice showed us into an interview room. Only this one didn't have a mirror, table, and metal chairs.

This room was warm and inviting. Two sofas, flowers, and a coffee table. It wouldn't look out of place in someone's house.

Oakley held my hand with a vice-like grip as we sat down, both having declined a drink. Anything I swallowed would probably come straight back up.

"Oakley, I'm Marie. Would it be okay to talk to me about what happened?"

Before addressing Marie, she turned to me. "Cole... I want to do this alone."

What the hell? I didn't want to leave her for a single second.

I blinked, shocked. How would she cope with going over it all when she completely broke down while telling me before? And I didn't have any details.

"Please, Cole, I don't want you to hear it all," she whispered, a tear trickling down her cheek. "Not yet, at least."

"Are you sure? I can handle it. If you need me to stay, I will." I absolutely couldn't handle it, but I'd do it.

"I'm sure. Not yet."

"All right." I leant over and kissed her cheek. "But I will be right outside."

"Thanks."

I left the room, closing the door, and my knees buckled. Shoving my hands in my hair, I gritted my teeth to stop me from shouting.

"Hey, are you okay?" an officer asked, crouching in front of me. He'd seen me with Oakley before we went in there. "Can I get you something?"

"No, I'm fine."

"You want to wait here for her... Let me get you a chair."

He disappeared into a room next door, coming out with a metal chair, and putting it against the wall.

"Thanks," I said, pushing myself up so I could sit on it.

"Shout if you need anything."

All I needed was for Oakley to be okay and Frank and Max to die.

As I waited for her, so many things passed through my mind. I tried to think of something, any little clue that I'd missed, but there was nothing. She never seemed scared of Max.

I ran my hands over my face, roughly wiping a few tears that I couldn't stop falling.

He didn't act any differently towards her. He was the perfect, worried, protective father, walking the line between concerned and letting her be herself.

The hatred I felt for him burned me from the inside out.

That's how he got away with it.

I gritted my teeth and hung my head. She'd gone through hell for years right under everyone's noses, and no one had known a thing. No one had helped her when she needed it.

When the door finally opened, I jumped up.

"Are you okay?"

She looked exhausted as she slumped against my chest.

"What happens now?" I asked, holding her close.

"We'll bring Mr Farrell and Mr Glosser in for questioning," Marie told me.

Glosser. That was his surname.

"I want to go now," Oakley whispered, gripping hold of my shirt. "Please can we go?"

I nodded reluctantly. There were thousands more questions that I wanted to ask Marie, but Oakley looked so defeated. I knew I needed to take her home... where she was going to have to go through it all again.

"We'll keep in touch. Call me if you need anything," Marie added, handing over a card. "You can take her home now."

I blew out a long breath when we got back in my car. "Do you want me to be with you when you tell your mum?"

"Yes," she replied. "But can we just drive for a bit longer?"

"Yeah, baby, we can."

Thirty minutes later, we turned down our road, and Oakley gasped.

Parked outside her house was a cop car... and Max's car. He must've come home thinking Oakley would be there.

To do what? Pretend everything was okay? Make up some excuse about how something had gone down at the camp and they could no longer stay there?

What excuse did this arrogant, sick fuck have that he thought he could turn up at home after she ran off and be able to control the situation?

She looked across at me with a horrified expression and whispered, "No."

"It's fine. We won't go in yet." I stopped the car at the end of the road, so we could wait until they left.

"They'll believe me, right?"

"Yes, of course, they will. I promise you, they will. It's going to be all right. We'll do it together. I'll be right there with you every step of the way."

I looked up at her house as the door opened. Max was being

walked to the police car with his hands behind his back in handcuffs.

Seeing him made me want to stick the car in drive and run him down.

Oakley shrank in the seat. She looked like a scared, lost little girl. Swallowing a lump in my throat, I squeezed her limp hand, trying to comfort her.

"Time to go in," I said when the police car drove off.

"I'm scared."

I was, too. I'd never been so scared in my life. All I could do was hold her. There was no magic button to press and make this okay. I couldn't fix it for her, and I couldn't stand that.

Parking outside her house, I said, "I know you are, but we're doing this together, remember? You're amazing—the strongest person I know. You can do this. I'm so in love with you, and I'm not going anywhere."

She looked over at me with tears in her eyes. "How can you still say that?"

"Hey." I grabbed her hand. "Nothing has changed for me, okay?"

"Okay," she replied, sounding more confused than she needed to be.

She took a deep breath and opened the passenger door to get out of the car. I followed.

I opened the front door to her home, and Sarah leapt towards us, sobbing her heart out. "Oh, sweetheart, you're okay," she mumbled, pulling back to look at Oakley. "Are you okay? Oakley." Tears rolled down her face. "Sweetheart, the police said..."

She wanted Oakley to deny it, to tell her that there had been a mistake.

I'd wanted that, too. But this was a nightmare we weren't going to wake up from.

I wanted to interrupt, but I waited to see what Oakley would do.

She stepped back from her mum, glancing between her and Jasper, who was back again to see Abby this weekend. Jasper's eyes widened.

"It's true," Oakley confessed in a croaky voice, barely above a whisper.

The room fell so silent, you could hear a pin drop. Sarah and Jasper stared on as they registered her voice.

Suddenly, Sarah gasped, slapping her hand over her mouth and gagging. She'd just realised what that voice was used for to admit for the very first time.

Sarah gulped. "No, no, no. Oakley... Oh, my God, sweetheart. No. Please, tell me it's not true. Please."

Oakley stepped back again, pressing her body into mine. "I'm so-sorry, Mum," she whispered, looking at the floor.

The hatred I had for Max doubled as *she* apologised. Oakley had nothing to be sorry for. We were the ones who should be apologising to her. *Eleven years* she'd been living with this, and we'd had no idea.

We'd all failed her so badly; I would never forgive myself for not seeing it.

"No," Sarah sobbed, her voice breaking.

Oakley sobbed as Sarah ran to the bathroom, crying hysterically, and gagging. She was going to throw up.

Oakley turned around and fell into me. "She hates me! He was right!" she shouted into my chest.

"Shh, no, she doesn't. Not you, never you. She's in shock but that doesn't mean she hates you."

Jasper jolted out of his own thoughts. "I'm gonna fucking kill him," he raged, turning red in anger. "I'm going to rip his fucking head off."

I reach out and grabbed Jasper just as he was about to run for the door.

"Don't, Cole. I'm gonna murder him. I'll murder him! I'll..." he said, tapering off as Oakley peeled herself off me and faced her brother.

"Jasper," she whispered.

"He touched you." Jasper's face crumpled in pain as he looked at his sister. "Oakley."

She shook her head.

"No? He didn't?" Jasper questioned. "He was arrested... you said it was true."

"Not me. It was Frank, his friend." she explained. Her voice cracked, and she coughed, rubbing her neck. "Dad just... let him."

Jasper's hand balled into fists. "I'll kill him."

Between the madness, my parents arrived, letting themselves in. "Is everything all right? The neighbour saw a police car outside."

Oakley stepped towards Jasper. He held his arms out, tears running down his face. "I'm so sorry," he muttered, pulling Oakley into his embrace.

Mum and Dad looked at them and then me. "What's going on?"

When Oakley nodded my way, still hugging her brother, I told my parents what'd happened.

"Oakley, sweetie, I..." my mum said, trailing off, unable to find the words. She wiped her wet face, smearing mascara across her cheeks.

Dad stared ahead, rage in his eyes at having been friends with someone like Max for most of his life. I knew him—he was going to ask himself how he missed it. He was going to blame himself for introducing Max and Sarah.

The bathroom door clicked open, and Oakley tensed. I

looked down to reassure her but stopped, open-mouthed, when I saw her peering up like a scared little girl. Seeing her like that was like taking a bullet to the heart.

Is that terrified expression how she'd looked up at her father when Frank abused her?

God, no, don't think of that.

I clamped my lips together as a wave of nausea swept across me.

Sarah walked over to us, and I had never been so nervous before.

You have to believe her.

She pulled Oakley out of Jasper's arms, sobbing, and they both sank to the floor.

"It's okay, honey," she whispered, soothingly stroking Oakley's hair. "Shh, it's okay. I'm here. I'm here." They cried together and clung to each other. "I'm so sorry. I'm so sorry. You're safe now, sweetheart. I promise. Oh, God, I'm so sorry."

I let out a breath I'd been holding. Sarah believed her. That was all Oakley needed to hear after being told she would lose everything if she ever spoke up.

"What happened?" Jasper asked. He dropped to the floor beside his mum and sister.

Oakley looked up and pressed her back against my legs. Clearing her throat, she slowly told her story, stopping to cough or to regain control. She explained that, shortly before her fifth birthday, Frank had started to turn up on their trips. She told us in as little detail as she could what had happened.

She explained that Frank sexually abused her, and the first time he raped her was when she was just ten years old.

Bile rose to my throat. I clenched my jaw together until it throbbed in pain. Taking deep breaths, I tried to stay calm, for her sake.

She was ten.

"It stopped when I was thirteen. Dad never explained why, and I didn't really care. At first, I was scared to go away again, but he said he wanted to..." She paused and took a deep breath.

Wanted to what? I stroked her hair, trying to give her strength I didn't even have inside myself.

"That he wanted our relationship to be how it was when I was little. *Before.* I wanted that, too. I thought maybe he would let me talk again if we'd repaired our relationship, so I went..."

She broke down again, her sobs replacing her words, and I felt like I was dying inside.

Chapter 31

Oakley

One week had passed since I'd spoken my truth.

Since I'd really spoken in eleven years.

My whispers in the shower didn't count.

Those seven days had been the hardest of my life. I'd relived everything I'd gone through to the police and my family. To Cole and his family, too.

I'd bled and wanted to hide, but I managed, somehow, to keep it together.

I stood up and proved my dad wrong.

They'd believed *me*.

A lot of things had changed in our house in that week. It looked completely different. Mum barely slept, she painted and decorated, threw out old furniture and bought new.

Every trace of Dad was sitting on a heap of rubbish at the recycling centre.

He'd been charged after the cops went through his computer. He'd never touched me, but he had victims.

It'd been a relief that there was evidence. It wouldn't be my word against his.

There would be a long investigation into his and Frank's

activities, apparently, but they were somewhere they couldn't hurt anyone else now. I didn't care how long it took for justice to be served.

I couldn't relax. Everything had me on edge. Being here was like drowning. I wanted to run now more than ever. Everyone in my village knew, and I couldn't stand it. I couldn't breathe, the claustrophobia gagging me every time I stepped outside the front door.

Mum was exhausted, devastated, and apologising over and over.

Jasper looked like he wanted to kill Dad.

Cole looked like he wanted to burn the whole world down.

"How are you feeling?" Mum asked.

I'd lost count of how many times I'd been asked that. Mum wanted to know how I was feeling every second of the day. I wasn't even sure how I felt anymore, whether I was even more broken or not.

"I'm doing okay," I replied. This minute, I was all right. It could change so fast, though. "You two?"

Jasper shrugged, gritting his teeth. He was going to grind them down if he kept that up.

"I'm okay," Mum whispered, but the tears in her eyes told me otherwise.

She was not okay, and that was one of the main reasons I'd kept quiet for so long. But I felt so much better that it was all out in the open and that my family had stuck by me—when they hadn't questioned if I was telling the truth. For the first time ever, I felt like it wasn't my fault.

The one who broke apart our family was my dad.

Cole had barely left my side. He was only at his house now because I needed time with my family.

"I want the sentencing to be over with," Jasper growled. "I

want to look that bastard in the eye knowing he is going to rot in prison for the rest of his life."

If he got life...

He hoped they would admit what had gone on. So far, neither of them had, and I didn't expect them to. I was fully prepared for it to go to trial, but I was *terrified*.

I'd have to stand up against my dad and the man who'd abused me for years. But I'd do it because I wasn't prepared to be a victim. No matter how hard being a survivor was, I was determined not to let them ruin my future.

"I don't think it'll be that easy, Jasper."

"He owes you that much!"

I got off the sofa and went to sit on the two-seater with him. He took a deep breath and wrapped his arm around my shoulders.

"He owes *all* of us that much, but that doesn't mean he'll do it. We'll be fine if we stick together," I said, drawing on the strength I knew my family needed.

"Will we?" he asked. "None of us can sleep in this fucking house, not even if Mum decorated it a thousand times over. Everything here is rotting. I want to get out, go somewhere far away. Neither of you can tell me you haven't thought the same. I see you both struggling just as much as I am."

Mum looked away, confirming that Jasper's observation was true.

If it were that simple, I'd have been gone by now. We couldn't just take off. We didn't have the kind of money it took to up and move so quickly. The house would have to be sold.

We could go somewhere, though. We had family... in Australia.

I almost didn't want to suggest it.

Cole.

Curling up, I rested against Jasper's side. I couldn't leave

Cole. I loved him so much. He was the one who'd given me the strength to carry on all these years. He gave me everything and made me believe that I could have a normal future.

I could tell everyone I was fine, and I could be strong and not blame myself, but that would never stop the memories. It wouldn't give me back everything that had been taken away.

I didn't ever want to be that little girl again.

There was an escape. A place I could go where I wouldn't be the abused girl across the road.

We could have a fresh start in Australia, a place where I would just be Oakley.

England is where you were abused.

This house is where you stopped talking.

I squeezed my eyes closed, my heart beating too fast. Each time I stepped outside the door, people would look. I couldn't go back to school and face everyone there.

Here, we were all stuck.

I couldn't stay here.

"We could go to Uncle Pete's," I said before I could stop myself.

Jasper looked at me with his mouth open, and I burst into tears.

I didn't want to leave Cole, but I couldn't watch Mum and Jasper breaking anymore. *I* couldn't break anymore, and we couldn't heal here.

We had to go.

Jasper was right. We could rip this house down and rebuild it, but it wouldn't stop being the place where our lives were ripped to shreds.

"Don't cry," Jasper whispered. "Right now, we've got to do what we've got to do. It wouldn't have to be forever. We all need a break."

A break for how long? A month? Two? A year?

I couldn't leave Cole hanging like that.

"Oakley, we don't have to go that far," Mum said, crouching down in front of us. "We can work something out. I have enough savings for a few months, and I could pick up work."

It didn't have to be, but Australia was about as far away from England as you could get, and that seemed *so* good. None of us could stay here, and in Australia, we had family.

A month. We could go to Australia for that long, let the gossip die down, and come back somewhere close. With everything that'd gone on recently, we didn't need to add money worries to it. I couldn't put that stress on Mum, too.

"Australia," I said. "Just for a little while."

"I think we should do it," Jasper said.

Mum nodded. "I do, too. We'd have to come back eventually, but my main concern is getting you somewhere you can heal. I don't care where that is or what I have to do to achieve it."

"Neither do I," Jasper said.

"You'd be giving up so much," I whispered.

As much as it hurt to be here and relive everything *all the time*, I couldn't make them leave their lives behind.

Jasper had uni, friends, and maybe Abby. Mum had a career, family, and friends.

"We stick together. I don't care about anything other than you right now," Jasper said. "The rest of it can wait."

Smiling through my tears, I gripped Jasper's arm.

"Okay," Mum said. "We do this *together*. We'll go to Australia for as long as we need. We'll heal there. I'll get us all through this. I promise, I won't let either of you down again."

The enormity of our decision hit me. I sobbed into Jasper's shoulder, my heart splitting in two, while Mum stroked my hair and cried.

Chapter 32

Cole

It had been twelve days since Oakley had spoken up about what'd happened to her, and twelve days since I had slept properly.

I spent every night at her house, holding her until she fell asleep. Some nights she cried, and the others she demanded we watched some shit movie.

Each night, she spoke to me.

It was Heaven and Hell.

But for the last few days, she'd been so distant, as if she wasn't really with me. We were together most of the time, but her mind was elsewhere. Whenever she looked at me, she had so much sadness in her eyes, it took my breath away.

I had to be patient with her.

We were waiting on the police to update us about the case against Max and Frank, but Oakley just wanted to forget about it until there were updates.

It was impossible, of course, but we stopped talking about it.

Oakley blamed herself whenever she saw her mum or brother upset. I'd told her a million times that none of it was her fault, and I'd tell her a million times more until she believed it.

She rolled over in bed and snuggled against my chest. Her long blonde hair was fanned out on the pillow behind her. When she slept, she looked so peaceful.

I ran my hand through that long, blonde mane of hers, and I kissed her forehead.

She was the bravest person I knew, and I was hopelessly in love with her.

With time, we would all heal, but the scars would still be there. We'd deal with whatever surfaced together.

"Good morning, beautiful. Are you okay?" I asked as her bright blue eyes fluttered open.

"Yeah."

It was a lie. I could tell by the pained look in those pretty eyes. She might be talking now, but I could still read the things she didn't say.

I lifted a brow, fear trickling down my spine. "Why can't you look at me, Oakley? What's changed? Are you angry? I know I should have seen what was going on. I know that, and I'm sor—"

She pulled back and pressed her finger over my lips. "Don't ever think that. Please, don't say that again. I don't blame you for anything. You're the reason I've had happy moments over the last eleven years. Everything good in my life involved you."

I kissed her forehead, my heart skipping beats with her words. That voice of hers was quiet and husky, and I wasn't sure if that was because she'd not used it in so long or if that was just how it was. Either way, I *loved* it.

Now wasn't the time to think about sex, but damn, that voice.

"Oakley, we slept together..." I trailed off, not really knowing exactly how to put it. I needed to know that she *wanted* to be with me, and I hadn't taken advantage of her.

She'd said yes, I knew that much. But did she mean it, or did she feel like she could never say no?

It would gut me if it was the latter.

She stiffened, and her jaw went slack. "I know. I'm sorry, Cole. I shouldn't have let you. It was really selfish." Her eyes filled with tears. "I should've stayed away."

Wait. She felt selfish?

Her words stole my breath. She didn't think I would want to after knowing the truth. More fuel to the fire of hatred that burned over Max and Frank.

"Fuck. Oakley, that's *not* what I meant. Baby, no. I hate what happened to you, and I want to kill them for doing it, but it hasn't changed how I feel about you. How much I love you and how much I want you. I was worried that you might not have wanted to."

A breath of relief blew across my face. "Yes, I wanted to. Being with you was something *completely* different to Frank. You made me feel safe and loved and special. It wasn't the same, Cole. It just wasn't. I'll never regret being with you."

I closed my eyes. Thank God for that.

"It almost feels like it happened in a different life," she said, and I opened my eyes again. "When I was thirteen, Dad said Frank was moving away and we wouldn't see him again. He said I shouldn't think about it anymore, so that's what I did. Well, not really. I tried to forget. It was always at the back of my mind, sometimes the front, but in a way, I did move on."

I nodded and ran my hand up her back to hold her closer.

"I felt like, because it was over, I could start being a normal teenager—or a sort of normal one. I still wasn't allowed to talk. I just couldn't go back to that place again, Cole. When I saw Frank, I knew what was going to happen. I couldn't do it."

"You shouldn't have ever had to. Your dad should've..." I took a deep breath, seething. "He should've done a lot of things. We all know that. I'm just so sorry you couldn't come to me."

"What did I say about blaming yourself?"

You don't have to be the strong one.

261

I kissed the tip of her nose. "I still don't know how you managed not to talk to anyone. I never understood why you didn't ever text me back."

"I didn't want anyone to get hurt. If I kept quiet, everything would be fine. If I started texting, you would have asked why I didn't speak, wouldn't you?"

I nodded. Of course, I would've. She cut off almost all form of communication to protect everyone else, no matter how much it hurt her.

"And I did reply every night. I just didn't send any of them."

She reached across me and grabbed her phone from the bedside table.

I took the phone and looked at what she was showing me. There was a huge block of text. A line of space between each one.

My breathing hitched as I scrolled up, reading each good night message, each declaration of love, each request for help, each time she told me she wished things could be different.

"Oakley," I breathed.

"Press send," she said. "I want you to have them all."

"Damn, baby." I couldn't function properly. My thumb trembled as I hit send and my phone dinged with everything she'd wanted to say over the last couple of years.

"I love you, Cole. I have for a very long time, as you'll see when you read all of those." She lifted my chin to meet her eyes. "Not now, though. That'll take a while."

She was right. I'd only managed to read a few.

"I love you," I replied, pressing my lips to hers.

I'd spent the afternoon with Mum and Mia while Oakley, Sarah, and Jasper spent some time together.

Now, I was in my room changing to go to Oakley's when Mia shouted up the stairs, "Cole, you need to come downstairs right now!"

Her tone, like the worst had happened, made my heart stop

I spun around and ran downstairs, petrified at what she would say.

"What?"

When I saw Oakley, Sarah, and Jasper by the front door, I froze.

They were crying... and so were Mum, Dad, and Mia.

"What's going on?" I asked, my eyes fixed on Oakley.

She took a deep breath and stepped towards me. "I'm sorry," she whispered. "We're leaving. Moving. Now."

"What? No, what do you mean?"

"We're going to my Uncle Pete's."

"Pete," I repeated.

Pete. Sarah's brother. The one who lived in *Australia*.

No.

"I can't stay here anymore. None of us can." She shook her head and added, "There are too many bad memories. I love you so much, Cole, and this is killing me, but I *have* to go." She sounded broken and desperate. It was like there was no other option but for her to leave.

The messages this morning... a goodbye gift.

"You can't leave." I shook my head, trying to make sense of what she was saying.

They were moving halfway across the world.

She was leaving me.

Pain cut through my chest, and I reached for her.

"Don't. Don't, please." I closed the distance between us, wrapping my arms around her and touching my forehead to hers. I didn't care who was with us. "I love you. You can't go. You can move in here if you can't live at yours, or we can go somewhere else. We'll go to a different town. Jesus, Oakley, you can't just leave!"

She clung to me, burying her head in my chest as she cried her heart out.

"I owe you so much, Cole. You gave me my life back, and I will *never* stop loving you. If there were a way I could stay, I would do it, but there isn't."

She pulled back, and I tightened my grip.

"No, no, no."

I couldn't breathe.

"Please. Don't do this, please. Oakley, don't," I muttered, holding her tighter, never wanting to let go. "I'll come with you, baby."

"Your life is here." She pulled away just enough to look me in the eyes, and she touched my cheek. "You can't give that up. Not for me."

I shook my head, frowning at how stupid she was being. "*You* are my life."

She sobbed and closed her eyes. Tears spilled over and poured down her beautiful face.

God, she was really doing this.

Pressing my lips to hers, I kissed her with everything I had.

She kissed me back and whimpered. "I love you," she whispered as she started to pull away.

"Don't do this."

Her hands gripped mine and pulled them off her. My vision blurred as tears filled my eyes.

Stop crying and make her see sense!

"Please stay."

This was happening too fast. I couldn't catch up with panic surging through my body.

She walked backwards and mouthed, *I love you*, before heading out with her mum and brother.

Mia gripped my shoulder and helped me stumble to the front door. I stared in horror as Oakley got into the car.

Neither of us looked away from each other as Sarah started the engine. I was vaguely aware of my parents and Mia standing close, but all I could focus on was Oakley curled up on the back-seat, crying as she told me she loved me with her eyes.

My legs gave out, and I fell heavily onto my knees. Mia crouched with me, holding me as I broke apart.

I watched numbly as their car disappeared and she was gone.

Watching her leave my life was an agony I had never felt before.

But I loved her so much...

Enough to let her go.

Cole and Oakley's story continues in Broken Silence

Acknowledgments

I first want to say a big thanks to my husband and two sons for being awesome.

Kim, thank you for reading this new version again! You're totally amazing.

To Sam, Elle, and Vic. Thanks for being there to kick my butt and spur me on.

Lou, you've done it again. The cover is perfect.

Vic, thanks so much for waving your editing wand over this!

To bloggers and my readers, thank you all for reading and spreading the love. It means the world to me.

Made in the USA
Middletown, DE
05 July 2023

34623347R10165